ChangelingPress.com

Styx/Ripper Duet
A Bones MC Romance
Marteeka Karland

Styx/Ripper Duet
A Bones MC Romance
Marteeka Karland

All rights reserved.
Copyright ©2023 Marteeka Karland

ISBN: 978-1-60521-869-4

Publisher:
Changeling Press LLC
315 N. Centre St.
Martinsburg, WV 25404
ChangelingPress.com

Editor: Katriena Knights
Cover Artist: Marteeka Karland

The individual stories in this anthology have been previously released in E-Book format.

No part of this publication may be reproduced or shared by any electronic or mechanical means, including but not limited to reprinting, photocopying, or digital reproduction, without prior written permission from Changeling Press LLC.

This book contains sexually explicit scenes and adult language which some may find offensive and which is not appropriate for a young audience. Changeling Press books are for sale to adults, only, as defined by the laws of the country in which you made your purchase.

Table of Contents

Styx (Salvation's Bane MC 10) 4
   Chapter One...5
   Chapter Two 25
   Chapter Three 40
   Chapter Four...54
   Chapter Five 68
   Chapter Six..80
   Chapter Seven 98
   Chapter Eight..107
   Chapter Nine 120
Ripper (Salvation's Bane MC 11) 143
   Chapter One..144
   Chapter Two 158
   Chapter Three 175
   Chapter Four...189
   Chapter Five 206
   Chapter Six..219
   Chapter Seven 239
   Chapter Eight..255
   Chapter Nine 267
   Epilogue 284
Marteeka Karland..289
Changeling Press E-Books 290

Styx (Salvation's Bane MC 10)
Marteeka Karland

Jolene: I've lived my entire life in the shadow of a feud that ended over a hundred years ago. But try telling that to my family. To them, the Hatfields and McCoys were never meant to mix. Or be in the same town, really. So, when I give my virginity to a Hatfield, my McCoy family disowned me entirely. And that Hatfield I trusted? He set me up to be raped by his kin. So yeah, my life's a shit show. Then another Hatfield picked me up out of a ditch and saved me. I thought he'd hurt me, too, but he turned out to be the kindest man I've ever met. Now, if I can just shake him long enough to get the revenge I need from those who hurt me. I just hope that, when I'm done, he'll take me back.

Styx: I just came for the car. A rare Mercedes Maybach the club intended to sell for a good chunk of change. I'd long ago left any family I had in this little hick town in West Virginia and only came back because I knew the area, and the man who had the car was my family's rival. Marshall McCoy had always been a swine. So, when I found his daughter in the ditch on the side of the road, beaten and bloodied, my first instinct -- and that of my MC brothers -- was that she was setting me up, but I couldn't leave her to the mercy of her family. When I found out how she'd been hurt and how she'd been treated her whole life, I knew there'd be hell to pay. I just didn't count on my sweet little hillbilly being hellbent on revenge. As I fall deeper and deeper under her spell, I find I can't deny her anything. Even if what she wants might break her.

Chapter One
Jolene

"Do you promise we'll be together forever, Avery Hatfield?"

"Absolutely, sweet Jolene McCoy. We'll be the only Hatfield and McCoy to ever have a till-death-do-us-part marriage. I swear it, Jolene."

I knew better. I'd seen Avery with at least three other women since we'd been together, but I guess this was his talent. He could make women fall for him no matter the consequences. And I was head over heels. I knew this was a bad idea, but I was doing it anyway. Maybe I just wanted to finally experience sex. I knew I didn't love Avery. Not like I should, to be doing this. But here I was. In a cheap motel with a man my parents forbade me to date because they hated his family. The feud of the Hatfields and McCoys might have officially ended in 1891 and then again in a symbolic gesture in 2003, but there were some who still carried that grudge into the modern climate.

"OK," I said, nodding and smiling at the man above me pressing me into the bed. "I trust you."

Avery shoved inside me, taking my innocence in one hard thrust. I cried out in pain, but he didn't stop.

"It'll get better, Jolene. Next time it'll be good for you." But not this time, was the implied ending to that statement. If he'd said it, he would have been right. Avery kept fucking me. Hard. He didn't kiss me or touch me other than to take his pleasure.

It took all of three minutes for him to get himself off and come inside me. I wanted to cry and probably would the second he left the room. I'd known it was a mistake from the start, but I'd kept moving ahead. I let him talk me into this, so it was my own fault.

"That was so fuckin' hot," he gasped out, his body weight heavy now that he'd completely collapsed on top of me. It was hard to breathe, but he wouldn't move. "Loved takin' that virgin pussy. Comin' in it."

Finally, he rolled off me and chuckled. "You bled. Guess my cock was too big for ya, huh?" Then he padded off to the bathroom.

What just happened? I mean, I hadn't really expected he'd hold to his promises. His goal had been to have sex with me. But this was…

When he came back into the room, he was dressed in his dirty jeans and stained T-shirt. He grinned at me. "Don't stay too long. I only paid for this room for an hour so you got maybe forty minutes tops. You better get cleaned up and get outta here or they'll charge you extra." When I just looked at him as he snagged his keys, he continued. "I paid cash so you can't charge it to my card. You'll have to come up with the money on your own." He opened the door and started outside.

"Wait! You brought me here. You're my ride!"

He laughed. "Well, call a cab. Or an Uber. I got shit to do. See ya 'round, Jolene!"

"Avery!"

He just shut the door in my face. I heard his beat-up truck start. He revved it a couple of times, making a bunch of noise since it didn't have a muffler, then peeled out of the parking lot. I was alone, Avery's cum still running down the inside of my leg.

OK. This had actually happened. It was far worse than I'd figured, but it was still manageable. Just… harder. And he'd probably tell all his buddies how he'd just popped my cherry. It would likely be all over town soon after. Which meant my parents would find out. Even if I bee-lined it home, I wouldn't be surprised if they knew before I got there.

I was so fucked. Literally and figuratively.

As I cleaned myself up, I heard my phone chime. At first, I ignored it. I wanted to get dressed and get out of here as fast as I could. But it kept going off. Putting on my shirt, I glanced at the screen when another chime went off. Social media notification. Didn't care. I wasn't a popular girl in school, but I had a circle of friends I connected with outside of class.

But then it went off again. And again. And again. Over and over.

Then I got a text. Then several texts.

Just as I was finishing up and walking out the door, my phone rang. I glanced at the screen. My stepmother.

No fucking way.

"Mom?"

"What the hell have you done?" The question was screeched at an uncomfortable volume.

"What are you --"

"Don't play dumb with me! You know what you did with that Hatfield boy. Is it true?"

"You're going to have to slow down. I don't understand --"

"Of course, you understand! It's all over the Internet! My friends at church saw what you did! It's bad enough you had to film yourself having sex, but to do it with a Hatfield? Your father is livid!"

I barely made it to the second-story railing along the walk before my knees gave out. "What do you mean?"

"Stop lying! You sullied yourself with a Hatfield, then put it up all over the Internet!"

"Mom, I didn't put anything on the Internet. Why would I do that?"

"Because I forbade you to see that boy and you just love flaunting how I ain't your real mom. I told you he was no good. But you knew better, didn't you? You just had to prove you could do whatever you wanted since you turned eighteen. Rubbing it in mine and your father's faces!"

"Mom--" This was spiraling out of control faster than I could keep up. I stopped just outside the motel room, leaning against the wall.

"I can't believe you did this! We'll never be able to show our faces at church again. All our friends will shun us! I can't believe you'd do this to us!"

"I don't even know what's happened!" I yelled. "Who told you about this? It literally just happened! And I didn't film anything! What are you even talking about!" The more my stepmother yelled at me, the more I yelled back.

"Haven't you been listening? Of course, you haven't," she scoffed. "That Hatfield devil sent the video of you fornicating with him to everyone in town."

"That's impossible, Mom. He's only been gone ten minutes, and he didn't video us. Besides, he said he loved me." I stumbled down the walk to the steps. If I didn't sit down, I was afraid I'd fall.

"You always were stupid." Then my stepmother mimicked me, her voice going higher. Her words sent a chill down my spine. "'Do you promise we'll be together forever, Avery?'" Then her voice went deeper as she mimicked Avery. "'Absolutely, sweet Jolene. We'll be the only Hatfield and McCoy to ever have a till-death-do-us-part marriage. I swear it, Jolene.'" I gasped, but my stepmom wasn't finished. "Little fool! Now you've ruined yourself and our family's reputation. I hope you're happy."

"This isn't about you, Mom! And why is it my fault?" I was sitting on the concrete steps as I argued with my mother. Tears threatened, but more than that, I was angry and hurt.

"Because you were a stupid little whore! Just like your real mother." She snapped the hate-filled words at me. It wasn't anything I hadn't heard from her before.

I was the middle of seven children from three different women. I either got lost in the pack or singled out for something I'd done to earn her displeasure. Sometimes, it felt like both my parents hated me and my siblings could give two shits. Maybe it was why I'd allowed Avery Hatfield to get close to me in the first place. Now, they might hate me forever, but at least it got me some attention. Too bad it was the wrong kind.

"Why are you calling me?"

"To tell you not to bother coming home," she said. "You've made your bed. You can lie in it!" The line went dead.

I whimpered. Had my stepmother just thrown me out of the house? Where was I going to go? How was I going to live? I had a job, but payday was still a week away, and Mom and Poppy made me give them most of my check for room and board since I'd turned eighteen.

Just when I thought the night couldn't get any worse, I was yanked to my feet by my hair. "Hey! Let me go!"

"There's the little slut!" Someone laughed as they shoved me back toward the motel. "Get her inside before someone sees us." I screamed, but they slapped a piece of duct tape over my mouth, dragging me back up the landing to the room I'd just vacated.

"Avery said we only got half an hour. Better

make it good, boys."

I gasped as I looked up at Avery's brother and five of his cousins. They shoved me to the bed and yanked off my pants.

They'd secured me so completely, they didn't have to beat me much. It must have been part of the fun for them because they still hit me. Though they didn't have a lot of time, they did plenty of damage in what they had. Strangely, Avery's brother pulled out a box of condoms and threw them on the bed beside me. They all used them. Probably to keep from leaving evidence of what they'd done that could link them to the crime. At some point, I checked out of reality. Sounds were distorted, my vision blurred. My body ached from the beating and the way they'd used me, but it wasn't as bad as I'd first thought. Or maybe I really had checked out.

I was found some time later when someone came to clean. The police and ambulance personnel got involved, but I just wanted a shower and to go home so I refused a rape exam. To me, there simply wasn't any point. I wasn't going to testify against anybody. Somehow, I was getting the fuck out of here and never fucking coming back. Even though I'd refused most everything offered, I'd allowed a paramedic to give me something for pain, which took the edge off. Tomorrow would be bad, but I'd figure out a way to survive.

Now, it was time to face the fact that I didn't have a home anymore. My clothes were in tatters, so the police got me some jail oranges. The motel manager allowed me to shower, and I dressed afterward. A policewoman had stayed behind to make sure I had a place to go. Which was really code for making sure I left the motel. At the time, I thought

Avery's information that he'd only paid for an hour was horrifying. He'd only intended to get what he wanted, then he'd blazed. Had planned on it all along. Now, I was grateful for it. I could have been there far longer. The damage much greater. Thankfully, it had only been three or four hours since the whole thing began.

But, now what? I had no idea how I was going to survive the night on my own. The pain medicine helped, but it wouldn't last. I knew I needed to go to my parents' house tonight if I was going to have a chance at all of getting some of my things. Once I had my stash of cash and some clothes, I could at least find a place to hole up and have a breakdown. Because it was coming. The pain was physical, but it was more mental, and once I allowed myself to feel it, I knew it would be a long, long while before I could get control again.

I lived in Williamson, West Virginia. Population under four thousand. My family, honest-to-God descendants of the Hatfield clan, pretended to be pillars of the community. They had more than one profitable business and helped bring in money into town. Rich. Influential. But they raised their children to do for themselves. I was their problem child. The likelihood of anyone believing my story or caring to help me was slim. If I told my parents -- especially my mother -- they'd just say I got what I deserved. So, yeah. I had nowhere to go. And I was in shock. Still, the officer saw me out and just… left. If a female officer wouldn't help me, who would?

It took me an hour or so before I made my way home. The doors were locked, but I still had my purse. Thank God, my parents hadn't thought to change the security code yet. I let myself in with my key and my code. The lights were off so I hoped everyone was asleep. It was almost three in the morning so I was probably in luck. All I wanted was a change of clothing and my stash of savings, and I'd be gone.

I crept upstairs and into my room. I thought I'd be alone, but my sister, Ginny, was awake, reading. In my bed. She shone the flashlight in my face, then scoffed.

"Thought Mom threw you out. She said I could have your room, so if you're back, you'll have to take my room."

"Just keep reading," I said as I went to my dresser. I grabbed my backpack and emptied it on my bed before stuffing clothing into it. Ginny may have moved in here to sleep, but she hadn't completely taken over things yet. Thankfully, my money was in the side pocket of my backpack, and I stuffed it in my bra just in case Ginny ratted me out and someone took the backpack before I could get out of here. It was a real possibility, because my head was still foggy from the pain medicine. I was upright because of pure grit. Once I crashed, I'd crash hard.

"You're not supposed to be here. I'm telling Mom."

"I just need some clothes, Ginny. I can't wear this bright orange jumpsuit all the time. Besides, I paid for everything I have here. It's mine."

"Mom!"

"Ginny, please! Stop!"

I knew she wouldn't. So I just zipped up the pack and hurried out. The light was on in the hall and my poppy stood outside the door to his and Mom's bedroom. He took one look at me and his face erupted in anger.

"Get your ass outa this house before I call the

fuckin' cops!" Without saying a word, I hurried down the stairs. "And leave that pack here! Little thief!"

No way I was complying with that. I might be homeless, but I needed clothes. I had enough money to get out of town and eat until I could secure a job and save enough for a down payment on an apartment, but I needed everything in that pack.

As I ran outside and across the yard, the deafening blast of a shotgun boomed in the night. I screamed but kept running. Another shot and dirt sprayed up from the ground just to my left.

"You ever come back here, I'll kill ya, ya little whore!" That was my father. Screaming at me even as he shot at me. I kept running. It was the only thing I could do. I had no idea where I was going to go or what I was going to do. But I'd figure it out.

I'd figure it out.

* * *

Styx

How could one place be so God-awful *redneck*? Always had been. Every fucking neighborhood in town had at least one car up on concrete blocks and numerous pink flamingos in the front fucking yard. Nothing had fucking changed since I was a teenager.

Red had a tip on a Mercedes Maybach that was supposedly being held in storage until the right buyer came along. In this fucking hick town. I had my doubts, but Red said it had been confirmed by our intel guy, Ripper. If Ripper said that's the way it was? Well. I'd gotten on a plane to fucking West Virginia, hadn't I?

My job was to scout. Using the little gizmos Red's woman, Rosanna, had developed, I had no doubt I could steal the car. The problem was getting it out of storage and into the enclosed trailer. Again, Ripper was on the issue.

Poison and Lock pulled up to the designated area about half a mile from where the car was being stored. They'd driven a nondescript Ford with a beat-up-looking trailer, and another, smaller car to act as lookout for the payload on the way home. *Smokey and the Bandit* style. The car was rough-looking, but souped up under the hood. Hopefully, the extra horsepower wouldn't be needed, but better to have it and not need it than to need it and not have it. Neither looked new, nor did they appear in disrepair. The vehicles were designed to blend in. To not stand out anywhere they went.

The plan was to load the car and get out of this place as quickly as possible. Use the app to give the thing a new VIN number and program our own FOB. Lose ourselves on the interstate, then the lesser-traveled highways off the interstates on a roundabout route back to Salvation's Bane and Red's underground garage. Once that was done, we'd ditch the truck and trailer and begin the rest of the cleaning process on the car. Which was the easy part.

I studied the area around the storage building from the remote screen provided by a drone. It wasn't more than a barn on the outside, but the reality was, inside the barn was a climate-controlled warehouse with state-of-the-art security. I knew the place well because it was owned by Marshal McCoy. I'd been poking my nose into the business of the McCoys since I was a kid.

McCoy was well off, having a legitimate business of some sort in the community. But his real money came from smuggling. This barn and a couple others like it were the reason for that success. From the outside, it looked like a big tobacco barn. Inside, the place was locked down tighter than a snare drum. Which was the beauty of it, I supposed.

Security outside the building was just as tedious. There were cameras all over the place. And traps. Thankfully, McCoy believed in electronics. Heavily. Always had. All the scouting we'd done had turned up a few rudimentary things, but nearly every single safeguard relied on electricity and electronics. Ripper had scoffed and told us it was too good to be true, that we needed to really recon the hell outta the place. We'd found a few pits and spikes and other simple shit that looked like it hadn't been well-maintained. We'd left that part until the evening we'd planned to do the job. Just in case someone did a manual security sweep.

Our planning was meticulous. Starting two months before we were ready to make our move, Ripper had messed with security at the same time he kept anyone interested in the car off the scent. If McCoy was going to upgrade things or do an extensive check, we'd know it well in advance. Ripper had the guy's entire place bugged. House, office and every car they owned. McCoy thought he was the smartest man in the room, but the fact was, he was on the verge of losing everything to a rival. Montgomery Hatfield.

Made me snicker to think about it. Generations of Hatfields and McCoys. They'd officially ended the feud in the eighteen nineties, symbolically in the early two thousands. But here in Appalachia, it was alive and going strong. Just... more civilized. At least on the surface.

Which was why we were here. Montgomery Hatfield was a half brother to my father, the bastard. While I didn't associate with that side of the family -- other than my half brother in Black Reign, Shotgun -- I did enjoy taking them down a peg or two. If I could take down Marshall McCoy while I was doing it? So much the better. Call it a character flaw.

"How's it going, Ripper?" I'd been touching base with the tech guy regularly. If there was a problem, we needed to identify it before we backed the trailer in.

"All's quiet. Same as always. They raised a fuss the first few times I blacked them out, but once they got used to their network coming back up, they quit worrying about it. Made a couple calls to the company, who charged them a bunch of money to go to each site and check on things. After that, they sent one of old man McCoy's boys out, and he's not the most thorough tool in the box. Last three times it's gone out, no one bothered to check."

"Good. Where is everyone now."

"Far enough away you'll have at least an hour before anyone could possibly show up." The man snorted. "Bit of a ruckus goin' on with one of his girls. Not sure what, but it's keeping everybody busy."

"So, we ready?" I was anxious to get moving. While I had confidence in the operation, something else was bothering me.

"Get into position. Once you're ten minutes out, I'll throw the switch." Ripper had everything bugged at Salvation's Bane, including all our vehicles. He said it let him know when one of us was in trouble. I figured he was just a control freak.

"Guess we're good to go, then." I signaled to Poison and Lock. "Move it out." My two MC brothers were in the truck pulling the trailer while I was in a separate truck we'd had waiting when we started scouting two months ago. Last thing we wanted was for the two vehicles to be seen together before the heist.

It was just past four in the morning. The darkest

part of the night. The moon was covered by clouds. The night was still. Even the nocturnal creatures were settling down for the day to come.

There were two routes into the place where we were going. Poison and Lock had taken a different route than me. Mine took me past the McCoy family home. Remembering that place from my early childhood made me want to fire my gun at the windows as I passed. I hated that fucking place. Old man McCoy was a fucking bastard. Always was. Being a Hatfield, I'd never actually been in the house, but I knew some of his kids. The boys were all bullies. Some of the girls, too. His wife had died a few years back, I'd heard. And now he was starting a whole new brood of kids to mold in his image. That massive house represented everything in Williamson I hated.

I'd gotten about six miles away from the house when something caught my attention. A small form huddled on the side of the road. I almost missed it. Looked like a boy or a small woman wearing a backpack. The figure was in an orange jumpsuit, which was the only reason I'd seen it.

I started to just go on. We didn't have a lot of time here. But, Goddammit, I couldn't just pass this person by.

"Guys, I've got a problem. Keep to schedule. If you don't hear from me in five minutes, abort."

"What's going on?" That was Ripper's voice. Of course, he was monitoring.

"Not sure. Switching on my body cam so you can see what I'm seeing. Get an ID on the guy."

"Guy? What guy?"

"There's someone on the side of the road. Could be someone in trouble," I said.

"Could be a fuckin' trap. What the fuck, Styx?"

Ripper didn't get upset too often, but when he did, he tended to go nuclear.

"Just keep an eye out. Give me five minutes. I'll either leave him or load him in the truck."

"Fuck!"

"Don't give yourself a nosebleed, Ripper. If it's a trap, I'll fucking kill the bastard."

"Take an earwig. I want to stay in communication every fuckin' second, Styx."

"Roger that," I said, putting the truck in park and stepping out. Though the truck's headlights shone brightly, I snagged a flashlight along with the gun at my hip. If this was an ambush, I wasn't getting caught with my fucking pants down.

The figure held up a trembling hand, blocking the light of the vehicle from her face. And I could tell by the small, delicate hand it was a female. I shined my light around the area but didn't see anything. Just to be safe, I turned my body, letting Ripper get a good look around in case I missed something. With his computer enhancement shit, he'd see danger long before I did.

"Don't see nothin'," Ripper murmured. I could hear him typing and flipping switches. "Can't say a hundred percent, but I think you're alone."

I eased toward the figure huddling in the ditch. "Hey, there," I called. "You good?" No response. "Girl?" Still nothing. The hand blocking her face from the light still fluttered violently. That's when I noticed the blood on her fingers and streaking her hand. "You OK?" The hand dropped, and there was a slight whimper as she lay still once more.

"Ripper?" I had a sinking feeling this girl was in a world of trouble. There was no way I could leave her. At this point, I was praying for an ambush, because I absolutely could not afford to be held up by someone in real distress. And I was certain that, if this woman was as hurt as I thought she was, she'd need medical attention.

"You've got four minutes. Get her in the truck."

I knelt down and looked into one startlingly blue eye. The other one was swollen shut. Dark auburn hair fluttered across her forehead in the breeze, and I brushed it aside gently. She flinched back but didn't move away from me.

"Girl, I ain't gonna hurt ya. But I can't stay. I can get you to help, but you gotta trust me." I could hear Ripper talking in my earwig, but he sounded muffled. Like he'd left the mic active but was talking to someone else. The girl just looked at me. Of course, she looked terrified, but she didn't offer any resistance. "I'm gonna pick you up. Put you in my truck." Still, she didn't say anything. "Fuck," I swore to myself.

"Two minutes, Styx," Ripper snapped. "Get movin'. I'm workin' on a plan for the girl, but you've got to get on the fuckin' road."

Carefully, I lifted her from the ditch. She whimpered, but didn't fight me or say a word otherwise. In fact, she didn't move other than to breathe. "She needs medical attention," I murmured to Ripper.

"I see that. Try to get her to talk, but if we're doin' this, we ain't got much time."

"Can Poison and Lock get the car out of the barn without me?"

"Yes, but you're their interference if they're spotted."

"Barn?" The girl spoke softly, like her throat hurt. I tried not to think it was because she'd screamed as she'd been hurt. Because, now that I had her more in the light, I could see she'd been beaten.

"Yeah, sweetheart," I said, the endearment rolling off my tongue when I hadn't wanted it to.

"You're after the Maybach. Aren't you?"

"Fuck," Ripper swore. "You're made. Everyone, get the fuck out."

"Just hang on, Ripper." I set her on her feet by my truck as I opened the passenger-side door. She managed to stay upright but leaned against me. Though her weight was slight, I could tell the only thing holding her up was the arm I had clamped around her back holding her against me. "You know about the car?"

"Marshall McCoy's my poppy," she said, her words slurred through her split lip.

"Mother fuck! Goddammit! Drop the bitch and get the fuck out!"

In my head, I knew Ripper was probably right, but there was no way I was leaving this girl in this kind of shape. Even if she was some kind of decoy, someone had beat the shit out of her, and I wasn't letting her go back to them. "You know I can't leave her, Ripper," I murmured. "She's hurt."

"She's probably fuckin' bait!"

"What's your name, girl?" I said, setting her in the truck. She clutched a backpack in her hands but looked at me fearfully. I reached behind the seat and pulled out an emergency blanket. It was warm out, but she looked like she was in shock.

"Jolene McCoy," she answered, though she didn't look at me. She kept looking at her lap. The name made me do a double take at her. I knew Jolene McCoy. At least, I knew of her. She was just a child when I left, but she was the only member of that whole sorry bunch, other than my half brother, worth helping. And if anything I'd heard about her over the years was to be believed, she was the last person who deserved this kind of treatment. That thought right there sealed this girl's fate. Because she needed a strong man in her life to protect her tender heart, and I was a ruthless enough bastard to take on the job and excel at it.

"Who did this to you?"

She shrugged, obviously not going to answer.

"How bad you hurt?"

Again, she shrugged, but she added, "I'll live."

"I'll get you help, but I've gotta take you with me."

"If you're taking the car, do what you gotta do. It'll piss Poppy off something fierce."

I grinned. "You got an issue with the old man?"

"I hate him," she said softly but with more than a touch of venom. "I hate all of 'em."

"Do you want me to take you to the hospital now?"

"No." She shook her head, then winced, pressing one hand to her temple. "Just get me out of this fucking town. I never wanna see this place again."

"Get to the site," Ripper said. "I'm making arrangements for a change of plans once you get the car. You can drop her off there."

"All right. Gonna be a hell of a ride. You up for it?"

"I'm up for anything that lets me see the last of Williamson."

"OK, then." I shut the door and ran around to my side. Hopping in, I put the truck in gear and took off.

"You're plus three minutes, Styx. Make up some fucking ground," Ripper ordered.

"Those pussies can last three minutes without

me," I bit out.

"What?"

I glanced at Jolene. "It's nothin', sugar. Just try to relax. Whatever you do, don't get out of the vehicle."

"I won't," she said, then turned her face away, looking out the passenger window.

I needed to assess her injuries, but she seemed like she was content for the moment. I also needed to deal with the fact that I'd just decided she was mine and she had no idea who I was. "You tell me if you hurt too much, Jolene. I got shit I have to do, but I ain't a complete bastard. I will do everything in my power to make you comfortable."

"I'll be OK," she said softly. "I just want out of here. If I'm along when you hurt my poppy, that'll make me comfortable." Then she muttered. "Wish I could kill 'em all."

"The McCoys?" I asked as I flew down the road. We'd be at the barn in a couple minutes. I had to be ready in case the boys needed my help. "I thought you McCoys were all about killin' Hatfields."

"I hate 'em all. Hatfields and McCoys. At least, I hate the ones I know. It was Hatfields who hurt me. I thought he loved me."

I glanced at her. She hadn't turned from the window, but I could almost feel her pain. Whatever they'd done to this girl, she'd lost more than something physical. She'd trusted her attacker. And he'd hurt her in whatever way.

"Just hang on for me. Let me get this done and get you safe, then we'll talk."

She shrugged. "Whatever."

I knew that tone. She didn't believe me. Not one little bit. I gripped the steering wheel. I was a bastard for continuing with this run, but she was safe and didn't appear in immediate danger. If that changed, I'd reevaluate.

"You almost here?" That was Poison.

"You should hear my motor. Cut the lights a while back, so you won't see me."

There was silence on the comm, then Poison said, "Hear you. We're opening the barn now. Should have the car out by the time you get here. All we need to do is do that thing with the VIN number and program the FOB. Once that's done, we can load and go. Get the fuck outta here."

"I'll lock up behind you," I said. "Then catch you on the highway."

"I've got new directions for you," Ripper said. "You're gonna take One Nineteen south until you cross the line into Kentucky. I'll guide you to Kentucky Eighty which will take you all the way into Somerset. You're gonna head to the Bones compound. Once there, you can regroup and head south again in a few days. That will give me time to assess the damage and you some time to backtrack and make sure the McCoys ain't invadin' Somerset."

Someone whistled low in the background. "Cain gonna be good with this?" That was Lock.

"Yeah. But only because of your passenger. You know he'd never turn his back on an innocent woman. It's a little over three hours there. If she needs help before then, Lock and Poison, you're on your own. I've got all the McCoy cars and phones bugged. I'll at least know if they take off after you and which direction they'll be coming from."

"Roger that," I said.

"When you get back to Palm Beach, Styx, you and I gonna have a fuckin' talk 'bout pickin' up strays."

"Talk all you want. You'd have done the same fuckin' thing."

"Don't mean I ain't kickin' your ass over it this time. Red's gonna be pissed the car's late. I'll let him fuck you up over that himself."

I glanced at my passenger. She'd laid her head against the window and closed her eyes, clutching that emergency blanket like a child might her security blanket. "Understood," I said, still watching Jolene McCoy. She turned her head. That one blue eye looked at me with such sadness and pain it made my chest ache. No matter what inconvenience it cost Red or the team, no matter how mad Ripper or even Thorn or Cain got at me, there was no way I'd regret picking up this girl. She needed help and, by God, I was gonna give her exactly what she needed.

Chapter Two
Jolene

My body hurt like a mother. I must have cried out in my sleep, because I heard the man who'd picked me up out of the ditch try to soothe me. His words seemed distant, but his touch on my arm was calming. Warm and safe. I had no idea why. He hadn't even told me his name. He seemed to be in communication with other people, because he constantly talked to himself. Whoever was on the other end didn't seem to like me much, judging by the one-sided conversation. But hey. I was used to it.

"Almost there, sweetheart. We'll get you some pain medicine and a doctor once we get to the Bones compound. Just a little longer."

The Bones compound. Whatever that was. It probably should sound sinister, but the guy wasn't being mean to me -- was trying to help me, in fact -- so I just let it go. The only thing that mattered was that I was far away from my family and that Godforsaken town in West Virginia.

The next time I woke up, it was with the guy's fingers tunneled through my hair, massaging my scalp while my head was in his lap. I lay in the front seat of his truck, the console flipped up so I was curled up on the bench seat with me facing the seat back. We seemed to have stopped moving, which was what woke me up.

"You awake?" He continued to pet me, playing with my hair, which had to be yucky and tangled. I thought I still had duct tape in my hair that I couldn't get out and had yet to cut, but I'd worry about that later.

"Yeah," I said, sitting up. That wasn't awkward

or anything. Waking up with my head in a strange man's lap. I shivered, scooting as far to the other side of the truck as I could and wrapping the silver blanket tightly around my shoulders. "We here?"

The guy just looked at me for long moments. Probably trying to size me up. "We ain't gonna hurt you, kid." I nodded, but I wasn't convinced. I'd made a stupid decision but, in my defense, I hadn't been in a good frame of mind. He sighed. "My name's Styx," he said. "Shoulda told you earlier, but we were in the middle of something, and I don't do well with niceties on the best of days."

"It's fine," I said, giving him a small smile. "Can I leave now?"

He opened his mouth to say something, then closed it. "Give me a minute," he said, then hopped out of the truck, shutting the door. I opened my door and climbed down gingerly. I was starting to feel every ache and pain of the trauma inflicted on me a few hours earlier. Before I got my feet on the ground, I felt Styx's hands at my waist.

"Take it easy. You got a bit roughed up. Let me help."

"I'm good," I said, turning and taking a step sideways to get him out of my space. "Where am I? I'll be out of your hair as soon as I can get an Uber."

"Fuck." Styx scrubbed a hand over his face and through his hair. "You need medical attention. I get the feeling you don't want people askin' too many questions, so let us help you. Mama is in her clinic. She'll take a look and fix what she can. If nothing else, she can load you up with pain meds to get you through the worst of it."

"Just need some over-the-counter stuff. I can get it on my own."

"Jolene," he said warningly. "You ain't leavin' here until Mama looks at you. I did you a favor lettin' you tag along. You're gonna do this for me."

That startled me. "Seems I'd be owing you double instead of repaying you."

"Nope. Gettin' you checked out is for my peace of mind as much as for your benefit. Callin' that one even. You're just submitting to it to keep me sane."

"Why do you even care?" I knew I sounded petulant, but I was at my lowest, and this guy was… strong. Kind. Not weak and broken like me. I was nothing more than an object of pity to a man like this.

Styx shook his head. He looked like he wanted to say something but couldn't put it into words. Then he gestured for me to come with him. "Just can't stand to see someone hurting. I can guess what happened to you. No one should have to go through that alone with no support. It could break you."

"I'm stronger than I look. Stronger people than any of those McCoy bastards have tried to keep me down." That was nothing more than bluster, and I was sure Styx saw right through it. If he did, he didn't say anything.

"Fine. I get you. But you're still gonna let Mama have a look at you. If you're gonna strike out on your own, you're gonna do it whole, Goddammit. Injured, you'll just get into trouble."

I snorted. "Trouble?"

"Yep. You can't defend yourself because you're hurting or not in the right frame of mind. Mama can help on both counts. And, like I said, I'll rest easier." He shook his head. "Don't like seein' you like this." He murmured the last as he reached out for the swollen side of my face, stroking it gently even as he winced. "You're a beautiful girl, Jolene. Don't let those pricks get the best of you."

"Fine." I stepped forward, and Styx reached out and took my hand. The contact was unexpected, but not unpleasant. In fact, I found myself clinging more tightly to him the closer we got to the big structure. "What is this place?" The racket coming from inside was off-putting. I was never one to turn down a party, but not right now. Not like this. I was battered inside and out. My trust shot. Except for this man. Maybe it was because he'd rescued me when it was painfully obvious by his one-sided conversation whoever was on the other end wanted him to leave me. Maybe it was just the fact that he'd taken me out of danger and hadn't pressed for what had happened. I had been at my breaking point. I might have lost my mind if he'd insisted on knowing what happened. Styx had just put me in his truck and brought me here. Wherever "here" was.

Which brought up another concern. "Where exactly are we?" I had to know if I was going to figure out what to do next.

"Somerset, Kentucky. This is the Bones compound." He climbed the three steps to the porch just outside the entrance.

"You said something about Bones before. What's Bones?"

"An MC. Motorcycle Club."

"Aren't those filled with thugs and outlaws?" I wrinkled my nose but didn't let go of Styx's hand.

He shrugged. "Some are, I suppose. We skirt the law sometimes, but I don't think we're thugs."

I looked at him for the first time. Really looked at him. He was older than me by several years. At least a decade if not more. There was some gray in his beard and at his temples, and lines fanning out from his eyes.

But he was fit. Muscular and lean. He had tattoos creeping down his arms and the side of his neck. He had on a tight black tee. I had to wonder if those tattoos decorated his chest or back as well. Or maybe his lean hips encased in denim. Were there tattoos hidden there too? He was beautiful to look at, but terrifying all the same. I loved the feel of his hand holding mine, but I wasn't fooled. This man would want a strong woman. Not one like me. Broken. Used. Scared. No. He'd feel pity. He'd want to be a white knight. Lord knew I needed one.

The second we walked inside the big room, a roar or greeting went up, and several men stepped forward with women at their sides. It was early in the morning. I estimated about seven or so, but the great room was full of men and women. The men all wore black vests with patches that indicated what looked like their names and rank within the club. One with the name *Cain* on one shoulder and *President* on the other stepped forward, offering his hand to Styx.

"Good to see you, Styx. Red keepin' you straight?"

"As anyone could, I suppose." Styx pulled me closer and put his arms around me gently. "This is Jolene. She could use Mama's care, if she's available."

Cain glanced at me then back at Styx with a raised eyebrow. Styx just leveled him with a steady gaze.

"Mama's been waiting for her," the woman at Cain's side said. She reached for me, pulling me from Styx gently but firmly. She frowned at Styx but said nothing about his proprietary gesture. "I'm Angel," she said. "Cain's my husband. He's president of Bones, but don't let that scare you off. He's always here if you need him. All the boys are."

"Why would I need them?" I asked, truly puzzled.

"To take care of… problems you can't otherwise solve yourself."

"I don't have anything like that," I said, getting exactly what she meant. "Anything that needs taken care of, I'll do myself."

Angel glanced up at Cain. "I'm sure you can," she said softly. "They just like to make it so you don't have to." Then she smiled gently. "Come on. The quicker Mama looks at you, the quicker Styx can relax."

"Yeah. I'm afraid he's gonna get an ulcer." I tried to make it sarcastic, but Angel just smiled. "They do tend to worry overmuch. How long have you known Styx?"

I shrugged. "Technically? Three or so hours. But I think I slept most of the way here, so… fifteen? Twenty minutes?"

That seemed to shock Angel. "Well. I can see why you're confused." Before I could question her further, she urged me farther inside. "Come along, dear. Let's get Mama to have a look at you, then I'll help you get settled."

Before I could stop myself, I glanced back over my shoulder at Styx. His gaze was fastened on me. Though I'd tried to have all this bravado, the thought of leaving the man who'd picked me up, kept me safe, and gotten me the hell outta Dodge sent panic flooding through my mind. I stopped dead in my tracks, my gaze clinging to Styx's.

"Go on, honey. I'll be right behind you."

"I… Can you just come on now?" I said it before I thought, then stiffened. "I mean… Never mind. I got this." I put my shoulders back and my head up. I could absolutely do this. I was going with a woman to meet another woman. I turned back to Angel. "There won't be any men, will there?"

"Pops is Mama's companion. He helps her sometimes, but if you don't want him there, he won't be."

All at once, sweat erupted over my body, and I started to tremble. A strange man. I tried to say something, to insist it was fine, but I couldn't. The words wouldn't come. I couldn't *breathe*.

"Styx," I whispered. My legs gave out, and I would have fallen on my ass, but strong arms caught me, pulling me against a hard, strong body.

"I got you, honey. I got you."

"I-I c-can't..." I sucked in air, trying to catch my breath.

"You gotta take slow, deep breaths, baby. You're hyperventilating." Styx scooped me up in his arms. I wrapped mine around his neck and held on for dear life, burying my face in his wide chest.

Then the tears came. And came.

I have no idea what happened next. All I knew was the whole night hit me. Hard. All at once.

There was a small prick to my upper arm that made me yelp. It didn't really hurt so much as it startled me.

"There," a slightly rough but feminine voice said softly. "Give the medicine time to work, and she'll calm down."

"I'd bet my last dollar she's gonna be pissed as hell when she realized what happened," Styx murmured softly above me. I was still wrapped tightly in his arms, clinging to him.

"Then it's your job to make sure she understands it's perfectly natural. Anyone can tell by looking at her she's been through a lot. You find who did this to her, and you make the son of a bitch pay. You hear me, young man?"

"I hear you, Mama. It will be my most sincere pleasure." He spoke low, but I could hear the intent in his voice even through my pain. He had every intention of bringing me justice. Which just made me cry again. Fuck. I needed to get a grip on myself.

"Crying never helped anything," I mentally told myself. It was something I often told myself when things got hard. I learned early on I was never going to be my poppy's favorite. I was his second wife's first child. The one she hadn't wanted because I "disfigured" her, as she called it. She'd been twenty when I was born, and very slight of body. She'd gained fifty pounds while pregnant with me and, apparently, my father never let her forget it. Instead of either fixing the problem or just leaving the bastard, she'd blamed me.

After that, she'd had another child before trying to skip town with a sizable bank account without my father's permission. He'd shut that down. Hard. And we never saw my mother again. His third and current wife had tried to make it hard on all of us. I was the only one who fought back. My sister meekly stayed in the shadows, doing little things for her to get in her good graces. Once she'd made herself indispensable to our new stepmother, she'd started taking her shots at me. Especially since Poppy's new wife had two more kids and there was real competition to be Poppy's favorite.

While his wife might technically get half his wealth when he died, he could -- and did -- make his will to suit his moods. The goal was to always be at the top. I was never going to be there and had realized early on I had no desire to be. Not if it meant groveling and submitting to his cruel whims. I'd watched more than one of my sisters be given to a business associate in payment of services or for one favorable deal or another. I never wanted that to be me. So I fought. Got physically hurt more than once. And crying hadn't helped any of it.

"No," the elderly female voice agreed. "But it can help you feel better. Especially when you have a big, strong male in your corner letting you get it all out."

I looked up. My one good eye was now puffy and probably red. The other one was nearly swollen shut from the beating I'd taken. "Did I say that out loud?"

She smiled kindly at me. "I won't tell if you won't." I decided right then that I really liked this woman. "Now. We haven't been formally introduced, but I'm Mama. I presume you're Jolene?" When I nodded, she continued. "If you let me look you over and maybe take a few X-rays, you can go rest."

"Did you give me a shot?" Not that it mattered, but I wanted to know.

"I did, child. Just a little something to help relax you. I'll give you something for pain, too, before you leave. No use suffering when I can make it easier for you."

"I... I only have a couple hundred dollars," I said. "But I'll pay you what I have."

"Nonsense," she said. The woman scowled at me. Much like a grandmother might if you were ever stupid enough to try to pay her for the chocolate chip cookies she made you. "You'll let me do this so I know in my heart your body will heal."

"You sound like him," I said, indicating Styx. "He blackmailed me into letting you examine me."

She glanced at Styx. "That true, boy?"

Styx just shrugged. "Ain't denyin' it."

"What'd you blackmail her with?"

"Just told her she owed me for the ride from West Virginia to Kentucky. As repayment, she had to let you examine her."

"Hum... not sure that actually qualifies as blackmail, but if it works, who cares." She grinned at me. "You let this one have his way in this, won't you?"

"I just don't want everyone putting themselves out for me. I may not look like it, but I'm a survivor. I'll make it through this."

"I have no doubt you will, sweetheart," Mama said. "And we'll all help you survive. That's what the men and women in this club do. We help each other survive. Thrive. Now. I have one question."

"What's that?"

"Do you want Styx to leave while I do this?"

Reflexively, my grip on Styx tightened. "I --"

Mama raised a hand and shook her head. "Your reaction is all I need. He can stay as long as you need him."

I looked up at Styx, expecting to see pity or something equally embarrassing. Instead, he just met my gaze with his steady one. "I'm here, Jolene. I'm not going anywhere unless you want me gone."

"I'm not used to having someone with me," I whispered. "Why do I need you with me?"

"Doesn't matter," he said immediately. "All that matters is that you want me here. I'm here. And I ain't goin' nowhere."

* * *

Styx

I wasn't sure if I was going to go back to West

Virginia to kill a motherfucker, or sit there and let Jolene rip my heart out with every new injury Mama revealed. Once Jolene threw her lot in with me, she was all in. She looked to me for everything. I could tell she liked Mama. Trusted her, even. But she always wanted my approval. Even when Mama asked to examine her privates, instead of making her own decision, she looked up at me with trembling lips. I knew she didn't want to do it, but I knew she needed it.

"It's up to you, baby. But you need this. If you're hurt or need medicine, Mama needs to know."

Very softly, she said. "I probably need a Morning After pill or something. They used condoms but I don't wanna take a chance. And yeah. One of 'em… The first time… He came inside me," she finally managed to whisper.

"I'll get you some antibiotics, too," Mama said. "Just in case. Will you let me have a quick look? If you have tears, we need to address them so you heal."

Jolene looked so miserable, I wanted to stop Mama from doing this. Instead I moved to set her on the exam table. I got a thick blanket from a cabinet and draped it over her lower body and sat beside her in a chair at the head of the table.

"I'm right here. I'll hold your hand, and I'll never take my eyes off your face. No one's gonna embarrass you. No one's judgin'. I'm your support. You take what you need to get through this from me."

She nodded several times, just a miniscule movement, but an affirmative nonetheless. Mama undressed her from the waist down while I talked to her, letting her hold my hand while Mama did what she had to.

"It's not as bad as I'd feared," Mama said. "Can I

wash you, Jolene? I need to put some cream on these lacerations, and you should be as clean as you can when I do." Jolene just nodded, closing her eyes as color swept up her neck to her face. The part that wasn't turning reddish purple pinkened in her embarrassment. "I'm going to give you some mild cleanser to use in a sitz bath. You need to do it every day at least twice a day for a week. Then you'll need to dry yourself carefully and apply the cream. You'll be able to feel the small tears. Wear loose-fitting cotton underwear and pants for at least a week." She smiled, patting Jolene's knee. "You're young. I think your physical wounds will heal nicely. You'll let Styx work on the emotional ones, won't you?"

"Yes, Mama," she said softly.

"Good. Now. All done. You need antibiotics and something to prevent pregnancy. I'll get both for you. You'll have to take the antibiotics for the next ten days, but they should cover most of the common things. If you start to have abdominal pain or excessive itching or pain or any discharge that shouldn't be there, let me know immediately, and I'll do a culture to make sure you're covered properly on medicine."

"This is so fucked up," Jolene said, her voice starting to quiver again. "I'm so sorry to put you to so much trouble, Mama. I'm sorry I wasn't brave enough for you to have Pops with you." She sniffed and cleared her throat, obviously trying to get her emotions under control. "I'm sure he helps so you don't have to do it all."

"Nonsense, child. You're no trouble, and I'm fine without Pops. The most important thing is for you to be comfortable and to feel safe. You're not ready for men to see you in such a vulnerable situation. And I understand how intensely vulnerable you feel. I'm just glad you recognize Styx is your protector. Let him fill that role for you."

Jolene looked up at me with a solemn expression on her face. "For now."

I raised an eyebrow, surprised at that. "For now?"

"I'm not weak. I just… this was a bit intense. Even for my family. I'll be fine in a day or two. Then I'll take care of those shithill Hatfields."

"Hatfields?" Mama looked up at me sharply.

"Not now, Mama. This ain't the time."

"You better make time, Styx. Now," Mama snapped.

"I got this. I promise."

Mama handed me a bottle of pills and Jolene a couple in a small paper cup along with a bottle of water. When she spoke next, Mama was calm, her kind, grandmotherly impression fully intact. "Drink up, dear. Then you get some rest. Today's Friday. You come see me Sunday, you hear me? I want you resting until then."

Yeah. Last thing I needed was Mama breaking the news to Jolene that I was a Hatfield, too. But she was also right. I needed to tell her. And I would. Just as soon as she got stronger. If I told her now, it would take away her safe place, and she desperately needed this safe place.

"You got two choices," I said, leaning down to stroke a lock of hair out of her face. She still had big hanks of duct tape matting her hair. It pained me to see all that beautiful auburn hair ruined. I wasn't sure how I was gonna fix that, but I knew I had to try.

"What's that?" She didn't meet my gaze as she asked but looked off to the side. I could almost feel the shame radiating off her.

"Ol' ladies got you a room deep in their territory of the building. You'll have privacy, and no one will bother you if you don't want them to. You'll have the protection of their men as well as all the officers in this whole place."

"What's the other option?" She shivered a little, still not meeting my gaze. So I cupped her cheek and gently turned her face to mine. When she still tried to gaze off, I moved so that I was in her line of sight whether she wanted me there or not.

"You come with me. I help you clean up, then watch over you while you sleep. You'll have privacy from everyone but me. And I'll make sure no one bothers you if you don't want them to."

She let loose a little sob, her gaze trying to slide from mine, but she was unable to commit to the action. The longer she looked at me, the more she seemed to cling with her gaze. She wanted me in her sight as much as I wanted her in mine.

"I -- I d-don't know w-what to d-do." Her bottom lip quivered, and I knew she was going to have another breakdown. And who could blame the poor girl. She'd been through hell.

"Do you trust me, Jolene?"

She seemed to think it over. Not answering right away, but not moving her gaze away from mine either. After long, long moments, she nodded. Then whispered, "Yes."

"Good." I scooped her up. "Mama, tell the girls to bring her some clothes. Tell them to put them in a backpack and set it outside my door. I want breakfast delivered in the morning."

"Ain't your Goddamned messenger, Styx," Mama groused. "Or your servant! But I'll do it for that sweet girl. After tomorrow morning, though, you're on your fuckin' own. And you better tell her everything she needs to know. Get me?" Yeah. Mama was put out. She had a right to be. But I'd tell Jolene. Just not right this minute. She'd had enough. She was done.

"Don't worry. I'll take care of that soon."

"You better. 'Cause if you don't, I will."

Chapter Three
Styx

"Bathroom's just there." I carried Jolene to my room and put her down in the bedroom next to the adjoining bathroom door. "There's everything in there you need for a bath or a shower. Take your pick." She looked up at me, then to the door, but made no move to open it. I sighed, then did it for her. There was a combination shower/bathtub in the corner. Not swimming-pool size, but large and spacious with plenty of room for a comfortable bath if she wanted to soak. She seemed to have lost her bravado, and I hated seeing her like this. I got the feeling the real Jolene was more like the woman who'd declared she was gonna "take care of those shithill Hatfields." This girl, this lost, broken girl, still needed to lick her wounds. I just wasn't sure how to help her.

"I'll be out here if you need me. You can leave the door open if you need to."

She nodded but only wrapped her arms around herself, moving to the vanity. She gazed at herself in the mirror. No secret she was a mess to look at. Mama had cleaned up the cuts and scrapes, but her face was bruised and swollen. Her hair was matted with duct tape, and she was still grimy. Glancing around, she opened a drawer and pulled out a pair of scissors.

"Honey," I said, moving to take the scissors from her. "Why don't we save that for last. I'll see if I can help you with it."

Without a word, she started hacking off hair above the tape. I winced and lunged for her, but she just threw out a hand to hold me back.

"I got this," she said softly. Then she kept cutting until all the tape was out. That left long hanks of hair that reached nearly to her ass. If washed and brushed, I was sure they would brush the delicate swell of her cheeks and beyond. But not once she got finished with it. She cut all the length, tossing lock after lock into the trash can beside the vanity. "Stupid hair just gets in the way anyhow," she muttered as she continued the grim task. Tears streamed down her cheeks with every single cut she made.

When she was done, her hair was almost in a pixie cut, cropped all over her head only a couple of inches long. She was trembling and silently crying, but she looked determined to not be upset about what she'd just done. She looked fierce, but vulnerable. The image she presented made me want to wrap her up and put her behind some kind of impenetrable defensive shield. But that was impossible. Didn't mean I couldn't use my own body as her shield. Between her and the rest of the world.

Once she set the scissors down, I picked them up along with a comb and snipped off strands of long hair she'd missed. She let me until I had everything cleaned up. Then I placed my hands gently on her shoulders.

"You need a bath, honey. Do you want me to run it for you?"

"I'll never be clean again, you know," she said, almost as if she were in a trance. "I'll always be dirty."

"You ain't dirty, Jolene. A bath will help you cleanse your mind. Soothe your muscles. But you were never dirty. They're the dirty ones. And they're gonna pay."

"They made me dirty."

"Wrong again, baby. They tried, but you survived. You were brave enough to let me bring you here and to let people you didn't know help you." I was silent until she met my gaze in the mirror. "Now you're gonna keep letting us all help. But most especially me. You're gonna let me fumble my way through this and let me be what you need me to be. 'Cause I ain't goin' away."

"Why, Styx?" she asked softly. "Why would you want to be with someone like me? I'm used up."

I shook my head. "You ain't. You're just a little broken. But you're strong. You have fire. I'm gonna help you heal, then I'm makin' you mine. You get me?"

She shook her head, closing her eyes. "Don't say shit like that. You don't want me, and I ain't gonna be a pity fuck."

"Ain't nobody said you was. And there ain't nothin' 'bout you to pity." I sighed. "Got some stuff to tell you later. But trust me when I tell you, I know the kind of person you are. You're special. In that whole clan of Hatfields and McCoys, you're probably the only one of 'em worth a good Goddamn. Never seen a more kind and giving person than Jolene McCoy."

Her lips parted. "You know me? I don't know you."

"Not personally, Jolene. But I heard'a ya. Heard how smart you are. How you didn't belong in that little town with all your kin. Also heard how your old man was a fuckin' bastard to you and your mom made your life hell. You didn't deserve none'a that then. And you don't now." I squeezed her shoulders, leaning in to kiss her temple. She didn't flinch away, nor did her gaze waver from mine. Her eyes were wide and, for the first time, I thought she might actually be with me completely in the here and now. "You want me to leave while you bathe? Said I'd wait out in the bedroom. You can leave the door open, so you'll know where I am."

She shook her head. "Don't leave."

I nodded. "Fine. Ain't goin' anywhere. I'm right here."

Carefully, she removed her clothes, keeping her back to me, though she didn't move away from the vanity mirror. I tried to keep my thoughts clinical, taking in every bruise and cut and scrape for the second time. While Mama had examined her, I'd memorized them all. I did again now, vowing I'd kill the pissant who did this to her.

As she stepped into the shower, she glanced over her shoulder at me. "You won't leave? You promise?"

"Not if you want me here, Jolene. I'm your protector as long as you'll have me." I meant it, too. It was more than I'd ever offered a woman. Not because I didn't believe in protecting women, but because it was too much like a commitment. Especially with Jolene. I wasn't big on commitment, but she was wrapping me up in some kind of spell, and I knew the offer was not only genuine, but as much a promise as it was a threat. I also knew that my promise earlier to make her mine was the same. I wasn't sure I could stop being her protector even if she wanted me to. And I damned sure was making her mine as soon as she was ready. Hell, as far as I was concerned, she already was mine. I didn't need sex with her to stake my claim.

"I don't want you to leave," she said, her voice trembling slightly. "I feel safe when you're with me."

I shook my head, holding my arms out to her. "I'm right here. Ain't goin' nowhere."

She nodded, then stepped into the shower. I leaned back against the vanity, crossing my arms over my chest, and tried not to see the woman in the shower. I needed to see the bruises and battered girl who'd been gang-raped and beaten, not the desirable woman she was. What I did was concentrate on every single bruise marring her fair skin and promised myself that the men who'd done this to her would experience every single injury she had. Including the rape. *Especially* the rape. She'd said Hatfields hurt her. I had an idea who it might have been because they'd done it before. No matter what, there were several people gonna die. But if it was who I thought it was -- if it was Avery Hatfield and his brother and fuckin' cousins -- they were gonna die hard. Very hard.

I watched as she slowly cleaned herself with my shower gel, then washed her hair. Every now and then she smothered a groan. Then she'd stop moving for a few seconds before continuing at a slower pace. The third time she did this, I couldn't take it anymore.

"You're hurtin'."

"Sore."

This was awkward. "Is there anything I can do to help?"

She was silent for a long moment. I knew she wanted me to do something but was hesitant to ask. I could guess it had something to do with me getting in there with her, but she was probably too terrified for a strange male to be in such an intimate position with her.

"You look familiar to me," she finally answered, her voice barely above a whisper. "You look like a guy I used to know when I was a little girl, though I thought you'd look older. So maybe I'm wrong?"

"You're not wrong, Jolene. It's what Mama was tellin' me I had to make you understand. Just didn't want you not to trust me 'cause'a my name."

"Ruben Hatfield," she whispered, her body shivering under the hot spray. "You gonna hurt me, too?" She sounded resigned. Fucking *resigned*!

I stomped the three steps to the shower and

shoved open the door. She whimpered and ducked into herself, her arms drawn tightly into her chest, her one good blue eye wide in fear. I took a calming breath before stepping in the shower with her. I was fully dressed while she was naked. It was the worst idea I'd ever had, but I couldn't seem to help myself. She needed comfort. I needed to give it.

"Ain't no one ever hurtin' you again, Jolene," I snapped. "Not fuckin' Avery Hatfield or his fucking family, not me. No one. You hear me?" I didn't sound calm at all.

She gave a terrified nod immediately, and I realized she didn't get me at all. And, sweet Jesus, she was so fucking beautiful it hurt. Even covered in bruises, her face half swollen, she was the most beautiful woman I'd ever seen.

"Fuck," I muttered, scrubbing a hand over my face to clear it of the spray from the shower. "I'm sorry. I ain't gonna hurt you, Jolene. And I'm gonna find my kin and take care of this shit."

"They're bad people, Styx," she said, not using my given name. Which I was fine with. "I knew they hurt women. Just guess I ignored it when Avery took a likin' to me. I thought he was different."

"He's rotten from the inside out. Just like the rest of 'em in that area. Both families, Jolene. At least, in Williamson. Met others in different parts of the state and country who are decent people. Ain't sure why this bunch is bad, but they are."

I stepped forward and urged her to turn around to put her back to the shower spray. "Lean your head back. I'll get the soap out of your hair." Surprisingly, she did it with no fuss. She still trembled a little, but I thought it was the aftereffect of adrenaline, both from the previous night and her fright now. Her body expected to have to make a run for it and hadn't yet caught up with her mind. "You ready to get out or do you need more time?"

"I'm done," she said. I got out before her and reached for a towel to hand her. She took it, wrapping it around her immediately. I sighed, then handed her another one.

"That was a dick move on my part," I muttered. "I don't like you seein' me same as my half-brother, but you don't know me. Why wouldn't you think I was like him?"

"You're not," she said softly. "You've been nothing but kind."

I snagged my own towel and pulled off my wet shirt, drying as I went. "You've got your backpack on the table. If you need anything else, there's another backpack by the door. Mama got the ol' ladies to bring you anything they thought you'd need."

I thought she'd scurry away from me, but she didn't. "You'll need clothes, too."

"Yeah. I've got some lounge pants in here."

"You're wet." She looked like she was in a trance as she looked at me. Her gaze was glued to my chest and, as she approached, she reached out to lay one small, pale hand over my heart.

"Yeah, baby," I said, my voice gone husky. This girl didn't need me like this. She needed tender and gentle. Someone to keep her demons away, but from a distance.

She met my gaze, her one good eye sparkling at me. "You're beautiful."

"Not me, honey. That's all you."

She flinched back like I'd struck her. "Don't lie," she hissed. "That's what *he* did."

"Ain't lyin', Jolene. You're a beautiful girl.

Always have been."

That made her gasp in surprise. "I was a kid when you were last in Williamson."

"Never said that. I seen you. From a distance, but I seen you. Didn't recognize you earlier 'cause of the beatin' you took, but I know exactly who you are. The only McCoy or Hatfield in the whole fuckin' town who didn't belong."

"No, I guess I didn't."

I was fucking this up. Royally. "You're special, Jolene. Everyone in town knows it, but they're too afraid of your family and mine to admit it."

"They show me favorable attention, they bring down the wrath of both families," she muttered. "Mine because they hate me. Yours because they hate McCoys."

"Pretty much, baby."

She would have dropped her hand, but I covered it with my own. I didn't force her to keep it there. I would have let her go if she'd tugged. But she didn't. She just looked up at me with that one blue eye. I reached out with my other hand and gently stroked the skin underneath her swollen eye.

"You have no idea how it pains me to see this." My voice was huskier than I wanted her to hear. "It's an abomination."

"It's life."

"Ain't neither." Fuck. I'd been in South Florida for years. I'd lost my accent years ago. Now, I sounded just like every Hatfield in West Virginia. "God as my witness, Jolene. This'll never happen to you again."

A single tear dripped from her good eye, and she stepped into me. I wrapped my arms around her gently, not wanting her to feel like she couldn't get away from me if she needed to. She was tentative, not sure of herself. Probably still half afraid I'd hurt her.

"I just wanted to know what sex was like," she said into my chest. The words were so soft I nearly didn't hear her. "All my friends had done it, but I was still a virgin. Ain't no one in that town would touch me 'cause'a my pa. When Avery said he wanted us to be together, I didn't really believe him, but I thought he at least liked me."

"Avery's a swine, Jolene. Can you tell me what happened? Is it too close right now?"

She shivered. "I'm cold." And her standing there with me in my wet jeans wasn't helping.

"Let me get out of these wet clothes. You get dressed. After that, we'll talk."

"I can't look at you when I tell you."

"What do you want, then?"

She buried her head in my chest, careful of the bruised side of her face. "Maybe you could hold me while I did? I mean, if it's not too much trouble. And you don't mind or nothin'."

I groaned. "Honey, I'll hold you all you want. You sure you want a strange man this close to you?"

"You ain't a stranger." Her statement surprised me.

"You don't know me, Jolene. I'd say that makes me a stranger."

She looked up at me. "I know you helped me when I thought I was gonna die. I was still on my poppy's land. He'd already shot at me. If he found me, I expected he'd've killed me."

My temper flared. I wanted to punch something, but I couldn't. What I could do was reassure the woman in my arms, though. "I'll get revenge for you, Jolene. Both your pa and that little fuck Avery and his crew. Always knew I'd have to clean out that place sooner or later. I ran to Florida to keep from it, but I can see now that was a fuckin' mistake."

"I don't want you to do nothin', Styx. Just…" She took a deep breath before meeting my gaze once more. "Please don't play with me like Avery did." Her voice was scarcely above a whisper, but I heard the pain and anguish there.

"Then best you tell me what he did to you, so I don't repeat his mistake."

"You probably already have." She stepped away from me, and I wanted to yank her back to me, but knew better. I would not terrify the girl. Instead, I used the time to strip out of my wet jeans and throw on some cotton pants.

Jolene walked into the bedroom, clutching the damp towel to her while she went through her belongings. Then she looked in the bag I'd asked for and pulled out a pair of cotton shorts and a long T-shirt, putting both on quickly. I raised an eyebrow as I recognized the shirt as one of mine. I could only guess someone had stolen it from my own bag, but I didn't care. She pulled the neckline to her nose and inhaled deeply, her eyes sliding shut. She turned fully to me then, meeting my gaze with her forlorn one.

"It smells like you."

"'Cause it's mine."

"Oh." She blinked rapidly. "I'll give it back --"

"Absolutely not. You wear it, sweetheart." I crossed to her slowly, reaching for her. She took my hand willingly. "Now. Where do you want to do this?"

She sucked in a breath, her gaze going to my bare chest. I knew what I looked like. I was tattooed and scarred and muscled. Most women couldn't get enough of looking at me. Or touching me. I could only hope I was as appealing to my little Jolene.

"I can't..." She shook her head and cleared her throat. "I can't have sex yet. I think it'd hurt too much."

I shook my head. "Honey, no one said you had to. I thought you wanted me to hold you while you talked about this? If you've changed your mind, that's perfectly fine. If you don't want to look at me when you talk to me, you can sit on the couch. I'll get you a fuzzy blanket, tuck you in, then sit on the floor behind you. I can hear you. You can hear me. But you don't have to look at me or touch me."

"No! That's not what I meant." She dug her fingers into my sides like she was trying to hold me to her. "Can we... can we maybe lie on the bed? In the dark? I'll tell you everything that happened, but if I'm gonna relive it..."

"I hear you." I caressed the uninjured side of her face. "Go crawl in. I'll get a shirt and turn out the light."

She nodded and crawled into the bed. I threw on a shirt and shut out the light. I shut the windows so the blinds could block out the late-morning sun. I did leave one window open on the opposite side of the room. It let in light, but not direct sunlight, thanks to a huge-ass tree just outside the window. I thought she might find the sounds and scents as soothing as I did.

Very slowly, to give her time to change her mind, I sat on the bed, sliding under the covers. To my surprise, Jolene reached for me, letting me wrap my arms around her as she settled her head on my chest. In that moment, I knew I could happily lie there forever. Nothing else had to happen. Sure, she was a beautiful woman. One I wanted with every fiber of my being. But I was more content than I could ever remember just holding her. As long as she was in my arms like this, no one could harm her. Least of all our fucking families.

I thought she might just lie like that, trembling in my arms. I knew she wept softly, but she held it in. All but the tears. There was no way I was going to force her to talk about this. Hell, I kind of preferred she didn't. Just seeing the evidence of what had happened was bad enough. If she started describing what happened, I wasn't sure I wouldn't lose my mind. She might not have been my woman then, but she was now.

"The men who did this to me were Avery, his brother, Clyde, and five of their cousins. Avery wasn't in on the rape, but he told them where I'd be, and they had to be quick about it because he'd only paid for the room for an hour." I tried to just relax. I petted her hair for comfort, trying not to spook her when I wanted to jump up and pace. Before punching something. "You know what happened with that. What you don't know is that Avery recorded us having sex. He even promised he loved me. That we'd be the only Hatfields and McCoys to ever make a permanent match. That's how he got me to agree to have sex with him. I knew he didn't love me. I didn't love him."

"But the words meant something to you."

She nodded, letting out one small sob. "Then he betrayed me."

"I'm claimin' you as my ol' lady, Jolene," I said. "I know you don't know what that means, but it's permanent in my club. We're as good as married. Even before I put my property patch on your cut."

"Cut?" She stilled in my arms.

"A vest. On the back, it'll have my club emblem. This is Bones. My club is a sister club in Florida. Salvation's Bane. You'll have that patch and 'Property of' above it and 'Styx' below it."

"Property of Styx?"

"Yeah, but it's not like it sounds. Talk to Angel tomorrow. She'll explain it better'n I can. But you'll be mine."

"What about you?"

"I don't cheat, Jolene. Not ever. If that's what you're worried about."

She was quiet for a while. I'd almost dozed off when she finally said, "What if I can't have sex with you?"

"Always been good at jerkin' off, Jolene. No reason I gotta stop."

Surprisingly, she giggled. Just a small sound, but she clutched me tighter. "I'll try. Since you're my hero and all. I mean, Mama always said if you touched yourself, you'd go blind. I don't want that."

I thought about it for a minute, pretending to give it real thought when I wanted to laugh, myself. "I mean, yeah. I'd hate going blind. Wonder how many times you have to do it before that happens?"

"Don't know. How many times have you done it?"

"Way more'n I can count."

"That many?"

"Yeah, baby. That many."

Again she was quiet for a bit.

"Maybe we should try it pretty soon. I mean, if you can't count that high, you've got to be getting close to the point of no return."

I did laugh then. She did too. I kissed her forehead gently, tightening my hold on her. "You rest now. I gotta meet with Cain and my brothers here, but I won't be long. Then I'll spend the whole day with you. We'll get to know each other. Talk about my masturbation habits and what you're willing to do about it."

"Please don't break my heart, Ruben," she said, her voice quavering. "You took care of me. Helped me. Maybe I'm focusing on you because of all that, but I know I never cared about Avery the way I care about you. You've made me feel safe like I've never felt before in my life. I can't… If you don't feel the same way, that's fine. Just tell me. Don't make me think you want me when you only want something from me."

"Care about you, too, baby. I'll never willingly hurt you. Not ever."

"Good. Because I'd hate to have to carve up your balls."

Again, I laughed. "You're gonna fit right in, baby. You're a biker's ol' lady through and through. And they're some of the fiercest women I know."

She snuggled even closer, her fingers clutching my shirt. Then drifted off to sleep.

Chapter Four
Styx

I woke coming harder than I could ever remember doing in living memory. Especially from a wet dream. Even as consciousness slowly made me aware of my surroundings, I was sure I was still in a dream. Because, lying over me, head between my legs, mouth working my cock with tentative movements, was Jolene.

"Fuck!" I bit out. "Did I come?"

"Um-hum," she answered, her lips still around me. She wasn't pulling hard or anything. Just, sucking softly, licking around the slit in the head of my cock. Cleaning me up.

I groaned. "Fuuuuck…"

She giggled before pulling away and sitting up beside me. "I wanted to see if I could at least do this for you. I mean. In the interest of you keeping your sight and all."

"Baby," I said, reaching for her. She came willingly into my arms. "Fuckin' never wanna let you go."

"Was it good for you? I mean, you missed most of it, but it didn't seem to take long…"

"Yeah. I loved it. Not sure I've ever come that hard, and that's the fuckin' truth." I waited until she snuggled into my side and was still before I continued. "You know, you don't have to do that if you don't want to. We can go as slow or fast as you like, but I want you comfortable with any kind of sex we have."

"I was comfortable," she said. "I wanted to try it by myself." I glanced down at her. Her brow was furrowed as she seemed to struggle to find the words she needed. "Without anyone holding me down or pushing back? Does that make sense?"

"I get you. Feel free to experiment all you like. Whenever you like. Ain't never turnin' you down when you wanna give a blowjob." I chuckled. "Fuck, girl!" Then it hit me. "Wait. Did you swallow my cum?"

She stiffened. "Uh, yeah? Was I not supposed to do that?"

"Honey, you can do whatever you want. I just didn't expect it. And you never *have* to."

"I never really liked it before," she confessed. "I mean, the couple times I've done it. But I like your taste."

She was killing me. I'd just come in what felt like a flood, and I was already hard again. Her soft hand closed around me again.

"You're still hard. Do you need more?" She looked up at me. Was that a hopeful look in her eye?

"Baby, I'll take what you want to give. But I was thinkin' you might want some of your own." At her blank look, I grinned. "'Cause it's time for your first sitz bath anyway. As long as I do not touch any sore spots, I can lick your clit as long as you want me to. Then you can soak so you ain't sore or uncomfortable."

She sucked in a breath, her eyes going wide. "You mean…"

I barked out a laugh. "Oh, yeah. I mean that exactly. Up to you, though. I don't want you uncomfortable, and more importantly, I don't want to scare you."

She thought for a moment. "What if…" She bit her lip and looked away, obviously uncomfortable with discussing sex this frankly.

"Tell me, baby. What did you have in mind?"

"Well, I mean, if you wouldn't mind me being on

top. I've never done it before, so it might smother you..." Jolene sighed, like she was defeated, but she also looked frustrated to hell and back.

"Are you talkin' 'bout a sixty-nine?"

Her head snapped up. "Yes! That! Only with me on top."

"Get your ass up here, little girl," I growled, pulling her toward me, urging her to straddle my face. "Do not let me hurt you. You hear me? You feel the first twinge of panic, you stop me. It burns you, stop me. Roll off me, bite me if I won't let you go fast enough. I absolutely will *not* have you hurt by this. You get me?"

"Oh, God," she responded as she settled herself. It took everything in me to not smack her ass. Which would have been a huge mistake. Instead, I gripped her ass tightly with one hand.

"Answer me, Jolene. I need to know you understand... AHH!"

She swallowed my cock like she was starving. I shuddered, gripping her ass with my hands. I had to be careful. With her positioned like she was, I could see the damage those bastards had done. It didn't look too bad, but it had to sting a little when her natural juices flowed.

"Stop, Jolene," I snapped, putting every ounce of command I could manage.

"Mmmm..." she moaned around my dick, sucking me down as she hummed. She wiggled her ass, over top of me, thrusting her hips at me in an instinctive move. When her pussy connected with my chin, she seemed to zero in on it and rubbed her clit over my face with small snaps of her hips. Her gasps told me she had the spot she wanted and, fuck, if she didn't keep moving.

Deciding there was no stopping this unless she did, I just went with it. My dick was pulsing in her mouth, on the verge of filling her with my cum. Her pussy was right at my face. Right where I could stick out my tongue and lick to my heart's content. She was the aggressor here. I was just along for the ride.

"Fuck it," I muttered, and found her clit with my lips and tongue. The second I did, she stiffened and let loose a muffled scream around my cock. Her pussy gushed, and I lapped her up eagerly, needing this taste of her. To devour her when I needed to be gentle no matter how lost in pleasure she was. I absolutely would not pull her out of this pleasure unless she became distressed. As I saw it, it was my job to see she *didn't* get distressed.

Then she did something completely unexpected. She took my cock deep until I felt her muscles massaging the head while she swallowed me down. Literally.

I wanted to hold her pussy to my mouth so I could lap up her juice, but the thought of hurting her, of making those small tears burn or sting in the middle of her obvious pleasure prevented me from it. Instead, I licked and sucked her clit, doing my best to keep her on the verge of coming without pushing her over, but when she reached that point, she took control, rubbing herself over my face. It was the most fun I'd ever seen a woman have during sex. Jolene took her pleasure and gave even more back to me.

It didn't take long for her to come again. Then again. She was dripping juices over my face, and I tried my best to catch as much as I could. She was wet, and her clit was swollen where I'd sucked on it and with her arousal.

When I finally felt her start to falter, her

enthusiasm waning, I let myself go.

"Gonna come, baby," I bit out. "You don't want it in your mouth, you're gonna have to let up." She took me deeper, swallowing over and over as if readying herself for the load to come. "Fuck!" I shouted my release as I came in a punishing rush. After the first round when I woke up, I never thought I could come this hard again, but Jolene seemed to have magic in her touch, because I came hard enough to arch my back and clench my muscles painfully. I couldn't do more than suck in a much-needed breath as she swallowed everything I had to give her.

Once I'd finished, Jolene let my cock slip from her lips and collapsed over me. I rubbed her ass and thighs, letting her take her time coming back to reality. Because, really, she'd plumb checked out, lost in her own pleasure. Her head lay on my thigh while she still straddled me, but it was a comfortable position. I could still smell her musky-sweet pussy, clean and fresh, making me want another taste when I'd just eaten my fill.

"We need to get you cleaned up, baby," I finally said, not really wanting to move at all. "The quicker we can get you well, the more comfortable you'll be. Those tears have got to be stinging."

"It does sting a little now. It didn't before." She sounded dazed and sleepy. Poor thing.

"You were enjoying yourself before. Didn't notice. Now you're feelin' it." I gently set her off me before climbing out of bed and reaching for her naked form. Seeing all the bruises on her body again gave me a visceral reaction. My chest tightened, and a surge of white-hot anger shot through my body. "Never met a woman as naturally sensual as you, Jolene," I murmured. "We shouldn't'a done that, but only thing I regret is you hurtin' now."

"It was wonderful," she said, her slender arms around my neck. She buried her face in my throat and kissed tentatively before abruptly pulling back .

"Why'd you stop?"

"I wasn't sure if it was allowed." She seemed to burrow deeper against me.

"Honey, you had my dick down your throat. Why in the world would you think you couldn't kiss me?"

"Well, when you put it like that," she muttered.

"Speakin' of which, you sucked me off, and I ain't even kissed you yet." I winked at her. "You know I gotta remedy that soon. Right?"

She shivered in my arms, clinging tighter to me. "I really want to do that," she said, turning her face up to me. "My lip's still busted."

"I know, baby. It's in my best interest to get you well so you can explore to your heart's content. I want you to do everything you've ever wanted. But I want you to do it with me."

She looked up at me, studying me. I needed to set her on her feet so I could help get her pan of water ready, but there was something about the expression on her face that made me pause.

"Say what's on your mind, sweetheart. We don't hold anything back from each other."

"Why are you bein' so nice to me, Styx? Your family and mine hate each other."

"I ain't doin' you like Avery did, if that's what you're askin'. That little fucker and his kin are gonna pay for that." I sighed. "Let me tell you somethin'. The people here don't know me well, except for Shadow and Cain. We work together sometimes, but mostly it's the members of Bane who work for ExFil I'm teamed with for missions."

"ExFil?"

"Yeah. Cain owns it. It's a paramilitary company. We're the guys the government sends in when they don't want an actual military presence somewhere. But we're also contracted out to do extractions of civilians being held hostage or lost in a dangerous area. We do stuff both sanctioned and unsanctioned by our government and others. We're really tight. Which is why Bane and Bones are sister clubs. Anyway, I want you to talk to Cain and Shadow. They'll tell you all my dirty secrets. I'll take you to the garage, too, once we get back to Florida. Talk to Red. He's my boss there, but also talk to his ol' lady, Rosanna. She can tell you what kinda man I am. And I'm not exaggerating when I say every single one of those people, especially Rosanna, will tell you the bad before they tell you the good."

"So it don't matter to you I'm a McCoy?"

"I could give a good Goddamn who your family is, Jolene. Beyond the fact that I'm gonna have a bunch a killin' to do."

"You don't have to do that," she said. For the first time, she pushed against me, wanting down. I let her go, but I didn't like it. "I'll take care of those bastards myself."

"Girl, don't go makin' me hard again. 'Cause the thought of you standin' over them boys, their bloody balls in your hand after you've sliced 'em off, turns me the fuck on."

She blinked up at me, her mouth open as if she intended to say something, but was unable to find the words. "You're crazy," she finally settled on, but her lips twitched.

"Never said I wasn't."

"I'm scared, Styx," she admitted. I could see that admission cost her, too. She turned her back to me. "You're nothing like I would have expected from any man, let alone a Hatfield. You're definitely not like your brothers or cousins."

"OK," I said, turning her to face me. I cupped her face in my hands. "You look at me, and you listen. Listen good." She obeyed, sadness and fear shining brightly, but I could see her pushing through it as hard as she could. "I'm not my family. You're not your family. We both fought hard to get out, and we made it. Now, we're gonna rely on each other. I'll help you. You'll help me. And when it comes time to cleanse the world of those motherfuckers, you're gonna let me take care of it. Me and my club."

"I can't ask you to do that."

"You ain't. I'm doin' it 'cause you're my woman, and nobody hurts my woman."

She sighed. "Styx, you didn't even know me before you picked me up on the side of the road."

"Did too," I said quickly. "Just didn't know you was gonna be my woman until I picked you up and put you beside me in my truck."

"And you're sure now? Because we don't know each other. I mean, what we just shared changed everything for me, Styx. And I mean everything." She met my gaze as boldly as anyone I've ever talked with. "After what happened, I never thought I'd enjoy sex. Ever."

"Didn't you enjoy it before?"

She shook her head. "Styx, I gave a few blowjobs for kicks, but I was a virgin. I gave that to Avery. Not because I truly thought he loved me, but because I thought he wanted me. I thought I wanted him, but I knew pretty quickly it was just an excuse. I wanted sex.

I wanted the experience of it."

I couldn't help myself. I pulled her into my arms and just held her. "You get better, baby. You let those fuckin' injuries heal, and I'll give you all the experience you want. Christ, you're breakin' my heart!"

"Just don't…"

"Ain't gonna let you down, baby. I got you."

* * *

Jolene

"Cain needs you, Styx. I'll take you to church." The man at the door was Carnage. I'd learned he used to be a member of Salvation's Bane but, due to Cain sending him on missions with men from Bones more and more, he'd been patched over by Bones and was now a member of this club.

"What's up?" Styx didn't immediately get up. I'd fixed taters and sauerkraut and wieners and cornbread for supper tonight instead of us joining the party in the common room. That was fucking *awesome*! But I'd just wanted some quiet time with Styx. Mainly, I'd wanted to show him I could cook and would be a good woman to him. I'd been trying hard since that first day. Keeping our room clean, washing his clothes, cooking when I had stuff. Basically, making a home when this wasn't his home. I felt kind of silly, but I had no idea what kind of expectations Styx had, and I was determined to anticipate his wants and needs.

"Just an update on everything. Figured since you were here you'd want to attend. You ain't Bones, but close enough." Carnage shrugged, his gaze straying to me slightly before returning to Styx. Instantly, Styx's whole demeanor changed.

"Give me five minutes."

"I have pie if you want to take it with you," I

said, turning to grab the pie plate where I'd made a butterscotch pie. "It was my Grandmother Rose's recipe."

His gaze zeroed in on the pie. "Butterscotch?" I nearly giggled when his tongue darted out to wet his lips and he rubbed his belly with his hand.

"Yeah. She said there wasn't a Hatfield or McCoy what could make a better butterscotch pie than her."

He reached for the pie with both hands, snagging a fork from the table. "Ain't promisin' I'll share, but I promise it'll get ate."

"Now, just a Goddamn minute," Carnage protested, taking a step toward Styx. "Anything goes to church at Bones gets shared."

"Yeah? Fuck you. How 'bout sharin' that?" Styx said, flipping the other biker off while curling his other arm protectively around the pie.

"I can make another one," I said quickly. "Share that one, and I'll have you a new one made by the time you get back."

Styx bared his teeth at Carnage. "Fucker. You know damned good and well officers'll take first dibs. By the time it gets to me, there won't be a fuckin' thing left."

"Well, come on, then. Let's get this over with, and your woman will have you one made all for yourself."

Styx sighed. "Fine." He glanced at me. "Don't like leavin' Jolene here."

"It's not like she won't be perfectly fine. I can get Cain to send Angel and some of the other ol' ladies over if you want."

"I'm fine," I said. "I'll just wait here until you get back." It had been two weeks since I'd come here with Styx, and I knew there were things going on I didn't know about. I got the feeling it had something to do with me, but Styx just told me not to worry about it. He said all I needed to do was let my body heal, and that he'd take care of anything needing taken care of. Which didn't sit well with me. If there was something going on with my family and the Maybach, then I wanted in on it. But really, the odds of whatever was going on being about that car were slim to none. These guys were super careful. Anyone could tell that. If my poppy was looking for that car, they would never find it here.

True to my word, I made another pie. I'd just pulled it out of the oven when I heard a commotion outside our window. At first, I ignored it. There was all kinds of stuff going on around the compound and not much of it quiet.

Then there was a gunshot. And the top of the window glass crunched as a bullet passed through the pane to imbed in the wall across the room. I shrieked, dropping to the ground and crawling toward the door.

"Jolene! You fuckin' cunt! Get your fuckin' ass out here a'fore I kill every single person in this fuckin' place!"

Poppy. Marshall McCoy. How had he found us? And how had he known which room I was in? Because there was no way he shot that window out by accident.

"Yeah, Jolene. Get your ass outta there and tell us what you done with the Maybach!" That was my eldest brother, Alex. So, they knew where I was but not the car.

No way.

I scrambled to my backpack and dumped everything in it out onto the floor. I was frantically searching the contents when the door burst open. I screamed and dove under the small table where Styx and I had eaten every day.

"Hey, hey," Styx called soothingly. He crouched down and reached for me. "You OK? You didn't get hurt, did you?"

I went to him immediately. Styx pulled me into his arms, holding me tightly. "No. But how did he find me?"

"Not sure." He glanced at my upturned backpack and the mess of stuff on the floor where I'd dumped the contents. "You think he put a tracker in your pack?"

"I don't know!" I sobbed. "It's the only thing that makes sense since he obviously doesn't know the car's here."

"Here," Styx took me back to the pack. "Put everything back in. Get anything you had in it when you got here and put it in there. Any dirty clothes, including those prison oranges. Put it all back in."

He helped me. Everything I'd brought with me went back in that pack. Then Styx shouldered it while putting himself between me and the window where my poppy had shot. Once outside our room, he snagged my hand and hurried down the hall through the compound.

On the way, Cain and Sword met us. "You good, Jolene? You didn't get hit, did you?" Cain looked me up and down as if expecting to find blood or something.

"No. I'm good. Just a little shaken up."

"Who wouldn't be?" Sword glanced at Styx. That one look scared me more than anything. I let go of Styx's hand and backed away from them.

To my complete and utter horror, I whimpered when I spoke. "Please don't make me leave. I know it's a lot to ask, but he'll kill me if I go out there."

Styx lunged for me, pulling me up against his big frame, and hugged me tightly. "Now you fuckin' listen to me, Jolene," he growled. "No one's gonna make you fuckin' leave. All we want to do is figure out how he knew you were here. You came to the same conclusion we did, thinking there was some kind of tracker in your backpack. Right?" When I nodded, he continued. "We can deal with that fuck Marshall and anyone he brought with him. Before that, however, we're gonna find how they're trackin' you and get rid of it."

"You swear you're not gonna make me leave?"

"Honey." Cain spoke gently, placing a hand on my shoulder even as Styx still held me. "Ain't no one gonna get to you. You've got this whole club standing between you and the outside. He thinks he's got the upper hand, but he's as good as dead for shootin' at our home. For tryin' to harm one of our ol' ladies, he gets to die hard."

"Oh, no! Did he hurt one of the women?" I looked up at Styx, tears spilling over my cheeks. "I'll never forgive myself if he hurt someone."

"Baby, he means *you*. You're *my* ol' lady. They'll protect you to the death. I told you we had your back."

"But -- but I'm not your ol' lady yet. Right? You said something about a vest or something. That 'Property of' thing.

"It's a formality," Cain offered. "Styx already told us he'd claimed you. He just has to get you home to get your patch ordered."

"I've actually already messaged Thorn. He said he'd have it ready by the time we get to Palm Springs." He leaned in and kissed my mouth gently. The cut there was almost healed, and he'd taken to kissing me very gently as often as he could. "But it doesn't matter. Already told you, honey. I got you."

Sword crossed his arms over his chest and gave Styx a hard look. "You need to build her up, Styx. She don't know her own worth."

"Workin' on it. She's had a hard life, but I intend to spoil her for the rest of it."

"Fuckin' whore! Get your ass out here!" There were more gunshots. Three. All three sounded like they hit where our room was just down the hall.

"That's it," Cain said, his face turning into a mask of rage. He raised his voice as he stalked down the hall to the great room. Me and Styx, along with Sword, were right behind him. "Men! You see a mark raise a weapon, you fuckin' shoot. Motherfuckers ain't leavin' this compound alive."

Chapter Five
Jolene

The club was going to war. Within a matter of minutes, they had the women who weren't built to fight and all the children locked down tight. One of the men, Shadow, had a woman who was readying for battle, as was her sister. Millie had hair that was black with teal blue streaks while Venus, her sister, had hot pink hair. And nails. And eyes. And was dressed all in pink. Apparently, somewhere on the grounds, was a pink Harley belonging to Venus. Rumor was, Millie had wanted to have a teal Harley made, but Shadow had forbidden it. Except that Millie had done it anyway and told him that, if he insisted on ordering her around, he should get used to her defying his orders whether she actually wanted to do the forbidden or not. She'd said it was the principle of the matter. I liked Millie.

Styx had tried to get me to go with the ol' ladies, but I'd refused. "If you're killin' my pap and my brother, I'm gonna be here." It wasn't that I wanted to watch them die, I just needed the closure. Or something like that. OK, maybe I did want to watch the whole thing unfold. Including watching them die.

Once everyone was gathered, Cain, Bohannon, and Sword left the compound's great room to stand on the porch and greet their guests. Every other member of the club present positioned themselves around the clan of McCoys assembled outside. That included Poppy, Alex, and several other cousins. There were eight men in all. All of them armed to the teeth, but I could tell just by the way the Bones men held their weapons, the McCoys were outmatched in every way.

"You harborin' that bitch, Jolene?" Alex, my

eldest brother, asked. "'Cause, let me tell you, whatever you gave her for the Maybach? She stole it. Now, we'll sell it to you, but only if'n you give us Jolene."

Cain just crossed his arms over his chest, saying nothing.

"That's my daughter," Poppy snapped. "You get her on out here now!"

"You just shot up our home," Bohannon said calmly. "And you're demandin' shit from us now? You do realize shit don't work that way here. Right?"

"Works same in Kentucky as it does in West Virginia, son," Poppy sneered, spitting on the ground. "Which means if you don't get Jolene out here, we're gonna fuck this place up."

Bohannon glanced at Sword with a raised eyebrow. "Told you it'd be the hard way."

"Thinkin' you men better rethink this whole situation you've found yourself in," Sword said, flashing Bohannon an irritated look. "You ain't got the men or the guns to win here."

Without warning, Alex drew his gun. I braced for the report of the gunshot, and I wasn't disappointed. Only it wasn't Alex who fired. It was someone from the Bones compound. Alex went down hard, a hole in his chest and an even bigger one out his back. The rest of the McCoys took that as permission to open fire. Poppy ducked behind the open door to his truck and climbed inside.

Every single McCoy who'd pulled a gun dropped seconds later. Poppy was the only one left alive, and he was trying to leave. Bohannon calmly took out a pistol and shot his tires, then put one in the front of the truck, hitting the radiator, for good measure.

"That should hold him," Bohannon said. Then he turned to Sword. "You owe me a hundred bucks, brother." A wide grin split his face.

"Fucker," Sword said, as he dug into his pocket and pulled out a hundred-dollar bill and shoved it at Bohannon. "Happy now?"

"Happier. Won't be happy till the last of these fuckers is bear bait."

"This all of 'em?" Cain asked.

"Data and Zora say yes. Their communication indicated they didn't consider us much of a threat. Seems we're too citified for 'em."

Cain's head snapped to look at Bohannon. "What the fuck is citified?"

Bohannon shrugged. "Beats me. Guessin' they thought they were more badass than us. Probably thought we were squeamish or somethin'."

"Nah," I said, coming forward slightly. Styx had his hand on my shoulder, trying to keep me from the doorway and any line of sight from my pap. "They just didn't think you would possibly shoot 'em. City folk are usually all talk and no action." I tried my best to explain, but that didn't really do it justice. "Poppy always thought of city folk as wantin' their guns but not really being willing to use them. I'm sure he thought a few shots at you and you'd all just lay down your arms and hand over anything they wanted."

Cain looked back to the truck where several armed club members had pulled Poppy out and were zip-tying his hands behind his back. Poppy was mouthing loudly all the way, especially when he caught sight of me.

"You bitch! Always knew you was a traitor! Ever since you's a kid when you tried to take up with that Hatfield boy."

"You mean me, old man?" Styx stepped out of the clubhouse. He tried to slip past me, but I wasn't letting him face my father alone. I snagged his hand and clung tightly. Surprisingly, Styx gripped my hand as well. "Am I the Hatfield she tried to take up with?" Styx sounded cold and deadly. What I could see of his face wasn't the man I'd fallen hard for. He was as big a killer as my pap. Looking from Styx to Poppy, I could see the similarity. It was frightening at first, but then Styx turned to me, his features softening before he whispered to me. "Go back inside. I'll take care of this."

"I'm not leavin' you, Styx. Poppy's --"

"Bein' an ass. You don't need to hear this shit."

"You fuckin' whore! Who is this bastard? He a Hatfield?" Poppy looked Styx up and down, narrowing his eyes. "You look familiar, boy."

"Should. I'm Ruben Hatfield. Your pa killt my pa."

"Then you killt my pa for his trouble."

I sucked in a breath, but kept my hold on Styx. "I remember that," I whispered. Styx squeezed my hand, a silent command to keep quiet.

"I did. Came close to killin' you, too, when you came after my ma."

Poppy snickered, then spit. "Bitch always wanted McCoy dick." He shrugged. "Just figured since she was widowed, I'd give the whore what she wanted."

Styx exploded off the porch, grabbing Poppy by the throat and slamming him back against the truck. For long moments he held Poppy like that. Poppy's face turned red, and he tried to struggle, but Styx was enormously strong, not to mention Poppy's hands were tied behind his back. Styx gave him a smile filled with hate. I could sympathize. After all, it had been done to me.

Cain stepped up beside the pair and laid a hand on Styx's shoulder. "That's enough, Styx."

Poppy smirked again, but this time, there didn't seem to be as much bravado, and he couldn't seem to decide if he wanted to keep his eyes on Styx or Cain.

"That's right. Call off your dog. Who the hell do you people think you are, anyway? You'll pay for killin' my kin."

"No, we won't," Cain said with a chuckle. "Didn't you think to look into the people you were comin' to threaten? When you go to war, son, you gotta know who you're fightin'. Now, you ain't gonna be makin' the ride home." Cain couldn't have been much older than my pap, if he was even that old. But him callin' Pap "son" was obviously an insult.

Poppy lunged at Cain. The other man didn't even flinch. Before Poppy got more than a few inches away from Cain, Bohannon struck out with his fist, connecting with my pap's jaw. Poppy crumpled to the ground, and Cain just snorted.

"Pick him up. Take him to the basement. We have questions that need to be answered."

"Ain't tellin' you nuthin'," Poppy said, his voice slurred slightly. When he stood, I could see him looking around warily. Like he only now realized he'd stuck his head in a viper's nest.

"Yes, you will," Sword said, grinning evilly into Poppy's face. "You'll be surprised how little time it takes, too."

They marched my Pap up the steps to the porch where I stood. As he passed me, Poppy spit in my face. His tobacco stung my eye and I cried out, stumbling backward until someone caught me. I wiped frantically at my eye until I could open it again. When I looked up, Poppy was grinning down at me.

"Fuckin' bitch. You disgust me."

I felt something solid against my palm where I tried to get my balance. I had no idea who had me, but I grabbed on to that object and pulled it free. Turned out, it was the hilt of a bigass knife. I flipped it around to lay against my forearm and scrambled to my feet. With a battle yell, I charged the three steps to my pap and slashed out, making one deep cut across his cheek, then one across his chest with the backward motion. I flipped the knife around to stab him, but Styx pulled me back.

"Easy there, baby. You'll get your chance to carve him up." Styx wrapped his arms around me tightly. Surprisingly, he didn't try to take the knife away from me.

"We still have questions for him, Jolene," Cain said, laying a gentle hand on my arm. "Let us get the answers we need, then you can do whatever you need to." He gave me a hard look. "Did he hurt you, Jolene? Growin' up?"

I shrugged. "Made my childhood a livin' hell. I managed to be problem enough he kept me out of his will, but not bad enough he sold me or just kilt me." I looked away, slightly ashamed of my outburst. "I hate him."

Bohannon and Sword shoved Poppy into the clubhouse none too gently. "He'll pay for everything he's done and then some before we're done with him, little sister," Bohannon said. "You want your piece, get Styx to bring you down. Just know it's not gonna be pretty."

"I ain't squeamish," I said defiantly. "He shot at me and woulda killt me. He said if'n I ever came back, he'd kill me."

"Then come with us," Cain said, reaching out to take my hand. "Stay as long as you want to. When you need to go, Styx can take you back to his room." Styx took my other hand and the three of us walked behind Bohannon and Sword as they escorted my pap roughly to the basement. I knew we were in for a long, bloody affair when I saw the tarp in the middle of the middle of the floor around a chair that looked like it had been bolted to the ground.

The two enforcers strapped Pappy to the chair, even used a long strap to secure his head to the chair's back. It reminded me of an old-time electric chair with its leather straps and sturdy, wooden frame.

"Now," Cain said. "How many more of your people are on the way to look for the Maybach?"

"Ain't none'a your Goddamned business."

Cain smiled and nodded to Bohannon. The big man made a show of putting on gloves before beginning to systematically beat the living shit out of Poppy. The sight should have repulsed me. Instead, I found myself smiling. How many times had my pap done this exact same thing to anyone who got in his way? It was why the whole town of Williamson was terrified to go against him. Even the law didn't mess with the McCoys. Hell, they didn't mess with the Hatfields, either, but the McCoys had made themselves an integral part of the financial community of Williamson. They might look and sound country, but they owned half the town.

It was a long time before Bohannon let up. The big guy wasn't even winded.

Cain waited several minutes, letting Poppy catch his breath. "You still with me, Marshall?" Poppy spat in response. "Good. I'll ask again. How many of your people are on the way for the Maybach?"

"You go'ta hell!"

"This is going to get tiresome," Cain sighed, scratching above his eyebrow with his thumb. This time, he nodded at Sword. Instead of beating him, Sword started removing fingernails. Then toenails.

He was getting to the third toenail when Poppy finally broke down and answered. "My second eldest! He's supposed to follow us here in a day or so if he don't hear from us. But we wasn't expectin' no trouble!"

"Good," Cain said. "That's good. Now. Tell me how you knew where to find us."

Pappy flashed me a hate-filled look. "Put a tracker in her backpack when she started showin' interest in that other Hatfield bastard. Knew she'd try to fuck me over. Figured she had somethin' to do with the car up and disappearin', too. We had security all over the fuckin' place, and she's the only one who knew anythin' 'bout it." Even as beat up as he was, Poppy still managed to spit in my direction. He hated me that much.

"Didn't know nothin' 'bout your stupid security," I muttered. "You just assumed I did 'cause you didn't think no one else knew 'bout that car."

"Unfortunately," Styx said, taking Poppy's attention from me and putting it squarely on him. "You can't steal a car like that and no one notice." He shrugged. "Well, unless you can replace the VIN number and reprogram the computer with new FOBs."

Poppy snorted. "Well, good luck, then. You got a car you can't sell, neither."

"Never said we couldn't do it." Styx gave him a chuckle and a grin. "This is our bread and butter, McCoy. The car's already reprogrammed. Got a new identity and a new pink slip. 'Cause, unlike some dumb hicks, we know what the fuck we're doin'."

Pappy yelled, struggling against his bonds. Sword just tsked and took another toenail. My pap was screaming now. And, Lord help me, I wasn't torn up about it.

As the Bones men continued to torture my Pap, I thought about my childhood. Never once did he offer a kind word to me growing up. Nothing was ever good enough. How many times did he backhand me for no other reason than I was in the wrong place at the wrong time? When I got accepted to Marshall University, he had his thugs make just enough of a ruckus they got me kicked out of school. Why? Because he didn't want any girl of his getting too uppity by going to a school that would let her make a living away from him. He needed every member of his family under his thumb, and I bucked that control. Which made me his enemy. Truth was, he was probably looking for a reason to kill me. He'd almost succeeded, too.

"When he shot at me."

Instantly, Styx turned to me. "Baby?"

"He'd been looking for a reason to get rid of me, Styx. All these years. He was just too chickenshit to do it. Claimin' I'd broken into his house. Stolen stuff from him. Maybe even that I'd threatened his daughter. That was his excuse." Saying it didn't hurt like I thought it would. But it was terrifying. "He didn't just shoot at me trying to scare me off. He really intended to kill me." I turned my gaze to my father. Or rather, the man who'd fucked my mom and gotten her pregnant. "Gettin' Mom pregnant was just an ego thing for you. To stake your claim. Having a girl must have galled you."

"Fuckin' useless," he muttered. "Only good for fuckin' and none of the dumbasses I threw your way could get the job done. No one wanted you. Too skinny. Too cold. Worthless to me." Marshall McCoy was barely conscious, but he kept talking. Like he was dreaming or in some kind of trance. "You always were smarter'n my boys." He shook his head. "Couldn't have that. You'd'a destroyed everything I built. Taken it all away and given it up."

"You didn't build nothin'," I said softly. "That was all Grandpa. Grandma told him he should set up a scholarship fund for kids in the area to go to college. Give them an incentive to keep their talent in Williamson. Grow the town. She said it could make the McCoy legacy in West Virginia one of buildin' up. Not tearin' down. But all'a'yas too blinded by hate. Even Grandpa didn't want to do it if it meant he had to help Hatfields. But he was gonna do it. 'Cause he loved Grandma."

My Poppy looked up at me and gave me a bloody smile. "Yeah. So I kilt the old man and the bitch. Wudd'n my kin anyway. Just your mama's. They wudd'n McCoys."

I clenched my teeth, willing myself not to show the grief and anger inside me. My grandmother had taught me more than merely making butterscotch pie. She'd taught me to love the person on the inside. Not the person you see on the outside. That was something my pap would never understand.

"You know you're gonna die here. Right?" I said, trying to keep my voice neutral. I took a deep breath and let it out slowly. "You're gonna die. Hard. Ain't got no idea how long they plan on keepin' you alive, but I'm gonna sit here and watch every little thing they do. I'm gonna pay real close attention." I took one slow step toward him. "Gonna learn how they do everything they're gettin' ready to do to you and how to do it so you stay alive as long as possible. When they finally decide to let you die, my face is gonna be the last thing you see. And I'm gonna smile and rejoice in my heart that you're on your way to hell."

"Jolene," Styx slipped his hand into mine. It was a tender gesture. One meant to pull me back from the edge of insanity. I wanted to scream. To weep. Mostly, I wanted revenge. And Poppy wasn't the only one who needed to pay.

"He's not the only one gonna suffer," I whispered. "I'm gonna make all of 'em pay."

"You leave that to me, baby. I'll bring every single motherfucker's head back to you on a silver fuckin' platter. But you let me worry about it."

I shook my head. "This was your kill, Styx. The others? Avery, Clyde, the cousins? They're mine. I'm gonna hurt them like they hurt me."

Cain stepped close to us. "Styx, take your woman out of here. She's stuck in the past. Bring her back to you."

When Styx hooked his arm around my shoulders and tried to urge me away from the carnage playing out in front of me, I resisted. "Not until it's finished," I said quietly. "Meant what I said. I want the last face he sees to be mine. Right before he crosses into the gates of Hell. So, I'm stayin, Cain. Until you're done with this. I'm stayin'. And I hope you see fit to draw it out as long as possible."

Cain looked like he was grinding his teeth in frustration. He also looked resigned. Then he nodded. "I'm given' Styx latitude on this one. Only thing I'm sayin' is, if you betray us, if this leaves the club, you answer to me. I don't torture women I know need to die, so it'll be clean, but the price for betrayal is still death."

Styx growled and tried to step between me and Cain, but I blocked him, taking a step closer to the Bones president. "I hear ya. And betrayin' the club means betrayin' men and women who've earned my respect. Your wife is one of my favorite people in the world. So's Mama. All the ol' ladies here have closed ranks around me since Styx brought me here. No one -- not even my own family of McCoys, who always defend their own from Hatfields -- ever protected me the way everyone here has. Especially Styx. I don't betray people like that. Good people. Y'all's good people."

"So be it."

Then Cain and his enforcers continued beating Poppy. With every hit, every groan and scream of pain from my father, I tried to find some empathy. To cringe or find a reason to ask Cain to stop it. Every time I thought that was what I should do, I'd remember how many times I went to school with a black eye. Or came home to him exploding in anger at me, shutting me out of the house in the dead of winter because I was late coming home. Taking my money so I couldn't leave home while telling me how he hated me and trying every way he could to make me leave. So I kept my mouth shut and watched. And didn't feel a Goddamned thing.

Chapter Six
Styx

I had to get Jolene out of there. She'd somehow shut down her emotions. Her gaze was intent on her father, holding his gaze when he could focus, letting him see her resolve to keep her word. And the bastard saw it. He seemed to want to look away from her, but couldn't. Her gaze was hard. Determined. Cain was right. She was lost in the past. Whatever she was remembering wasn't pleasant, and it didn't include *anything* positive. I glanced at Cain, who looked at Jolene, studying her for several seconds. After a brief glance back at me, Cain stopped the torture.

"Bohannon," Cain said softly. The other man, who'd been letting Sword take his turn working McCoy over, raised an eyebrow at Cain. Cain nodded.

"Knife or bat?" Bohannon asked.

Cain shook his head slightly as if he really didn't want to give the order. I knew it was more that he didn't want Jolene to witness this than that he cared at all how he ended it. Then he did something that surprised me even as it infuriated me. He moved next to Jolene, watching her watch her father for a long time. Jolene's stare was fixed on McCoy like a cat watching her prey. I knew what was coming. Wanted to rebel against it. But I knew she needed this choice.

"I've never even considered doing this for anyone in my club. We have enforcers for a reason. Men I've known and commanded in battle. I never want just anyone taking this responsibility unless I know they can handle it and are willing to take it on. But if you want this kill, Jolene. It's yours."

Without a word, Jolene moved forward, going to Bohannon. She didn't take her eyes from her father.

For a long time she stood there waiting. For what, I didn't know. Her father managed to open his eyes. For several seconds they were unfocused, then they seemed to find Jolene. The man whimpered. There was a pleading look in his eyes, like he expected she'd take up for him. Stop the torture and the upcoming killing. I almost intervened, but she finally broke her stare on McCoy.

"He shot up your home. He was shootin' at me, but your families were in here too. If you want the kill, you can have it. But if you need me to do it as insurance I don't rat you out, I got plenty of bills that need collectin' from my pap."

Cain shook his head. "No, honey. If I didn't trust you, you wouldn't be here in the first place. You know the price if you betray us, but I believed you before when you said you respected my ol' lady and my club. This is for you if you need the closure."

"I got my own killin' to do," she said softly. Then McCoy moaned softly, a pitiful sound if anyone still had pity inside themselves. I didn't. He sounded almost relieved. Like maybe he thought Jolene was giving him a stay of execution. That noise brought Jolene's full attention back to her old man. Her mien grew hard, and she muttered, "Fuck it," before snagging a baseball bat leaning against the table next to Bohannon and stepping toward her father. "See you in hell." McCoy whimpered. Then Jolene swung. Hard.

There was no doubt McCoy was dead. The blow shattered his head like it might a melon, splattering blood and brains and bone everywhere. Jolene flung the bat at McCoy's body, spitting on him before turning and heading toward the door.

Cain shook his head, obviously not liking that he'd given her the choice to end her father. "Girl's either evil to her core or has bigger balls than I do."

"You know she's not evil," I said softly. "Ain't got her to talk about her childhood much, but I'm willing to bet that man traumatized her her entire life."

"Probably right. Still goes against everything I believe in. Women should be protected from violence like this. Not encouraged to engage in it."

I raised my eyebrows. "Like Venus isn't encouraged to engage in it? Or her sister, Millie? Jolene's just as hard as they are when she needs to be. She grew up hard and still managed to have a good and gentle heart."

Cain gave me a withering glare. "She ain't like Venus and Millie. They were both trained in what they do. That girl learned strictly to survive. Like Rain. Rain can fight with the best of them, but she's not like us. Neither is Jolene. I don't want this life for her. You need to coddle her and pamper her and teach her how much she's worth to you just the way she is."

"Fully aware. And, believe me, I'm working on it."

"Take her out of here."

I nodded and followed Jolene out the door, intending to take her back to our room so I could bathe her, then take her to bed and make her forget all about the violence of the last few hours.

"On it, Cain. And thanks for the shelter and protection. Sorry this whole mess disrupted life here, but me and Jolene as well as Salvation's Bane appreciate the help."

"Any time."

I had to trot to catch up with Jolene. She was headed in the direction of our room, but she didn't look like her mind was on where she was going. I fell into step beside her, not touching her for fear of startling her.

"Jolene," I said softly, needing her attention focused on me. She said nothing. "Come on, sweetheart. Talk to me." Her gaze remained fixed ahead, her face a hard mask. I wasn't even sure she registered I was talking to her.

To anyone who didn't know what had just taken place, it probably looked like she was angry with me. I knew better. The men knew better. The club girls? *Sigh*. Not so much.

"Aww, Styx." I thought I'd seen the woman around but had no idea what her name was. Didn't fuckin' care. "The little hillbilly mad at you? Come see me if she puts you on the couch. I got a nice warm bed you can share with me." Then the woman actually approached me, stepping in front of me and throwing her arms around my neck.

Which was when Jolene snapped into the here and now. Her head whipped around until her gaze clashed with mine. Then to the woman whose arms I was struggling to pry off me.

"What the fuck?" Jolene kept looking back and forth between me and the woman. I was starting to panic even as I kept trying to get her away from me. It wasn't easy. It seemed like she was all arms and legs. Like an octopus. The longer Jolene looked from one of us to the other, the more angry her expression.

"Get the fuck off me," I bit out.

"I got you, sweetie," she said, completely ignoring Jolene. "You just let that dumb hick go on her way. You come with me, and I'll take care of you."

Before I could say anything, Jolene attacked. And I mean, she *attacked*. One second I was prying the woman's hands from around my neck, the next Jolene had her on the ground pounding the fuck out of her.

The fight started mere seconds before, and already there was blood splattered all over the floor and nearby wall. Had this been Salvation's Bane, I'd have let the fight go on until I was certain the club girl had learned her lesson, but I had no idea how Bones worked in this regard. I'd never actually seen a club girl cause trouble with the ol' ladies in Cain's outfit.

I wrapped my arms around Jolene's waist and pulled her off the other woman, whipping around to put myself between Jolene and her target. Jolene screamed like a wounded animal, the sound as much grief as it was anger, and I knew I had a huge problem on my hands.

"What the hell's goin' on here?" Cain stepped from the door leading to the basement. He was at the other end of the hallway, having just left the carnage in the basement of the compound.

"Cat fight," someone said, grimly. "Queenie picked the wrong man to try to steal."

"You good, Styx?" Cain didn't step in so much as he was trying to feel out the situation.

"Not sure. She's not in any kind of shape mentally for this."

"Fucker!" Jolene screamed. "If you wanted that bitch why'd you make me think you loved me? You swore you were different! And I fuckin' believed you!"

"Jolene, stop it! Look at me!"

"Fuck you!" She fought to free herself of me, but I held on doggedly.

"You don't have to put up with this," the woman -- Queenie -- managed to get out through panting breaths. "She's a rabid animal in need of putting down!" She put her hands on my back, sliding one around my neck and the other around my waist. "Let Cain take care of the bitch and I'll take care of you."

She tried to make her voice a seductive purr, but it just grated on my nerves like nails on a chalkboard. Then she tried to pull my head around for a kiss and I lost my shit.

"Cain, I know I'm a guest here so I'm tryin' to not break the rules too much. But if someone don't get this fuckin' bitch offa me and out of my woman's sight, I'm'a fixin' to throw her a beatin'!"

Bohannon sighed and pulled Queenie off me while I scooped up Jolene. She still fought like a madwoman, and I suppose she was exactly that. Mad. Angry.

Hurt.

But not at me. Not really. Once I got her calmed down, she'd see this for what it was. No. Jolene was grieving. For the loss of a father who never loved her. For killing a man in cold blood. For the loss of her innocence and then of her body. She'd lost everything in life. Sure, she had me, but she didn't know me. Not really. We'd had a couple weeks together and had been forced together by circumstances rather than because we'd wanted to be. But I loved her. And I knew she loved me back. She'd remember that after she got out all the grief and negative emotions she'd held in check her entire life. And maybe that was the surface reason for this outburst. She saw another woman with her arms around me, taking what Jolene thought of as hers. Hell, I *was* hers. No question of it. So, once she calmed down, I'd remind her. It was time. If she was ready -- and I thought she was -- it was time.

"Not your fault, brother," Cain said, using the reference in regard to me for the first time. This wasn't my club, but Cain was my boss. He knew me inside and out. Just like he did everyone in his employ. "Tell me if there's anything you need. Take care of her and help her back to the present. Don't give up on her."

"Never," I growled. "She's mine. She always will be. Good or bad."

I made it to our room before letting her down. By this time, Jolene was sobbing uncontrollably, though she still fought like a banshee.

"You bastard! I trusted you!"

"You still can, baby. I ain't goin' nowhere."

"How can I possibly? That woman --"

"Ain't part of this. She's gone."

"You were hugging her!" Jolene yelled at me, tears streaming down her face. "You tried to kiss her!"

"You know that ain't right. I'd never do anything to hurt you, and I know that'd hurt you worse than just about anything." I wanted to tell her to calm down, but I wasn't completely stupid. She had to do that part on her own. But I'd be here for her no matter what.

She still sobbed, wrapping her arms around herself and turning away from me. "I hate this place."

"No, baby. You don't hate it here. Up until today, you've been doing wonderful. So let's talk about what changed."

"*You* changed! You got another woman!"

"You know better, Jolene." I kept my tone gentle when everything inside me wanted to vehemently deny it.

She stood there for long moments, tears streaming down her face. Her face scrunched, as if she were really trying hard to think back. "You weren't hugging her back," she murmured. "You didn't kiss her when she tried to kiss you."

"No, baby. I didn't. You know I'd never do that, because you and I are a team. We have been since the beginning."

Nodding slowly, she said, "Yeah. You saved

me."

"And I'll always save you, honey. Just like you'll save me." She met my gaze, then gave an anguished cry as she launched herself into my arms. "I gotcha, baby. I gotcha."

"I killed him, Styx," she said in a shaky whisper. "I killed him, and I didn't feel a fuckin' thing." She looked up at me even as she clung tightly. "Does that mean I'm a horrible person?"

"Not at all. Got a feelin' that bastard made your life hell."

She nodded slightly, then winced. "Yeah, but was it worth killin' over? I mean, I survived. It wasn't easy, and he never loved me or tried to protect me, but that didn't mean he shoulda died."

"He didn't die just 'cause'a that. He shot at you. How many times?"

She shrugged. "Few times. That night. And over the years."

"And you said yourself he tried to kill you before. Well, he did the same thing today. Only, this time, he not only put you in danger, but this whole club. Including the kids in here. And he didn't care one fuckin' bit who he hurt. So, I had no problem with him dyin'. I just wished you'd'a let Cain take care of it and left with me instead of watching the whole thing and takin' the killin' blow for yourself."

"I wanted that, Styx. Wanted it with every fiber of my fuckin' being." She ducked her head. Which wouldn't do. "I guess it all just built up."

I lifted her chin to force her to look at me. "I'm proud'a you, honey. You made him pay. You made him *see you*. Got a feelin' he never considered you a strong offspring. Probably mistook your capacity to care as a weakness."

"Maybe. Or maybe he's just an asshole who hated me 'cause I made my mama ugly like she always said."

That didn't compute. "Now... what?"

"Mama was young and slender and pretty when she got pregnant with me. Gained a lotta weight during the pregnancy. Always knew she blamed me from my very first memory of her. Only time I've ever felt loved and wanted was before my grandma and papaw died. She taught me how to bake. Papaw taught me how to hunt and fish. Then they died."

"He said he killed them. You believe that?"

She nodded. "I was there." Her voice was barely above a whisper. "He knew I saw, and knew I'd never tell anyone because I was afraid of him. But that wasn't the reason." She took in a shuddering breath. "I didn't tell 'cause I knew no one would believe me. Then he'd just kill me, too. Always wondered why he didn't."

"Who knows what reason his twisted mind came up with?" I hugged her tighter, rubbing her back to comfort her as much as I could.

"Probably thought he'd find a way to use me like he did my older sisters. Probably had someone special in mind and was biding his time until he needed me. Unfortunately, with me hooking up with Avery, giving him my virginity..."

"It made you less useful, and he decided to let his temper have its way." I expected her to look... I don't know. Hurt? Angry? Something. Instead, she gasped, her eyes going wide. Like it was a revelation. Something she'd been trying to put together for a long time and hadn't been able to figure out.

"That's the only thing about my life that actually makes sense." Then she looked ashamed. "I'm so sorry for attacking you, Styx. You're the only person who's ever shown me the least bit of kindness, and I was so mean."

"Not a word, baby. Not one more fuckin' word." Then I pulled her to me and kissed her.

She let me have her in the sweetest surrender. Jolene opened her mouth and let me kiss her the way I wanted to. Following my lead, she met my tongue thrust for thrust. I still tasted her tears, but now I could tolerate them because I knew she was with me. In the present. She knew I had her back and hadn't betrayed her. So help me God, if it was the last thing I ever did, she'd learn she could trust me with her heart. I'd never risk losing her for any reason, especially not for a fucking club girl.

"Styx," she sighed into my mouth as she explored our kisses, finding what she liked while still following my lead. "You're wonderful to me. So very wonderful."

"Not nearly as wonderful as you deserve, but I'm gonna get better."

"You really didn't want that woman?" She sounded vulnerable, and I knew she was. She was honest in her reactions, not trying to hide her emotions. What I saw was what I got.

"Baby, I never want a woman other than you. You're it for me."

She whimpered as she tunneled her hands under his shirt, caressing his skin with a light touch that became bolder the more she touched me. Her hands moved around to my chest, rubbing over and over my pecs. I wasn't certain if she was fascinated with the muscles or the way my chest hair abraided her palms, but she seemed to love something. I peeled off my shirt and tossed it to the floor, watching closely as her gaze zeroed in on my chest. She licked her lips and leaned in like she'd been going to kiss my skin. Or lick it. Then she pulled back abruptly, snatching her hands away and looking up at me with wide eyes as if she'd been caught doing something naughty.

I chuckled. "Go on. Touch what you want. *Taste* what you want."

"Fuuuuck," she groaned, then gave up her fight. Again, she reached for me, her little fingers curling against the heavy muscles of my chest. She leaned in and kissed one of the tattoos over my left nipple. When I circled my arms around her, petting her hair and urging her closer, she ran her tongue over my skin, then lower to close her mouth around the flat nub and lap softly. Her hands slid around my chest to my back and, again, she clutched me to her. When she looked up at me, her eyes were bright and filled with lust. "Styx?"

"What is it, baby?"

"I want..." She cleared her throat. "That is... I mean... will you make love to me now?"

I grinned at her. "Baby, just been waitin' until you were ready. Much as I want you, much as I fuckin' *ache* for you, the most important thing to me is that you're comfortable. In everything."

"Please, Styx," she pleaded, looking up at me with those luminous eyes. "I know I was a bitch earlier, but I need this."

"Honey, you weren't a bitch. I doubt you have a bitchy bone in your body. You were hurting. You're still hurting, but I understand the need to have that physical connection with someone. I'm glad you picked me."

I reached for her shirt and tugged gently until she pulled it off the rest of the way. Without prompting from me, she took off her bra and stepped out of her shorts and panties. Jolene's naked form was the most erotic, most beautiful sight I'd ever seen. I knew her from before I left to work for ExFil. When I lived in Williamson with the rest of our fucked-up families, she'd been a young girl. Bright, bubbly, and cute as a button. Now, she was all woman. Soft curves and supple limbs. Pouty lips. Beautiful, radiant innocence.

"How the fuck could anyone hurt you?" I said, not really meaning to ask the question out loud, but there it was.

She shrugged as if it were no big deal, but I could tell it was. She was so vulnerable in this situation. No doubt thinking about the last man she gave herself to. Much as I wanted her whole being focused on me, I knew it was impossible. So I'd get it out of the way now. Let her know my plans. Then I'd proceed to worship her body in the best way I could.

"I guess no one thought I was worth anything before." She looked away. "Avery sure didn't think so."

"'Cause he's a stupid-ass motherfucker. And a waste of oxygen." I held her gaze for a long moment before I told her my intentions. "You know he's gonna die. Right?"

She shrugged. "Ain't gonna pretend to be outraged or to beg you to not hurt him. If he did that to me, how many other women did he do it to?"

"Ain't even lookin'," I said, shaking my head. "All I care about is that he did it to you. For that, he's gonna pay."

"You know, I can deal with him." She let her gaze drift off to the side, and her expression turned hard and fierce. "Gonna kill him and his kin."

I grasped her chin and turned her gently back to

face me. "You focus on me, Jolene. Really look at me." I knew I could be intimidating, but this was for her own good. And mine. "You're gonna do exactly what I tell you to regarding those motherfuckers. And that is you're gonna leave them to me. Once we get back to Florida and Salvation's Bane, I'll take this to Thorn, and we'll put a plan in motion. That way, we control what happens and, most importantly, you're safe."

She met my gaze. She wasn't defiant or bold or even resigned. Jolene just gave me a steady look of her own and shook her head. "Cain't promise you that, Styx. I love you. I'm certain of it. I'll do anything for you and love that I can give you what you need. But I'll never lie to you. Not for any reason. And this, I can't give you."

I groaned because, Goddammit, her fierce bravery, along with her complete honesty, turned me the fuck on. With one hand, I undid my jeans. With the other, I took her hand and shoved it inside my boxers and urged her to cup my hardening cock. "Gonna do my best to change your mind about that, but fuck, woman! That bloodthirsty streak you have is the sexiest Goddamned thing I've ever seen in my fuckin' life."

With a little sob, Jolene lunged for me, squeezing my cock and hooking an arm around my neck as she found my lips with hers. She was as aggressive as I'd expect from a woman who'd basically told me I could boss her around if I wanted, but she'd make up her own mind if she did as I told her. Though her kisses were unpracticed, she took what she wanted, still gripping and squeezing my cock.

"Fuck me, Styx," she whispered against my lips. "Fuck me and show me how to enjoy this."

I grunted, lifting her so she wrapped her legs

around my waist, though she didn't let go of my cock. Carrying her to the bed, I fisted a hand in her hair and cupped one cheek of her ass with the other. Somehow, I got us in the bed, her beneath me, doing her level best to make me lose my fucking mind. She was succeeding.

Somehow, I managed to pry her hands off me and pin them above her head with one of mine. She whimpered and mewed much like a kitten as I kissed her neck and growled against her shoulder.

"God, you smell good, Jolene. Wanna eat you up."

"Yes," she sighed as she thrust against me. "Styx! Oh, God!"

"Tell me what you're feeling, baby."

"I'm burning up inside! I need you!" Her pleas were almost a sob. She'd cried enough today. From here on out, I only wanted her to have pleasure.

"I know. You felt how hard I am. I'm burning too, Jolene. We're going to take care of each other. You get me?"

She nodded slightly, her eyes wild with need. I wanted to worship her body like she deserved, but she didn't look like she could take much more without losing her mind. I reached for a condom on the nightstand, but she whimpered and shook her head, struggling to free her hands. Immediately, I let her go, not sure what was wrong. But she just pulled my hand back to her and kissed my fingers.

"No condom," she said, shaking her head. For emphasis, she snagged the one I had in my hand and threw it over the side of the bed.

"Baby." I didn't really care, though I'd been willing to use one for her benefit. But she seemed to be having a really strong negative reaction to this.

"I felt them. Before. I don't want to feel that again. I just want you." She closed her eyes for a moment, tears leaking from her eyes. I wasn't sure if it was from fear or frustration, but I got the sense it was a little of both. "I'll take responsibility if... if..."

"Honey, I'm in this regardless of what happens. I'm always gonna be with you. I was only going to use one to protect you. I never want you uncomfortable with sex. Not with me. And you ain't having sex with anyone else, so you need to explain what's going through your beautiful head."

"The latex," she said, unable to form the words she needed.

"You didn't like the way it felt?" I could understand that, but surely there was more.

She nodded, then added, "It was like nails on a chalkboard, only in touch. Not sound."

"Is that your only objection? You're not scared of me, are you?"

"NO! No, Styx. I want this. Need it. Need you!" She was back to clutching at my shoulders and back, pulling me to her. Holding me tightly.

"OK, then. We do this bareback. Do you want me to pull out when I come?"

"No," she said. "Not unless you want to."

"This is for you, sweetheart. I want you to have what you need. I'll give you anything you want."

She sobbed then, so many emotions flitting over her face. If she'd hadn't responded so genuinely to my touches and kisses, I'd have called a halt to this. But the only time she seemed to be in the here and now and not in the past was when I gave her pleasure. When she lost herself in what I was doing to her, she seemed to know exactly who she was with and wanted to be there as much as I wanted her there.

"Then please, come inside me, Styx. I don't want any part of me to belong to anyone but you."

As much as I knew she was hurting, I also wanted to howl with pride. She wanted me. She wanted to belong to me.

"I've never come inside a woman without a condom, Jolene. Once I do this, there's no takin' it back. Not for you or me. Already intended on makin' you my ol' lady, but this is your one chance. If you don't want to be with me forever, you tell me now."

"I want you, Styx. Not because I know you'll protect me. But because I love you so much it hurts!"

"All right, then."

Before I fucked her, I needed to make love to her. Needed her back in this and with me and out of the past that would probably always be just one bad thought or nightmare away. So I petted her body. Kissed my way to her breasts and suckled both of them, taking my time. Tasting her. Praising her and her response to me. When I got to her pussy, I nibbled and sucked and licked until she came over and over again, thrashing against me, rubbing her sweet little cunt over my mouth to ride out her orgasm as long as possible. After the third time, she tugged my hair, pulling me up her body.

"There's my greedy baby. You ready for my cock now?"

"Yes! Give it to me! Now!"

"Fuck, yeah," I bit out, knowing she was in exactly the right frame of mind for this. She'd found her way to the pleasure and left behind the pain. At least for now. "Gonna make you feel so fuckin' good, Jolene. Look at me. Don't you dare look away."

She obeyed, gripping my arms as her gaze clung to mine. With a deliberate movement, I entered her pussy one slow inch at a time. Her eyes widened and her lips parted.

"Styx," she whispered, her breathing coming faster and faster. "Fuck! Oh, God!"

"So fuckin' tight, baby. Can you feel how fuckin' tight we fit?"

She shuddered in my arms, clawing me as she wiggled beneath me. At first, I thought she wanted free, but all she did was adjust her hold, place her feet on my calves, and then met me with a thrust of her own. Before I was ready, I was completely inside her, my dick throbbing like a son of a bitch and on the verge of coming.

"Mother of God," I bit out. "I ain't comin' before you do, Jolene! I just fuckin' ain't!"

She arched her back, thrusting her hips up and fucking herself with my cock. I tried to make her hold still, but there was just no way to keep her from it. She was firmly in control even though I tried desperately to wrestle it from her. Not fucking happening.

Finally, I realized all I could do was just hold on for the ride. Jolene was the most demanding lover I'd ever had. She saw what she wanted, and she went after it. It was going to be fun trying to tame my little hellcat.

I surged forward, meeting her bucking hips with ever-increasing thrusts of my own. Soon, we were coming together hard, our bodies slapping against each other. The sound was loud in our room, accompanied by our grunts, groans, and shouts. I was as loud as she was, reveling in the staccato rhythm we made together.

When Jolene screamed her last orgasm, I shouted my own, our cries mingling as the sound of flesh slapping flesh finally stopped. I came deep inside her, reveling in the fact that she was now mine. Wholly and completely. I couldn't wait to get back to Florida and give her the vest I'd ordered for her with my property patch on it. Once she was mine in the eyes of my club, when she was safely behind Salvation's Bane walls, I'd go hunting. My first call would be to my half brother in Black Reign. Shotgun would want to be in on this. Once we got the logistics worked out, we'd track down Avery and Clyde and the cousins. Once we did, we'd kill the motherfuckers.

End of story.

Chapter Seven
Jolene

The ride to Palm Beach was enjoyable in the extreme. Styx, Poison, and Lock arranged a meet with their boss, Red, and a "road crew" halfway between the Bones clubhouse in Kentucky and the Salvation's Bane clubhouse in Florida. Cain offered five of his men to ride with us until we met up with Styx's club, so it was like a big convoy of motorcycles. I'd never seen anything like it.

"This is awesome!" I felt like a kid with my head hanging out the window looking around at all the wonderful, foreign sights around me. I waved cheerfully at the men on the bikes surrounding us.

"Get your head back inside the window, you little brat!" Styx growled at me. He wasn't put out, though. I could tell by the way his lips twitched.

"I'm just bein' friendly. If I ain't friendly, your friends might abandon us."

"You're friendly enough. Do me a solid and roll the window up." The truck we were using was the tits, too. Leather interior, all kinds of bells and whistles. The thing still smelled new!

"But the breeze is wonderful! I love feelin' it blowing my hair everywhere." I couldn't help but giggle. If I'd known short hair felt this good, I'd have cut it years ago.

"I know, but there's something important I need from you. Now roll up the fuckin' window."

With a pretend pout, I did as he asked. Truth was, if there was anything Styx needed, I'd give it to him. "What is it you want?"

"You. Naked. I want you to turn and put your back against the door and put one foot on the floor, the other on the center console. Now, strip."

I gasped, before giggling like a loon. "I can't do that! Everyone will see." But I unfastened my seat belt and started stripping anyway.

"Windows'er tinted. Ain't no one seein' but me. Besides, even if they do see, they'll just know I'm the lucky bastard you're showin' off for."

I mean, honestly. How could a girl say no to that? No one in my life had ever made me feel as wanted and treasured as Styx did. He took ribbing from his brothers, but they were all unfailingly nice to me, congratulating me on confiscating Styx's man card and everything. Styx always had an arm around my shoulders or a firm grip on my hand when we were together. Always touching me. Always laying a caveman-style claim on me. I loved every fucking second of it. It was all the quiet reassurance he gave me when we weren't having sex that gave me the confidence in him that he wouldn't betray me. So yeah. I was giving him this.

I positioned myself the way he wanted, then cupped one breast and slid one hand between my legs. "Well? What now?"

"Just keep doin' what you doin' there, sugar." He glanced at me as he drove. I could see his cock getting hard as his eyes raked over my bare body. "Play with your sweet pussy."

I dipped my fingers into my opening, then rubbed all around, swirling my finger around my lips before circling my clit once and starting over again. "My pussy's wet. Can you see?" I continued to rub and play, spreading my moisture around and around.

"Oh, yeah. You're drenched. I think you like showin' off for me."

"You make me want to do any little thing you

ask me, Styx."

He glanced at me, his eyes intense before he looked back to the road. "I'm glad, Jolene. I will never betray that trust. Anything we do, we do together."

I smiled at him, dipping my fingers inside my pussy once again. "I know that. Don't think I've not paid attention to everything around me. I've been kind of self-absorbed at times, but I know the club we just left would kick your ass if you betrayed me like Avery did. I also got to know the men you had with you from your club. Get the impression they'd do worse than kick your ass."

Styx snorted. "You could say that. Suffice it to say, I'm not the only one plannin' on goin' after Avery and his clan. And yeah, we all thought about how there are probably other women out there they'd done this to, but it's just an afterthought. They're all solidly in your corner, babe. So yeah. They'd fuck me the fuck up if I hurt you. Keep that in mind if I do anything you don't much like. 'Cause they'll probably do it without any proof just 'cause you're a woman and I've got a reputation for being a horny motherfucker."

That made me laugh. "You're crazy. Why would you tell me that? I could just make something up to get you in trouble."

He nodded. "Yep. And there's nothing I could do to convince them you were lying, neither. So yeah. I want you to always feel safe, Jolene. Even from me."

"Which you've accomplished or there's no way I put myself in this --" I stretched my arms wide, indicating myself, stretched out naked, sitting in the seat next to him, "-- situation." I went back to stroking my pussy lazily.

"You're absolutely beautiful, Jolene. The most stunning woman I've ever seen. I love the way you give me what I want."

"So, what do you want me to do now?"

"Taste yourself," he whispered. "Finger your pussy, then suck off your juice."

I shuddered as I complied, stroking my pussy as he commanded. When I pulled my hand away from my sex, my fingers were glistening in the sunlight filtering through the windshield. Very slowly, I brought them to my mouth, closing my eyes in bliss as I tasted myself. It tasted musky and slightly salty, but there was a sweetness I found appealing. So I did it again.

"Fuck… me…" Styx seemed torn between watching me and watching the road. "I'm gonna fuckin' wreck," he muttered. He punched a button or two before turning his attention to me, reaching out to caress my calf where my foot rested on the center console. He didn't turn back to the road.

"What are you doing?"

He shrugged, "Driver Assist. BlueCruise or something like that. Cain has the best shit money can buy, thanks to ExFil. We're on the interstate, the brothers around us. Ain't recommended, but I'm willin' to risk a little danger to watch you come like this."

His hand caressed my calf, then moved up my thigh while I dipped my fingers back to my pussy, stroking lazily. "I love the feel of your hands on me, Styx. I love how big you are."

"Good. 'Cause I'll be touchin' you every fuckin' day for the rest of our lives. You're mine, Jolene."

"You're mine, too." I lifted my hand and leaned toward him, offering my gleaming fingers to him. He grasped my wrist, pulling it to his mouth and sucking my fingers.

"Mmm." His growl was a sexy sound. "Love your taste. Do it again." I did. "Mother fuck!" An alarm beeped, and Styx returned his gaze to the road before reaching for me. He leaned in to swipe his fingers through my pussy. I scooted my ass forward, making it easier for him to touch me in the spacious truck interior. The second I pulled my hand back, he replaced it with his own. Styx sucked my juice from his fingers as I brought my fingers to my mouth. Instead of sucking on them, however, I painted my lips until I knew they shone like I'd coated them with lip gloss.

"Kiss me," I begged, moving forward to lean against the center console. He reached out for me, cupping the back of my neck with his hand as my lips met his. Tasting me as he kissed me seemed to make something click inside Styx. He held me closer, the grip on my neck almost painful, but it only fed my own lust.

"Takin' everything everything I got to not just yank you over the console and pull that sweet pussy down on my cock."

"What does it taste like when you kiss me, Styx?" I asked against his lips.

"Like the sweetest honey. Do it again." I kept kissing him, sliding my hand down to my pussy only to bring it between us and paint both our lips with my juices. "Fuck me," I muttered as I licked his lips.

"God, I want to!" He sounded pained. One glance at his crotch told me he was hard for me.

I pulled back, getting my legs under me until I was on my knees in the seat. I painted each of my nipples in my intimate moisture before offering them to Styx. He greedily sucked first one, then the other. I needed more.

Turning, I scooted my ass onto the center

console, lying back and pulling my knees up to my chest. "Eat me," I demanded. I knew there was a very real possibility there was no way Styx could manage this, but I was rapidly losing my mind in a lust-filled haze. And, really, he'd started this adventure.

The fucking alarm telling him he needed to keep his eyes on the road chimed again, and I wanted to groan. With a scowl, he turned his head to focus on the road before turning back to me and burying his face in my pussy. I screamed, reaching around my thighs to part my pussy lips. I wanted him in as deep as he could manage in the awkward positioning. His tongue inside my pussy. His fingers. Whatever he could manage.

"Fuck, Jolene! So fuckin' good!"

"Need to fuck you, Styx," I whimpered.

"I know baby," he bit out between licks. "Need you too." Lick. Slurp. He groaned between every suck almost as loudly as I did. "God! You're so fuckin' wet!" He slipped his fingers inside me, curling them to rub against the sweet spot inside me. The instant he did, I came in a hard, wet rush. I screamed, my lower body contracting with my orgasm. The stupid alarm chose that moment to trill again, and I groaned my frustration. Styx chuckled as he pulled his fingers from my weeping cunt to lick them clean and make eye contact with the road as well as steadying the steering wheel.

Fuck this shit.

While Styx was distracted with his driving -- *funny*! -- I slipped one leg over his lap and settled myself on top of him.

"Jolene..."

"Need you inside me."

"But..."

"Please, Styx." I was working to get his cock out of his jeans. When it sprang free, we both groaned. With me between him and the windshield, he had to look over my shoulder to look at the road so the truck would stop its stupid alarm.

"Get me inside you, baby. Then lay your head on my shoulder so I can see the road. You'll have to do most of the work."

"Don't care." I whimpered. "Just need to fuck you. Need your cum inside me."

"Son of a bitch," he gasped as the head of his cock kissed the opening of my pussy. "Put it in, baby. Get me the fuck inside you."

It didn't take me long to comply. When I sank down fully on top of him, another orgasm hit me, and I threw my head back and cried out as my pussy squeezed his dick.

"Goddamn! Jolene! Fuck!" One of his big hands gripped my ass, holding me still. "Don't you fuckin' move, girl! Not one fuckin' inch!"

"Styx," I whimpered, trying to rock my hips on him no matter his warning. "Need your cum in me."

"You're such a hot little thing." Styx said as he fisted my hair and brought me down for a kiss. I let him have what he wanted. His tongue carried my taste with it, and I moaned, loving our mingled tastes and scents. "Gonna give it to you, babe. All my cum. Deep in your hot little pussy." He urged me to move on him, so I rocked back and forth until I found a fast but steady rhythm.

Styx shouted, lifting his head and letting it fall back onto the seat. "Fuck! That feels fuckin' good!"

"Yes," I whimpered, kissing him again and fucking him as hard as I could. Styx wrapped his arms around me, keeping my head out of his line of sight.

Just like he'd told me, my head was on his shoulder, and I just fucked him. It didn't take long before he gripped my ass in both hands, directing my movements, using me to fuck him the way he needed. "You ready, baby? Ready for me to come?"

"Yes!" My whisper was more like a demanding hiss. I needed this so much. Needed him. Styx.

"Then take it!" He roared, his hips surging up to fuck me the last few strokes as he came. His cum was hot. Scalding. Like a brand deep inside me I couldn't get enough of. "Fuckin' take it!" His orgasm, the feel of his seed inside me, triggered my own orgasm. I cried out, milking his cock for every last drop.

I collapsed on top of Styx, my naked body draped over his fully clothed one. He kept one hand firmly around me, holding me to him. I assumed the other one was back on the wheel.

"I love you so much, Styx," I whimpered. I hadn't really meant to say it, but there was really no way he didn't know. And if he didn't, I wanted him to.

He sighed, hugging me tighter. "I know you do, baby. I love you, too. You good?"

"Yeah." The single word was drawn out on a sigh. I didn't want to move, but the air conditioning was chilling my bare skin. "I'm afraid I made a mess on you, though."

"Honey, it was me who made the mess. And I ain't worried about it."

Tentatively, I moved, knowing I needed to move back to my seat. "That probably wasn't the safest idea, huh?"

Styx barked a laugh, tightening his hold on me. He even let go of the wheel to wrap his other arm around me. "No. Can't say it was. Or that I would recommend it to anyone else." He fisted a hand in my hair to pull my head back and tilt my face up for a kiss. "Can't say I won't repeat it, either."

With a happy sigh, I maneuvered off Styx and back to my side of the truck. Thankfully, there was a box of tissues in the back seat. I cleaned myself and disposed of the tissue in a plastic sack used to contain trash over the long ride. Now that the adventure was over, I felt a little foolish.

"Hey," Styx snapped. His gaze was fiery hot as it fastened on me. "None of that. You're a beautiful, passionate, hot-blooded woman. Mine. I happen to love that side of you as much as I love everything else about you. Don't doubt yourself." He reached out and took my hand, squeezing it. "I wouldn't want you to be any other way, Jolene. I hope you're always as eager for sexual adventure as you are now." He slid me a cocky grin. "If you are, we'll have one hell of a time together."

I smiled, a relieved laugh bubbling to the surface. "It is an adventure. Isn't it?"

"The greatest." He pulled my hand to his mouth and kissed my fingers.

Chapter Eight
Styx

We rolled into the Bane clubhouse just before dark. Jolene had made the trip the most eventful, exciting trip from Kentucky to Florida I'd ever experienced. In addition to the first time we'd fucked while barreling down the highway, she'd had her way with me twice more, and had sucked me off another two. I was completely, thoroughly, wonderfully spent. So was she. She'd brought herself to climax more than once. And she'd come several times when she'd fucked me. Just thinking back to that trip had me smiling. My Jolene was a rare treasure.

Once inside the compound, Thorn, Havoc, and Red met me as I was climbing out of the truck. "Did you get it?" Red crossed his arms over his massive chest. "'Cause, if you didn't, you can just drive that son of a bitch back to West Virginia and get my fuckin' car."

"Red, stop being such a grouch." The short, willowy redhead who'd let Red claim her hurried to catch up with the other three men. Rosanna was one of the best mechanics I knew, and she'd been itching to get her hands on that car. "There's more important things than that Maybach. Styx brought home a woman." Her comment made me grateful I considered her a friend.

"You're can be a fuckin' son of a bitch sometimes, Red," I muttered. "I have no idea why Rosanna puts up with your sorry ass. Got shit to discuss with Thorn 'bout Jolene and her kin."

Red jerked back like I'd struck him. "What the fuck's with the accent? You sound like you stepped out of a Hatfield and McCoy movie. That girl gettin' to you already?"

I grinned. "Well, we *are* Hatfields and McCoys." With a shrug I waved him off, the bastard. "I fought hard to rid myself of that accent when I left for the Army. But I loved Jolene's accent so much, I guess I fell back into the habit."

"Where is she?" Rosanna looked around, obviously wanting to meet my Jolene.

"She's asleep in the truck," I said, not even trying to suppress the grin.

"Oh? Did you have an eventful ride?" Rosanna looked worriedly from me to Red.

"Definitely had an eventful ride."

"Well, it's gettin' ready to be more eventful." Ripper, the intel guy for Salvation's Bane walked into the yard, a hard look on his face. "You've lost your fuckin' mind, Styx." Ripper sounded as angry as hell as he approached us.

"Me?" I probably looked as confused as I sounded.

"Yeah, you bastard. There's a contingent of fucking hillbillies headed this way. What'd you intend to happen when they got here?"

"Hillbillies," I snapped. "What the fuck do you mean?"

"I mean, your fuckin' half brothers and his cousins are on their way here. For your woman."

"Is Shotgun comin'?"

"Oh, yeah. He was the first one I called after Thorn. Got here a couple hours ago. I think him and his ol' lady are in the clubhouse, partyin' with the rest of the club." Ripper scowled in the direction he'd indicated. "Man don't take nothin' seriously."

"He does. He just likes to play." I grinned, thinking of my half brother. Shotgun had left West

Virginia when he was just a boy. He didn't remember much about life in Williamson.

"Well, this ain't the time. Better get your girl tucked away. Crazy bastards stopped just outside of town. Figure they'll be here either tonight or tomorrow. Dependin' on how fuckin' stupid they are."

"They're pretty fuckin' stupid, Ripper. How'd they find us? Are they after Jolene or the Maybach?"

"Oh, they're after the girl. What'd you expect to happen when you tagged them on fuckin' social media with a big ole fuck you to 'all your kin in West Virginia'?" Ripper made air quotes as he berated me. "I mean, you posted a picture of the two of you obviously havin' sex, for fuck's sake!"

OK, that got my attention. "I never took no picture like that, Ripper. If Jolene finds out, she'll lose her shit."

"Yeah," Rosanne said, slipping her hand into Red's and looking up at him. "We heard about what your other brother did. She's gonna take that hard."

"Take what hard?" I turned around when Jolene spoke. She was out of the truck looking adorably sleepy as she rubbed one eye. Had the situation been different, I'd have smiled at her. Instead, I knew I needed to be careful. "Hey, baby," I reached for her, pulling her into my arms. "We're here."

"Yeah," she said, rubbing her face against my chest like a contented cat. "I see that."

"Why don't I take you to my room, Jolene? We need to talk."

"Uh-oh," she said, pulling back from me slightly. "What happened?"

"Fucker," I said, throwing Ripper a killing look over Jolene's shoulder.

"Just tell me," she said, sounding resigned. "You

don't want me anymore. Do you."

"Honey, there is no way you believe that. Let's just do this in private."

She looked up at me, a bewildered look on her face. "I -- I don't under -- understand."

I sighed, pulling her back into my embrace. "Honey, Avery's in Palm Beach. Him and his kin." Jolene stiffened in my arms. "Stop," I said next to her ear. "Just take a breath. I've got you. I'm not goin' anywhere, and I'll always protect you."

"I know that," she said against my shoulder. "We always protect each other."

"That's right, baby."

With another shudder, she pulled back and looked up at me. She must have seen something in my face, because she closed her eyes and sagged against me. "Just tell me what you don't want to say, Styx."

"Apparently, there's a picture of us. On my social media."

She looked confused. "You took a pic of us? Why is that bad?"

"I didn't take it, honey. And I didn't post it."

"But, isn't that what people do when they're together? Post pics of themselves? Together? You know, as a couple?"

"All true. And I'll gladly take any picture you want and post them everywhere with a caption proudly proclaiming you my ol' lady. But this one…"

"What about it?"

"Apparently, it was of us makin' love, baby." There was a long silence. Jolene had gone perfectly still. "Talk to me, honey."

"I did it," she said softly. "I posted the picture and tagged your brothers and cousins, Styx. I wanted them to come here. So I could kill 'em. 'Cause I ain't goin' back to West Virginia for anything ever." She took another breath. "And, 'cause I wanted to replace that other video with something of my choosin'. If shit like that's gonna be out there 'bout me, I'm pickin' the pics, and I'm pickin' who it's with." The more she explained, the stronger her voice. She was trying to take back her life in the only way she knew how. Had she stuck me with a dagger through the heart, I couldn't have been more shocked.

"Well," I said. "Wasn't expectin' that."

"Why would you do that, Jolene?" Thorn didn't look mad, just thoroughly confused. "We know what they all did to you. How you were betrayed, then attacked. Why would you taunt them like that?"

She took a breath, then turned to face everyone. "I'm sorry I put y'all in a bad position. I just wanted ta face 'em where I'd be strong."

"Baby, I told you I'd take care of 'em."

"I know. But I wanna do it." Her expression grew fierce. "I'm *gonna* do it."

Thorn shook his head, grinning slightly when he met my gaze. "Girl's gonna be a handful. You sure about this?"

Jolene gasped, then pushed away from me. "I ain't trouble! I'm takin' care of my own fuckin' mess is all. Just thought it'd be safer to do it in a controlled environment."

"Relax, baby," I said, pulling her close once again. "I'm sure 'bout us. Thorn knows it too. He's just givin' me shit like he does everyone else. All our women are handfuls. That's why y'all put up with us. Just wished you'd given me a heads-up."

"You'd'a just tried to talk me out of it. Or, worse, gone'n done it without me." She had this adorable, stubborn look on her face as she looked up at me. Like me going into battle without her going with me was the most unreasonable request she'd ever heard.

"Well, yeah," I responded. "Ain't never lied to you, so I ain't startin' now. I don't want you near the mess that's gonna go down. If you'd'a told me, we could've been ready to meet 'em head-on."

"I'm ready," she said, her eyes fierce. In that moment, I saw how much Jolene needed this. "You don't have to go with me. I got this."

"Honey," Thorn said, pinching the bridge of his nose. "I'm not doubting you, but there's more involved than just killin' the bastards. I mean, they deserve it, and they're gonna die fuckin' hard. But I like to have a plan in place if possible so we can mitigate the damage. I've had to move the clubhouse once because of it, and my wife is rather fond of this one."

"Wait," I said, something just occurring to me. "You never took pictures of us having sex."

"Yeah," she said, looking slightly ashamed. "It was when we were in the truck."

"No…" I said slowly, trying to think back. "I'm pretty sure I wasn't that far gone," I said. "I'd have remembered if you took a pic or vid. I mean, that's pretty hard to miss."

"You fucked her in the truck?" Ripper said, a big grin on his face. "I hope that was at a rest stop or something. 'Cause, yeah."

I couldn't keep the grin off my face. "Nope. While I don't recommend it, I'll definitely do it again."

"Dude! That's a hundred-and-twenty-five thousand dollar vehicle! Cain's gonna kick your ass!"

"Why?" I shrugged. "No one died, the truck is in one piece, and so's the car we were hauling. *And*, no one got a ticket. No harm, no foul."

"I mean, he's not wrong, Ripper." Rosanna

grinned before asking Jolene, "Big thumbs up on the Tesla Challenge! So... How'd you take the pictures? I mean, if you didn't actually take the pictures?"

"Susie. I asked her if she could hack the cameras inside the vehicle and take something." She looked up at me, her eyes wide. "But I swear, I told her to just get me. Not you. I didn't want your face to be in the picture at all, and she promised she wouldn't. That way you could deny it if you wanted."

"She's right," Ripper said. I was sure that was more to reassure Jolene than me. "Your face wasn't actually in the pic. Knew it was you 'cause of your tats."

"Honey, I could give a rat's ass if you got me or not. I'd actually prefer you did. That way those punkasses knew for sure who they were dealing with." I wrapped her up in my arms again. "How long'd you say we had? Later tonight or tomorrow?"

"If I had to guess," Ripper said, "I'd say they'll come callin' tonight." He shrugged. "Couple hours, maybe. Once I figured out who they were and what was goin' down, I started finding active ways to keep an eye on them. Right now, they're holed up in a roach motel on the highway. Don't look like they're lookin' to settle in for the night."

"I didn't want to make it difficult for you, Styx," she said softly. "I was gonna hide outside the compound and take them out one at a time."

"You didn't exactly make it difficult. I mean, they're pissants. We'll just squash 'em. I just don't like it that you planned on doin' this without tellin' me. We're a team. Remember?"

"And how'd you get Susie to do this without tellin' us?" Thorn asked. "She really shouldn't have done that."

"I might have told her I'd told Styx?" She winced, looking up at me to gauge my reaction.

I wanted to look stern but couldn't manage it. Instead, I might have chuckled a little. "You're gonna get your ass busted for that, little girl."

"I -- what?"

"You heard me," I grinned. "Gonna spank your ass till it's red." Then I leaned in and whispered at her ear. "Then I'm gonna fuck it."

She shivered in my arms and let out a little giggle.

"You could use something that's gonna correct her behavior instead of encourage it," Thorn groused, but I could see his amusement.

"So, have I really caused you guys a bunch of trouble?" Jolene didn't look intimidated, but anyone could tell she was contrite. Her question was sincere. "I really just wanted to take care of it myself."

"No one here does anything by themselves," Havoc said. "Not even Thorn. We're a team. That means you, too." He looked squarely at me. "Something your man there should have explained to you."

"It's not his fault," she said quickly. "He told me he'd take care of it. I just wanted to... I don't know. This is my problem. Not y'all's or his. Didn't wanna get nobody hurt on account'a me."

"And you've already been hurt enough, baby," I said. "Ain't lettin' you get hurt again."

"Jesus, Styx," Red muttered. "Could you sound more like you're actually from the sticks? Where'd the fuck did that accent come from?"

"You didn't honestly think I meant to spell my name S T Y K S, did you? Was supposed'ta be be S T I C K S for that very reason."

Havoc barked out a laugh and Thorn chuckled. "You ain't right, brother," Havoc said, still laughing.

"No," Thorn agreed. "He ain't. Doubt anyone from the hollar is. But we all got our own brand of crazy." He shook his head, grinning. "Now get your woman upstairs and give her a good seein' to. You wear her out enough, we can get this done so she can wake up and it all be over and done with."

"Don't want that," she said. "I realize you can't be like Cain and give me the kill. That's too much for any club like yours. But I still wanna be there."

"Wait," Havoc said. "What did you say?"

Thorn swore, looking from Jolene to me and back again. "I'm gonna have a word or three with Cain next time I see him." His gaze finally settled on me. "Is she shittin' me?"

"Afraid not. I wasn't altogether for it. Neither was Cain. But we both realized she needed it. I think she might need this, too. Though, last time was almost too much for her. This time's gonna be worse."

"You know I'm standin' right here. Right?" Jolene frowned, pushing away from me again. "I know what I want to happen to every fuckin' one of 'em. And I *can* take it." She lifted her chin, meeting Thorn's. "I will."

I could see Thorn knew there was no way he was winning this battle outright. But I could also see that he didn't intend to let Jolene anywhere near my kin. I was with him on that. Mainly because I knew that whatever Jolene wanted to do to them would ultimately break her. She was fierce, but she had a tender heart. I'd nearly lost her to grief after she'd killed her father. I wasn't about to get that close to losing her again.

"Come on, baby," I said, taking her hand. "Let's get ready. If we're going to fight, we need to be rested.

Been a long drive."

"I'm goin' with you, Styx. Ain't hidin' in my room like a coward."

"You're the bravest person I know, Jolene. Don't ever think otherwise." I scooped her up into my arms, carrying her. She wrapped her slender arms around my neck and buried her face there. I didn't think she really wanted to be part of this, though she tried to convince herself she did. But I'd give her what I could. If she needed to face Avery again, I'd make sure she got to. But she was absolutely not going to be there when he died. I was sure she needed something from her father when he died, but it had taken something from her. Far more than she could afford to give at the time. I was pretty sure I'd given her love to fill in the gaps he'd stolen from her, but she still wasn't whole.

As I carried her to my room, she settled against my chest, nuzzling my neck and kissing softly. Once inside, I took her straight to the bed. I didn't even bother with our clothes. Not yet. She needed love more than sex, though the sex would come later. I settled myself between her legs, my arms wrapped tightly around her. Her arms wrapped just as tightly around me.

"My beautiful, sweet Jolene." I stroked her hair and kissed her softly. "You are everything to me." My words were whispered but as fierce as I could make them. I needed her to understand and believe in me. "There's no one in this world who means as much to me. No one in this world I'd protect as viciously and violently as I'll protect you. You... are... *everything* good in my life Jolene."

She let out a small sob, tears leaking from the corner of her eyes to streak down her temples. When I kissed her, I took her cries inside me. I could almost feel her pain as sharply as I imagined she did. Jolene put up a brave fight, but the coming battle was more than she could handle. I knew it as well as I knew my own name.

The longer I kissed her, the more she responded until she was consumed by the need inside her. She cried out several times, begging me to let her come, but I wouldn't.

"Not yet, baby. You're not nearly ready enough."

"You're killing me!" Her cry was anguished. More tears flowed from her eyes, and I kissed them, lapped at them gently before kissing her some more.

"I'll never get enough of your kisses. When you kiss me, Jolene, nothing else in the whole fuckin' world matters."

"Styx." She said my name on a sigh, and she surrendered to me. Her legs came around my hips, and she held me to her. We still kissed, but it was more for comfort than to arouse. She needed it, but I thought I needed it more than she did.

We stayed like that for a long time. Just… kissing. Holding each other. Not thinking about anything but being in each other's arms. I praised her. Told her how much I loved her. How much I admired her courage. I bared my heart and soul to her and did my best to comfort her when I knew she didn't want it. Not really. As I saw it, my job wasn't just to give her what she wanted. Sometimes, I had to find a way to give her what she needed.

"What are you trying to tell me, Styx?" she said, cupping my face in her tiny hand. Before answering her, I kissed her once more, taking my time so she knew it really meant something to me. That what I was about to ask of her was important to me.

"Baby," I said, stroking her delicate cheekbone

with one finger. I remembered how she'd looked when I first found her. She'd healed. At least on the outside. "I need you to let me do this. With my brothers."

"But --"

"Shh... Just listen to me. You did what you had to with your pap. If you really need to face Avery and his ilk before they die, I'll see what I can do. But I don't want you there until I say. And I need you to leave when I say. Can you give me that?"

"Styx," she sighed, meeting my gaze with a determined one of her own. Then she sighed, giving me a soft smile. "You really do love me, don't you?"

"I do, baby. With all my heart and more."

"I want to see them before they die. I should be a good person and ask you to just beat the shit out of 'em, but I want all of 'em dead. I ain't askin' you or your friends'ta kill 'em. That's too much to ask of anyone."

"Honey, you ain't askin'. I am. And I'll be the one doin' the killin' this time. Not you. Cain shoulda never given that to you."

"I needed it."

"This time, I need it," I said. Meaning it. "So, I'm askin' you to give this to me. I need to unleash hell on those bastards, and I don't want you there when I do it. I can't have you watch it."

"But I did before."

"Yeah, but I wasn't doin' the beatin' that time. I'm gonna be front and center this time. Please, Jolene. Let me have this."

"All right." She pulled me down for another kiss. This time, I made love to her. I stripped her naked and worshiped her body for the better part of two hours. As always, Jolene gave as good as she got, taking me to a bliss so complete, I wondered if I'd ever come down from it. And I wasn't sure I ever wanted to.

When the text came from Thorn, Jolene was sound asleep in my arms. There was nothing more I wanted than to stay with her, but I had work to do. I was about to vanquish the last of her demons, and it wasn't going to be pleasant.

I gently extracted myself from her arms and dressed. Before I left, I took one more look at her beautiful, angelic form. I was about to sell a large chunk of my soul. Torturing a man took a toll. And I was going to torture seven. If I'd had more time to prepare, I'd have been creative. I wanted them all to suffer exactly like they'd made Jolene suffer.

Leaning down, I gave her one last gentle kiss, careful not to wake her. Then I headed out to meet my president. We were getting ready for war, and I couldn't fucking wait.

Chapter Nine
Styx

Shit was about to get real for Avery and the rest of those little fucks. Leaving Jolene now was the hardest thing I'd ever done. Except for looking at her as Mama examined her that first day. Seeing all those bruises on her body, knowing what she gone through at the hands of my fucking brother filled me with even more rage now than it did when it was fresh.

I stalked down the hall into the common room, that rage building inside me with every step. It must have shown on my face because when Queenie, who I remembered from the Bones compound in Kentucky, approached me with a triumphant smirk, I met her gaze and she stopped dead in her tracks. Her face paled, and her hand went to her throat defensively. I shook my head slowly, and she backed away before turning to leave the room. She didn't even go to another biker in the room. Just left. Yeah. I wasn't in the mood to be fucked with.

"You ready?" Shotgun approached me with a grin. The man looked like he didn't have a care in the world, but it was mostly an act. He was always lighthearted and fun-loving, but when it came time to fight, there was no man I'd rather have in my corner than Shotgun.

"I am. They all come or did some of 'em stay back in West Virginia?"

"Nope. All here." He gave me a puzzled look. "Since when do you talk like a hillbilly? What the fuck, Styx?"

I rolled my eyes. "Is that the most important question you got? Really, Shotgun?"

My half brother shrugged. "Well, yeah. I mean,

you lost your man card to a McCoy, that's one thing. But I'm not sure I can claim you as my brother with that accent."

"Fucker," I muttered.

"They're just outside the gate," Havoc said as he leaned against the bar, nursing a beer.

Beast strode through the room. The big man was as intimidating as they came. His leather vest showed off his powerful arms, chest, and tats. Yeah. There was a reason he was the club's enforcer. Beast was one scary bastard. Well, to everyone other than his wife, Lucy. One look from her, and the badass of the club turned into complete mush. Until he looked away from her. Anyone smirking might or might not live to see the next sunrise. He nodded to Thorn, an indication everything was ready.

"Everyone's on lockdown until further notice." Thorn's voice boomed in the cavernous, two-story, open main room. "Everyone not a patched member has five minutes to get to a room and stay there." There were no consequences specified, but no one would dare defy the president when he had that look on his face. Everyone but patched members hurried out of the room and to the various suites in the rest of the building. The clubhouse was actually a converted firehouse. Salvation's Bane had been building on to it and adding smaller buildings throughout the land we owned. There were plenty of accommodations for everyone currently here.

For the full five minutes Thorn had given everyone to secure themselves, we all stood in silence. Everyone watched Thorn, waiting to take their cues from him. Thorn watched me.

"You do exactly what I tell you, Styx." His voice was deceptively soft. I knew he meant business. We weren't close to the city, but we'd invested far more in this clubhouse than the one we'd abandoned several years earlier when Thorn's woman had been attacked and she'd killed the bastard.

"I ain't gonna do nothin' to put the club in jeopardy, Thorn. But these fuckers gotta die."

"No one's sayin' different. I'll let you put some emotion into this, but Doc has strict control over all... activities, and I decide when it's time for the kill. You got your woman secured?"

"She's in our room asleep."

"And when she wakes? She comin' after you?"

I shook my head. "I got her to agree to let me have this. I promised her she'd have the chance to confront them before they died if she chose, so I'd respectfully request that you allow me to give her that option."

Thorn snorted. "Don't think I didn't notice you *promised* her before you *asked* me. But OK. I can give you that. You know what your woman can handle and what she needs. If Cain let her have anything during the other interrogation, then he trusts her."

"*I* trust her, Thorn. She's the genuine article. My woman."

"I've read up on the file Ripper gathered on these fuckers. All seven of 'em. They've earned everything they're gettin' ready to receive. I also got an in-detail description of what happened at Bones with Marshall McCoy from Cain. This is gonna make that pale in comparison."

"I'll let you know before it goes beyond what I think she can handle."

Thorn gave me a crisp nod. "Good, then. Let's get this business done. Fuckin' bastards have lived too long as it is."

***

Jolene

I knew Styx had gone to take care of his kin. No. I didn't think of them that way. Avery and his bunch weren't Styx's kin. They might share blood, but Styx had no kinship with men like that. He'd given me any little thing I'd asked for since he met me. He'd taken care of me. Seen to my injuries. Most importantly, he'd taken my shattered heart, soul, and body and rebuilt it stronger. I loved Styx. Ruben Hatfield. And I never wanted to let him go. For that, I'd give him what he asked. I'd do what he said regarding Avery and the rest of them. I wasn't sure I wanted to go through it all again anyway. I thought I'd need the closure, but now I wasn't so sure. In fact, I thought that, if Styx walked back through that door and told me they were all every one of them dead, I'd take his word for it and never mind the visual proof. Styx hadn't lied to me yet, and I didn't believe he'd start now.

As if I'd conjured him, the door opened. I looked up from where I sat at the window looking out at the ocean. Instead of Styx, however, Queenie entered before shutting the door securely behind her.

"What the fuck?" I stood, fully prepared to kick the other woman out when she waltzed in and plopped down on the couch in front of the TV. "Thought you were back in Kentucky."

"Thorn only gave us five minutes to secure ourselves," Queenie said with a shrug. "I don't have a permanent place here, so I went to the room I'd been in last." She gave me a smug grin. "Styx had me follow him down after he got back to Bane. I mean, I followed him from here to Bones on his orders. He told me to come back a couple days after he returned here." She shrugged. "I'm sure Styx won't mind me being in here now. I mean," she grinned, "it's *his* room, after all. He told me so when he showed me around."

I wanted to grind my teeth in frustration. I wanted to throw her out. But she had a point. This wasn't my room. It was Styx's. I had no idea if he'd mind her being there or not, especially if she really had nowhere else to go.

"Stay out of my way," I finally settled. "And don't make any noise. I need to hear anything going on."

The other woman shrugged. "You won't hear anything. They keep club business to themselves. You'd know that if you'd been with Styx long."

I had no desire to converse with the woman. I just wanted solitude. I needed to think about something other than Styx and this woman in an intimate position, because that was all that was spinning in my head.

She stretched out on the couch, moving her body sensually over the leather. "I think my favorite time with Styx was when we broke in this couch," she said with a merry tinkle in her laughter. "Never had a man fill me so full of cum as he did those three days."

"Three *days*?" I hadn't meant to rise to her bait, but I couldn't seem to stop my stupid mouth. And hadn't Styx told me he hadn't ever come inside a woman?

"Oh, yeah. We'd have gone longer, too, except he had to leave to help Red." She shrugged. "Guess it was when they went to steal that really expensive car in West Virginia. Just a couple weeks ago. That where he found you?"

I nodded slowly. "Yeah. Car was my pap's."

"Pap? What's a pap?" She wrinkled her delicate

nose even as she stretched more, showing off her flat belly and the little navel jewelry hanging from her piercing. Her tits were barely contained in the halter she wore, and her hips and ass were hugged in leather boy shorts. The knee-high boots she wore had insanely high heels. I cringed as she propped them on the arm of the couch. That couldn't be good for the leather.

"My dad."

She snickered. "Oh. So, hillbilly for dad." She gave me a wink and a smile. "Gotcha."

I turned back to the window to hide my wince. I guess my dialect wasn't up to standards around here. There was no way I could stay here. Not like this. Not with one of Styx's former lovers in the same room with me. He hadn't said he didn't know her when we were at Bones, only that he hadn't wanted her attentions. I wanted to kick her out but wasn't sure I could. I mean, if she sought out Styx to complain, then I'd have driven her right into his arms. Then I sighed. I'd lived my whole life with people making me miserable. I could manage for a few hours more. Surely. I'd just grown used to being so comfortable with Styx, it shoved home how much my life had changed in the last few weeks, and I didn't want to go back.

"I saw the pics you took in the truck," she said, ignoring my order that she be quiet. "I can't wait to do Styx one better when he takes that truck back to Kentucky."

That got my full attention back on the bimbo on the couch. "What?"

"Oh, yeah. Didn't he tell you? I'm going back with him to return Cain's truck. I'll get a full video of us instead of just one stupid picture. You missed your chance, honey. Men around here love to do one better. Ain't often you'll get a chance to fuck in a vehicle like that, and you blew your chance to record it."

"What do you want, Queenie?" I bit out. "He's with me. Not you."

She shrugged. "For now. He'll get tired of the little hillbilly act you got going on soon enough. When he does, I'll be waiting for him."

"No one said he'd get tired of me. Styx is with me. Me! He's mine."

"Don't see no property patch on your back."

Hadn't Styx mentioned something about that? "He said he had it ordered."

"Don't mean nothing until he gives it to you. I know lots of guys in the club who told a woman they were gonna make them their ol' lady but never gave them a patch. That's the only way it's official."

"He told me it was a done thing. Patch or not, the club knew he'd claimed me."

Queenie laughed and gave me a pitying look. "Oh, honey. I can't believe you fell for that. I take it he's still not given you a vest?" When I said nothing, she continued. "Yeah. He'll be done with you soon. Probably sooner than he thought. He's just trying to keep you on a while longer. Probably once he can't shock you anymore he'll throw you over. Once he does, I'll be waiting for him."

"You're lyin'," I said, trying to hold back the tears. I tried to put as much confidence as I could into my denial, but how sure was I? This woman had been in the club for years. My experience was exactly two weeks and three days. And most of that I'd been healing. Not actually interacting with the rest of the club. Well, other than a few of the ol' ladies. But no one had indicated I wasn't exactly what Styx said I was.

She shrugged one shoulder. "Don't take my word for it. Ask any of the other girls. They'll tell you the same thing. A property patch is like puttin' a ring on it."

"Whatever." I turned back to the window. I needed Styx. Needed his reassurance. I believed him, so if he told me she was lying, I wouldn't question it. But right now, I was raw. Probably because the men who'd turned my life upside down were in this very place where I needed to find refuge. If it weren't for Styx, I'd be running as hard as I could go back to the Bones compound. I wouldn't have Styx, but I knew they'd let me have a home there if I needed it. And no one there had tried to take Styx from me except for this fucking bitch.

But I was built from sterner stuff than that. I might not be what my pap always wanted me to be, but I was Styx's woman.

Raising my chin I pointed to the door. "I want you out of here. This may not be my room, but I'm living here until Styx says otherwise, and I don't want to share the place with you."

She laughed before sitting up. I winced when the heel of her boot scratched the leather of the couch. "Why don't you *make me*? Fucking hillbilly."

Oh… it was *on*.

* * *

Styx

The confrontation with my half brothers and cousins went better than I'd hoped. That is to say we got them inside the compound almost immediately and carted their asses to our interrogation room. It didn't take long for them to be sobbing like little babies. I was in great shape, but beating the shit out of seven men was more than I was physically capable of. So all my brothers took a turn. Including Thorn. In fact,

Thorn did most of the heavy hitting. He left the little stuff -- like removing fingernails and toenails -- to Beast. I'd never seen the man relish a task so much.

"I'd normally spare you this kind of shit," Beast had told one of them. Couldn't remember his name. Tried hard my whole adult life to forget that branch of the family tree. "But any man who takes a gang of men to rape a single, helpless woman deserves every fuckin' thing we can throw at him. And believe me. What I'm doin' is a cakewalk compared to what the women are gettin' ready to do." He actually chuckled. "And that man over there?" He pointed to Doc, who stood leaning against the wall with his arms crossed, a little grin on his face. "He's here to make sure you don't pass out or die before we're ready." Yeah. The whimpers and pleas from the seven men were music to my fucking ears.

Then Venus had her turn. She tag-teamed with Millie, Shadow's woman, even though she and Shadow weren't patched members of Salvation's Bane. Venus was a patched member, and the three of them were very close.

Ripper had laid out what he'd dug up on the men, including their rape of Jolene. That included the rapes and deaths of several more women. Apparently, one of the cousins worked in law enforcement in Williamson. He'd managed to steer any investigation away from them, so they'd gotten away with dozens of rapes and more than a few murders. All them women and older girls. Venus hadn't been as kind as the rest of us. Millie watched on with a bored expression on her face. She supplied the commentary to Venus's action, recording the entire thing. Not that we'd ever put up evidence of this on the Internet. She just wanted to humiliate the bastards like they'd humiliated and hurt other women like Jolene.

Millie and Venus cackled as they watched the video when Doc called a momentary halt to let them recover with some fluids. Millie had made fun of the men as they described what they looked like in vivid detail.

"Oh, look," Venus said with fake sympathy in her accented English. "He's bleeding. I bet that hurt."

"Did baseball bat hurt, little man?" Millie grinned as she taunted Clyde, my other half-brother. Venus and Millie had taken the serial raping very seriously. They'd said they couldn't make them experience over and over what it was like to be raped, so they were doing it all at once. The man just whimpered. Blood dripped from his mouth to pool on the floor. Because me, Beast and Poison had pulled out all his teeth. One at a time.

Venus snorted. "Nyet. He can take it. Hand me bat I made special. I think he's ready for that."

Milly chuckled. "This should be fun." She turned to one of the cousins. I think it was Jacob. Hard to tell, he was beaten so badly. "I know you can't see with your eyes swollen shut, but since your ass is next, I thought you might want to know what's coming." She snagged a wooden bat from the stack of implements.

"Little kinky, but I'll take it," Venus said. Millie tossed Venus the bat, and she proceeded to penetrate Clyde. The man screamed an unholy sound. He sobbed and begged for Venus to stop. The woman just laughed. "How many times have you heard that? Did you grant request when you heard it? No? Well, you get same answer."

Millie kept up the dialogue, reminding Clyde of all he'd done to at least a couple dozen women we'd found out about. "Not having good time, little man?

But we've got so much more to do before you die."

"Please," he whimpered, his throat raw from his screams. "Just let me die."

"Oh, you'll die," Millie said. "Just not right now."

Thorn stepped beside me. "This has already gone too far for Jolene," he murmured. "Hell, I'd have thought twice about bringing Venus and Millie if they'd been in her position." He said that about the time Millie cut off Avery's dick with a pair of trauma shears to the sounds of Avery's blood-curdling screams.

"What?" she asked, giving Avery a feigned puzzled look. "It's not like you'll need it after this is over." She held up the appendage before Avery as she cackled. Blood was everywhere. Thank God she and Venus were dressed in fluid-proof coveralls -- as we all were -- but it was still a disgusting mess.

Venus and Millie had more blood and gore on them than the rest of us, but they'd known it going in. Had happily agreed to it. Venus had said, "Least we can do for your woman. She's one of us now." Looking at the pair now, I wasn't sure how I felt about that.

"Yeah, they're both real delicate feminine flowers," I said dryly. But I knew he was right. If I was honest with myself, I'd done it on purpose, not wanting Jolene anywhere near this. I'd just tell her it went too far too fast. Hopefully, she'd understand.

There was a knock at the door. Havoc glanced at Thorn before going to the door and opening a panel that let him see who was there without unlocking it. I heard Havoc grunt, then he walked over to me.

"You're needed in your room."

My gaze snapped to him. "Jolene?"

Havoc shrugged before glancing at Thorn again.

"Let's just say she ain't as delicate as you two dumbasses want to believe."

"Fuck." I stripped off my coveralls, dumping them in the burn barrel before heading back up to Jolene. I took the steps two at a time. The closer I got, the more commotion I heard.

"What've you done?"

"Someone get Marianna."

"Are you kidding? Thorn'd kill us if we brought his ol' lady up here to see this!"

"Well, we can't just leave her here. What if… what if she dies?"

"Oh, God!"

"Who gives a fuck. She's a Bones girl. Not Bane. She shouldn't be here in the first damned place."

There were women talking over each other, but the gist was clear. Someone was hurt pretty badly. My mind flashed back to the night I'd first found Jolene. She was beaten and bloody and broken. If something had happened to her in my own club, woman or not, I was killing who ever'd hurt her.

"Jolene!" I yelled as I reached the top of the stairs. There were club girls everywhere. Then I saw the blood sprayed up the side of the wall. "Jolene! Where the fuck are you!"

The crowd parted, and Queenie sat in the middle of the hallway. Blood dripped steadily from a wound on her forehead. Just when, exactly, had that woman gotten here?

"I told you to get the fuck outta my fuckin' room, and I fuckin' meant it!" That was Jolene. And she sounded pissed as all get out.

"But Styx --"

"Ain't fuckin' here!" Jolene stood over Queenie and kicked out, landing a blow to the other woman's side. "I asked you to leave nicely, then you had to go and be a bitch about it."

I couldn't say anything. I just stood there staring at my brave, fierce woman while she put a club girl in her place. Forcefully.

"He ain't claimed you! Not yet!"

"Yeah? Well, maybe I fuckin' claimed him! Ever think'a that? Don't you come back here. I don't care if he invites you or not!"

"Jolene?" I shoved my way through the club girls to get to my woman. "What happened?"

"I'll tell you what fuckin' happened! Your fuckin' bitch happened!"

"Baby, she ain't mine. You know that."

"Huh. Funny thing happened, Styx. She had a key to get into your fuckin' room. Said somethin' 'bout Thorn tellin' everyone they had five minutes to get inside somewhere, and she didn't have a place of her own other than your room."

"OK," I said slowly, looking from Jolene to Queenie and back. "So you threw her out." I shrugged. "Got no problem with that. But I promise you, baby. I never gave her a key to my room." I gave Queenie a hard look. "That's somethin' that'll need fixed, but I ain't got time for that shit right now." I looked around until I found Isadora. She was a club girl, but also a Domme at the BDSM club owned by Salvation's Bane. By default, she was in charge of the club girls when shit went down. "Take Queenie to Blade. Let him patch her up, then put her in a holding room until we're ready."

Isadora nodded her understanding, then rounded the other club girls up. "Get back in your rooms. We're still on lockdown. I see anyone else out of their rooms, you'll join Queenie on her way out."

"What?" Queenie looked stricken as she looked from Isadora to me. "No! I don't have anywhere else to go!"

"You can go back to Bones," Isadora said, unruffled. "If they'll have you. Once Cain hears about this little stunt, you may be on your own."

Queenie looked back at Jolene. "Look, I'm sorry, OK? Styx is yours. You won't get no push back from me anymore."

"Fuck you," Jolene spat.

"After everything's secured, I'll get some of the girls to clean this up," Isadora said as she helped Queenie to her feet. "For the record, your girl put up with Queenie longer than I would have. I saw her enter the room when this all started hours ago."

"You knew she was in my room and didn't come get me?" My temper was about to redline. I had more important shit to worry about than this.

"Hey. Your girl is perfectly capable of taking care of herself. Not sure what Queenie said to set her off, but once Jolene was done, she was *done*. She physically tossed Queenie out. When Queenie wouldn't stop…" Isadora shrugged. "Things got a bit more physical. Queenie swung at Jolene. Jolene shoved her head into the wall." Isadora gestured to the blood spatter on a wooden support.

I couldn't help but grin. "Good goin', baby!"

"Don't you call me baby!" Jolene bit out between clenched teeth. "If you didn't give her a key, how'd she fuckin' get in?"

"Stole it. Probably made a copy of her own."

"Is this how you guys work around here? 'Cause I don't want any Tom, Dick, or Harry walkin' into my home without permission."

Had the situation been different I'd probably

have laughed my ass off. But I had a small window, and it was rapidly closing.

"Come with me, Jolene," I said, putting my arm around her and leaning in to kiss her temple. She halfheartedly batted at me but allowed the contact. I took her into our room and shut the door.

"Don't bother lockin' it. Women just come and go as they please around here. I'll probably walk in here one day, and you'll be in bed with one of 'em but, oops, baby! I don't got no idea how she got here. Must'a stole a fuckin' key!"

"Honey, come sit with me a minute." I sat on the couch in the living room, but Jolene seemed even more agitated.

"Yeah, if you notice a few scratches in the leather, that'd be your girl out there and her freakishly high heels."

"Jolene." I tried to keep hold of my temper. She didn't need it, but I was struggling. It wasn't her I was getting agitated at but the situation. I absolutely did not need this drama with a club girl right now. "Just sit with me."

She continued to pace, her arms wrapped around her as she did. I thought she'd continue to fume over Queenie, but she didn't. She just paced back and forth for a couple of minutes. While I didn't have the time for this, not letting her work through whatever she was upset about wasn't even an option. Finally, she turned to face me. The tears streaking down her face hit me like a sucker punch.

"Baby," I said, jumping up and going to her. I pulled her into my arms and let her cry. What else could I do?

"Are they dead?" She asked the question so softly I almost didn't hear it.

"Not yet, baby." I scooped her up and went to the window seat I knew she loved because it overlooked the sea. She sat on my lap, her arms around my neck, clutching my shirt. "I told you I'd give you the choice to see them if you wanted. I also told you I'd give you that choice before it went too far." I shook my head. "It's gone too far. They're a fuckin' mess."

She sucked in a breath, looking at me with large, wide eyes. "Tell me everything," she demanded, her voice strong, not wavering one little bit even as her chin trembled.

So I did. I glossed over parts of it, but told her they'd suffered every pain she'd suffered. As many indignities we could reasonably manage. Obviously, we couldn't put out a video of them getting raped or us beating the shit of them, but something similar had been done, and they were in their last hours of life. Maybe even their last few minutes.

"OK," she said softly. "Do you want me to stay here? To not confront them?"

"No, baby. I don't want you confront 'em. I want you to just let me and my brothers finish this. Venus and Millie did a better job than any of the rest of us ever could. When I tell you they suffered, I mean they fuckin' suffered."

"OK," she said again. "Go finish this. I'll stay here."

"Dammit, Jolene." I hugged her tighter. "Do you need to see them? I mean, really need it? 'Cause I'll give that to you even though it's the very last thing I want for you."

"No, Styx. They're dying. That's good enough for me."

"Ain't gonna argue with you 'cause I'm gettin' what I want. But I'm not leavin' you alone while I finish this."

"I'll be fine. Just go do what you need to, then come back to me."

I took out my phone and shot a text to Thorn, asking for him to send his woman to Jolene. It wasn't long before there was a knock at the door. I stood to open it and Lucy, Mariana, and Fleur stood outside the door. I stepped back to let them in. All three women went straight to Jolene.

Mariana looked back over her shoulder at me. "You go on. We'll stay with her."

To my utter and complete horror, Jolene dissolved into tears. Yeah. Once again, the confrontation hadn't been about what was on the surface. She was hurting and probably scared. Her tormentors were under the same roof as she was. They might not be in good shape, might be actively dying, but they weren't dead yet. And she was scared.

"Jolene."

She sniffed, wiping her eyes angrily while muttering, "I'm such a wuss."

"Baby, if you need me here --"

"No," she said, lifting her chin and meeting my gaze. "You go finish those bastards. Just come back to me when it's done."

I stared at Jolene hard for several seconds. Tears still streaked down her cheeks occasionally, but she was strong. Her features reflected that. She wanted me to finish this. Get it done, get home, tell her she was safe.

"I won't be long, Jolene. We'll have to take care of the remains, then debrief with Thorn, but I'll be back as quick as I can. You need me, you text me. Promise."

"I promise, Styx." She waited, holding my gaze with all the power of any dominant I'd ever met. "You get this done. See those motherfuckers dead." Her voice broke, but she held my gaze. "You do that for me, Styx."

"Consider it done, baby. Consider it done."

* * *

Jolene

It was about three hours before Styx returned to our suite. The women were solidly with me the whole time. They tried to keep my mind off everything happening in another part of the clubhouse, but it was a losing battle. Styx was with the other patched members of this club, systematically destroying my nightmares.

The second he walked through the door, I shot to my feet and flung myself in his arms. He clutched me to him as tightly as I held him. He thanked the women as they made their way out. I wanted to thank them, too, but my throat seemed to close up, not letting sound out. Once we were alone, Styx tugged me with him to the bathroom.

"Shower with me."

I could tell this had taken something out of him. "Was it that horrible? Did I do wrong in leading them here?"

"NO!" He was vehement in his response. "You absolutely did the right thing leading them here." He pulled me into the shower with him. "Don't ever think we didn't want to take care of this ourselves. I'm not gonna tell you I didn't wish you'd done it in a different way, or that I wouldn't have wanted a heads-up ahead of time, but I absolutely wanted this club to be the ones to bring justice to those motherfuckers. Jail was too good for them." I sighed. "Baby, we knew there had been other women, but these guys, my kin, were serial rapists and murderers. Ripper found dozens of women. Those men deserved every single thing done to them and more. Unfortunately, we just didn't have the stomach to continue any longer."

I wrapped my arms around Styx, kissing his chest while the water pounded our bodies like a heated massage, or maybe a cleansing summer rain. I could see in Styx's face he needed to wash himself clean. Knowing that, I reached for a bottle of shower gel. Squirting some in my hands, I rubbed them together before beginning a sweep over his chest and back. I knew it was more just being physically dirty. What they had done to his family had affected him. But he'd done it because it has been the right thing to do.

"I'm so sorry," I said as I continued to wash him. "I never wanted this for you."

"What?" He looked thoroughly confused. "You never wanted what for me?"

"For you to have to do all that to your kin a 'cause'a me."

"Honey, I did that gladly. And those fucker's shoulda suffered more. It's just that, after a while, it becomes pointless. What we did today ain't something I'll ever regret." He sighed. "Before it all began, we had to recount all the things Ripper found on 'em. Including what they did to you. So, yeah. I needed you naked in the shower with me so I can see for myself you're all healed."

I gave Styx what he needed. I gave him my body. I let him look his fill, then he made love to me. It started out slow and gentle. He kissed much like he had before this all began. Just... kissed me. Over and over, his kisses drugging me with exquisite tenderness. He lifted one of my legs over his hip before guiding himself inside my pussy. I sighed as his cock stretched me with every slow, incredible inch he slid inside me.

"Love you so fuckin' much, Jolene," he whispered against my lips. "Ain't never lettin' you go."

"Ain't lettin' you go either," I said. "Don't matter how many club girls want you, I ain't givin' you up." I smiled against his lips. "Maybe I'll get you a property patch."

He chuckled. "I'll wear it proudly, baby. And, I gotta say. That scene out there when you were standin' over Queenie, tellin' her what for, will be the subject of many masturbation sessions for me."

I grinned. "I thought we'd already discussed that. You're far too close to goin' blind for you to masturbate anymore."

"True. So… you gonna help me with that?"

I clenched my pussy muscles around his dick. "All's you gotta do's just slide your cock inside my pussy. I'll take care'a ya."

Styx's eyes flashed at me, hot lust shining brightly. "Fuck," he hissed as he started moving in earnest. He found a hard, driving rhythm as he hooked my leg over his arm, then lifted me to do the same with the other leg. Once he had me where he wanted me, spread wide with his arms locked securely around me, he fucked me like there was no tomorrow. It was a rough ride -- his cock slammed into me, and I was helpless to control anything. So I just locked my hands around his neck and held on.

It wasn't long before I came. My scream was long and loud, my pussy seizing up tightly around his dick. Nothing had ever felt so good. At least, until Styx came deep inside me with his own war bellow. His cock swelled inside me until cum exploded in one hot jet after another. His body jerked, his legs quaking until he sat down abruptly on the bench, his cock still firmly seated in my pussy.

"Fuuuuck," he groaned, giving a little laugh.

"I know," I said, smiling as I kissed him again. "I'm so glad you found me, Styx. No one in my life has ever treated me as good as you do."

"I always will, baby. Findin' you was the best thing that's ever happened to me." He pulled my forehead to his. "You always stay as fierce as you are, you hear me? You take what you need from me and bust my ass when I need it."

"Oh, don't you worry about that." I grinned. "I was a little broken when you found me, but you put me back together better than I ever was. Besides, I got more than a little hillbilly in me, so I don't take a whole lotta shit. At least, not anymore."

He snorted. "*Hell*billy is more like it. You can be a fierce little thing when you need to. I'm glad of it. Turns me the fuck on."

"Good. 'Cause I ain't givin' up anything else I want. And I want you."

"You know," he said, looking a little wary. "There's one thing we ain't discussed."

"Yeah? Let me guess. You're gonna try to be all hung up over our age difference." I grinned at his shocked expression. Then he grinned.

"Well, I'm definitely older'n you. Gonna guess about twenty years. You ain't much more'n eighteen."

"Nope. And you're in your thirties. And I don't give a fuckin' shit, Ruben Hatfield. So shut up about it and fuck me again." I tilted my head at him, scrunching up my nose. "Unless you can't get it up again that fast."

His eyes widened. "Oh, no, you didn't."

I smirked. "Sure did."

He set me off him, turned me around and swatted my ass again before scooping me up in his arms. I squealed as we exited the shower. He dried me off as he tickled me.

"I can so get it up again." He actually managed to look indignant, but the gleam in his eyes said he was enjoying the challenge. I knew I'd be enjoying it in a minute.

"Oh, yeah? Prove it!"

He tossed me onto the bed. I tried to scramble away with a laugh, but he snagged my ankle. "No, you don't. You wanted to get fucked again? Now you're gonna get it."

I was on my belly when he settled his weight on top of me. Styx wrapped his arms around me, one just beneath my breasts, the other crossed over them, his hand gripping my shoulder.

"I'll never get tired of this," he murmured beside my ear. "Every time I slide into your slick little cunt is like a fuckin' homecomin'."

Then he slid in. Just like he said. His contented sigh was a balm to my every fear and worry. Styx. He'd plucked me out of my old life and given me a new one. My very own biker ready to defend me with his last breath. An adventurous lover ready to give me every pleasure imaginable. And a few I'd never even dreamed of. He'd slain my demons. Given me a home and a family.

And I loved the fuck outta him.

"I love you, Styx," I said, my words broken as he pounded into me with increasingly harder thrusts. "Love you so fuckin' much!"

"God, Jolene! Fuckin' love the fuck outta you! Fuck! Fuck! *Fuck*!"

My pussy clamped down on him as an orgasm

rushed through me. I screamed and thrashed beneath him, needing to milk him once again. I wanted his cum inside me. Wanted him to feel that same rush of pleasure he'd given me.

"Gonna fuckin' come, Jolene! Fuckin' come in your pussy!"

"Please, Styx! Please!"

With another brutal roar, he did. His cock pulsed over and over, filling me full and putting a big smile on my face. My man. My protector.

My lover.

Styx was… my everything.

He groaned as he left my body, his cock sliding free wetly. He cleaned us both up, then pulled me with him under the covers and held me against his chest. I was exhausted, the emotional and physical toll finally catching up with me.

"You good?" His voice was a little husky. Probably from all the noise he made.

"Yeah." Mine was too. Same reason.

"Good. Tomorrow we start fresh. No looking back. Only forward."

"Sounds good to me." I was just about to doze off when a thought occurred to me. "Do we have to take that truck back to Kentucky?"

He was silent a moment. Then his cock stirred, poking my thigh where I'd rested against him. "Yeah, actually. We do."

I grinned. "I vote we take the interstate. I hear the Nav system works better on those types of roads."

"Definitely takin' the interstate."

Challenge accepted.

Ripper (Salvation's Bane MC 11)
Marteeka Karland

Emmanuell: Once upon a time, I was a princess. OK, so maybe I was just an heiress who stood to inherit nothing. But my father was still rich and powerful. He just believed I should be able to stand on my own. To make my own way in the world. All that ended the night I left with a man I hardly knew for a quick getaway and a one-night stand. That one night turned into several months and I found myself reeling at the tragic turn my life had taken. Little did I was about to find my salvation in the most unlikely of places.

Ripper: Never did I ever expect to find a woman I wanted for my own. My life was about the club. The job. Then this little pixie showed up on the clubhouse doorstep looking for her baby daddy. Turns out, she's heiress to a fortune, and the subject of a statewide search for a missing person. There's no way Salvation's Bane doesn't end up in a world of hurt if she's found here. There's just one tiny problem. The second I see her, I know she's mine. I'll take over her care. I'll take responsibility for her. And I will reign down hell on the man who left her homeless and on her own. I just hope I'm up for the task because this is one pregnancy that doesn't go as planned.

Chapter One
Ripper

August in Florida was damned miserable. The party at Salvation's Bane had migrated outside the second the sun started to set, and I just wanted to be inside where I could fucking breathe. I'd only followed everyone away from the paradise that is blessed air conditioning because I was on first watch tonight -- eight PM to midnight. My job was to monitor the party and make sure it didn't get too out of hand. There were several visitors, and while everyone was there to have a good time, sometimes newbies couldn't handle their alcohol. Or whatever drug they'd chosen to imbibe. As such, I had to stay sober and babysit. Which meant no women for me, either.

Honestly, I didn't mind that last bit. The club girls, while a pleasant distraction, weren't my thing anymore. Sure, I fucked one occasionally, but it had been so long since I'd had a good time doing it, I just didn't bother much. If I needed relief, well. One of my legs might have been left back in Afghanistan, but I had two perfectly good hands.

Nursing the Coke in my hand, I looked out over the party. Everyone was having a great time and generally behaving themselves. The club girls only had one altercation over a guy but that had been settled when the guy in question had fucked both of them. Problem solved.

"Ripper, we got a problem." The voice came from behind me. I turned to see one of the prospects, Slash, approaching me, concern on his face. "You're needed at the front gate."

"Ain't Dazz on guard duty?"

"He is, but he says this needs a patched member,

and you're in charge of the party."

"That ain't part of the party."

"Dude, you're the ranking member here. Everyone else is either deployed or gone to the Black Reign thing with El Segador's woman. Takin' all the kids to Disney World."

"Shit. I forgot about that." With a sigh, I drained the last of my Coke. "Stay here," I said. "Keep an eye on things. Text me if there's a problem."

Slash nodded and leaned against the wall, his eyes automatically sweeping the area. Confident everything was under control here, I hopped on my bike and headed to the front gate.

The property was fenced off, the acreage growing every year. We'd started building a small community inside the fence, offering housing outside the main clubhouse for the members with families. Currently, we were four houses ahead with room for several more. Which was good because all the brothers with ol' ladies had started having or expanding their families.

The ride wasn't long, but I welcomed even short spurts on the bike. Besides, it was urgent or Dazz wouldn't have sent Slash for me. When I approached the gate, I wasn't certain what I was seeing.

A small woman, obviously pregnant, was arguing with Dazz. It wasn't a violent argument or even a loud one. She just seemed to be trying to get her point across. I couldn't hear what was going on until I shut down the bike.

"I just want to talk to Devan and maybe get a bottle of water," she said. "It's not like I'm going to hurt anyone. If you want payment for the water, I can't right now, but I'm good for it. I'll pay you back once I get a job. Or look around the water fountain in town.

There's always change in city fountains." Spoken like a girl who'd gone looking in those public fountains a time or two.

Dazz just looked at her, his arms crossed, not saying a word. A muscle in his jaw ticked like he was pissed off in the extreme and trying not to take it out on the poor girl.

"What's going on?" I asked, walking over to stand by Dazz. The woman, who obviously just wanted a bottle of water and to talk to Devan -- whoever that was -- looked like a vagabond. She was clean... ish... but her clothes looked like they were falling apart and were stretched over her belly where she'd obviously outgrown them and hadn't bought maternity clothing. And she was heartbreakingly beautiful. A mane of nut-brown hair, pale skin slightly burned from the sun, and a delicate frame were only a few of the things that drew me to her. I got the feeling she was way more than she appeared, yet there was no artifice about her.

"Nothing," the woman said, backing away, her eyes going wide as I approached. "I -- I was just leaving." She looked disgruntled but afraid. I couldn't blame her. Both me and Dazz were big men and I was scarred, my face sporting the remnants of burns and shrapnel on one side. A woman alone in obviously advanced pregnancy would never have been in our presence unless she knew us. This one didn't look like she was in much shape to fight us. She looked like she was fucking dead on her feet.

When she started to leave, Dazz barked out, "Stop." She froze, a little whimper escaping her. "Found her sitting next to the fence," Dazz said. "Says the Devan she wants to talk to is a member here." He glanced back at the girl before back to me. "If she's tellin' the truth, and the man she's lookin' for is a brother here, there's gonna be hell to pay. Why I bothered you instead of just lettin' her in."

"You got a last name on your Devan, girl?"

She looked down at her feet before shaking her head slightly. "Pretty dumb, huh?"

"You sure he belongs to this club?" I wasn't addressing her embarrassment. At least not yet.

She shrugged. "I'm just going on what he told me. He mentioned Salvation's Bane a lot. Said he worked as a bouncer at Salvation's Angels. I went there, but they wouldn't let me in." She indicated her state of dress before putting her chin up proudly. "Apparently, I'm not dressed appropriately to visit a strip club." The girl was an enigma. She obviously lived on the streets, but she spoke like someone who had money.

"This Devan your baby daddy?"

Keeping her head high, she seemed to dig deep for every ounce of courage she possessed. "He is. So, if you're telling me he's not here, I'll just be on my way."

"Girl, do you even have anywhere to go?" I was rapidly losing my patience. The more I looked at her, the more I saw the woman underneath the guise she presented. I was certain she was homeless, and that she hadn't been that way long. She was adjusting, but she was still trying to pretend she *wasn't* homeless. And I was drawn to her so strongly it hurt my fucking heart.

"I do," she said decisively. "I'm sorry to have disturbed you."

"Girl," I sighed. "Get the fuck in here. I'll take you back to the clubhouse and get you a hot meal. Then we'll talk."

Her head snapped up, her eyes going wide before she cleared her throat and squared her shoulders. Was that because of the prospect of food? She had so much pride, those sparkling hazel eyes of hers so fierce while at the same time her lower lip trembled. "Um... that would be... that is, I'd appreciate it. If it's not too much trouble, that is." Then she quickly added, "I'll find a way to pay you back."

"Got a cage on the way, Ripper," Dazz said softly. "It ain't safe for her to ride a bike, and I don't think she can walk that far. She's done."

"C-cage?" Her voice went high and she backed away from us, tripping on the uneven sidewalk. I reached out and grabbed her arm before she hit the ground, pulling her against me. "P-please," she cried, trying to shove away from me. "D-don't hurt me! I-I'll just go! I'll figure this out on my own!" She was trembling, her body breaking out in sweat, obviously terrified now. She didn't smell bad, but it was more obvious with her in my arms that she had challenges bathing and washing her clothes. If this was all she had -- and it looked very much like it was -- she would have had a really hard time.

"Relax, girl. No one's gonna hurt you." I made sure she was steady on her feet before I released her completely. Even then, I stayed close to her. I didn't want her to run off because she was afraid. She needed to be taken care of. Not running away because we were obviously not the straight and narrow kind of men.

"I don't want to be in a cage!"

"It's not what you think." I looked at Dazz, raising an eyebrow. He'd started this. He could give her the fucking explanation she needed.

"A cage is just an enclosed vehicle. Most of us prefer to ride bikes. Uh, motorcycles. Got another prospect bringing a truck to take you back to the main clubhouse." Dazz looked uncomfortable. "Shouldn't we contact Thorn? I mean, it's not like she's leavin' anytime soon. Girl's exhausted." Again, she whimpered. I was ready to beat the fuck outa Dazz, but it wasn't his fault. He wasn't a man to explain himself much. In fact, this was the most he'd spoken to me this entire week.

"My name's Ripper," I said to the girl. "I'll get you settled, then we'll find the man you're lookin' for." And beat the fucking shit out of him for leaving her to fend for herself. Then a thought struck me. "He know you're pregnant?"

"Yes," she said, looking away. "He doesn't want me." She turned back to me quickly. "And I'm OK with that. But he has my purse with my identification and social security card, as well as my bank card and insurance card. I need those to get a job and to go to the doctor and to buy… stuff." She trailed off as she finished, obviously not liking that she'd given me so much information. "I had a suitcase with me, but I left it with my purse in his truck. He said I wouldn't need them."

As she finished, a Bronco rolled up, and a prospect hopped out. Beaner was his name. "Need me to take your bike back to the clubhouse?"

"Devan!" The girl called out. I turned, and she had her eyes on Beaner, a wide-eyed, hopeful look on her face. That look told me this girl was as naive as they came. "I'm sorry to bother you, but I have to have my purse and suitcase. I swear you won't have to see me again, just please. I need my ID and my insurance card. The bank card, too."

Beaner did a double take, his eyes going wide. Yeah. Kid knew her. Then he schooled his expression, trying to pretend he didn't know she was talking to him.

"I'll park it in your usual spot," he said, completely ignoring the girl.

"You gonna answer the lady?" I gave Beaner my most intimidating expression. I would most definitely be getting to the bottom of this, but judging by what I'd witnessed so far, I was beginning to believe the girl wasn't acting.

"Huh? I thought she was talking to you." Beaner wasn't the sharpest knife in the drawer and couldn't lie for shit.

"My name ain't Devan," I said, taking a step toward Beaner. He took a step back.

"Mine ain't either. Who knows who she's talking to? She's probably crazy. I mean, look at her. Obviously lives on the streets. I bet she ran away from a mental hospital or something."

The girl gasped. It wasn't loud, just a sharp intake of air. I turned my head and saw the sharp look of disbelief on her face. "I'm not asking for anything that's not already mine, Devan. My purse and suitcase were in your truck when you left. I assumed it was a mistake, but then I wasn't expecting to be left in upstate New York when we left from Miami. I need my purse because it has all my identification in it."

I looked back at Beaner. The kid was sputtering, obviously trying to come up with something to say. When he glanced my way, his eyes got wide, panic taking hold.

"Told you she's crazy," Beaner said. "I have no idea what she's talkin' about."

The girl lifted her chin. "I'm not crazy! We met in Miami six months ago at a party my father was hosting to raise money for foster families in the Miami/Dade area. You told me you were raised as a foster kid, and that you hoped to be a foster parent someday, too. I was supposed to ride home with my dad, but you talked me into going out for a drink." Her lip trembled now, and her eyes filled with tears she tried to hold back. "Dad's car ran off a cliff on the way home. I'd have been killed, too, if I'd gone with him. You said it was fate. That we were meant to be together!"

I remembered the event the girl was talking about. From what I recalled, it was determined he was run off the road. No one was charged, but there were speculations money was the motive. The man's wife had died from cancer several years before, and his daughter was the only one named in the will, but she'd disappeared...

"Emmanuell Stanton?" Dazz voiced what I was trying to wrap my mind around. The girl looked from one of us to the other, her eyes wide with fear and indecision. Then she gave a small nod. Like she wanted to lie but couldn't commit to it.

"Everybody in the fuckin' state's been lookin' for you for months." And she'd turned up on the doorstep of an MC. Right. No problems there. None at all. My gaze snapped back to Beaner and rage enveloped me. It didn't take much to put two and two together. "*You little fuck!*"

Beaner didn't even reply, just dashed out of the compound gate like the hounds of hell were after him. Well, they were about to be. I nodded to Dazz, who growled before hopping on his bike and taking off after Beaner. The chase didn't last long. In fact, it took Dazz only seconds to catch up, then he spun the bike around, taking Beaner down with his back tire. Given the way Beaner squealed, I was pretty sure something was broken. That was a problem for later. Right now, Salvation's Bane had a more pressing fucking problem.

"Come with me," I said, holding out my hand.

"You need food, a bath, clothes, and about twenty-four hours of sleep in a soft, warm bed."

"W-what's going to h-happen to me?"

"You? Nothing. We're gonna get you fed and clothed, then you're gonna go see Doc and make sure both you and the baby'er good. After that, we'll see. Do you have someone you need to contact? A next of kin? A lawyer?"

She looked away. "My mom died from brain cancer three years ago. Dad was all I had. My grandparents are dead. Neither of my parents had siblings. I couldn't get anyone to take my calls at Dad's lawyer before. When I was stranded in New York. So, I don't think there will be any help there."

"All right. Come on." I led her to the passenger side of the Bronco and opened the door. She balked, stepping back as she dropped her head.

"I don't think I should get in there," she said, not meeting my gaze.

"Why not? You can't walk back. I mean, you could, but it's a good hike, and you don't look like you're capable at the moment."

She took a deep breath, then closed her eyes before looking up at me. "I stink. I'm dirty. This is a brand-new vehicle. I don't want to mess it up."

That didn't even warrant a response. I just picked her up and set her in the seat, shutting the door before she could protest. Girl was gutting me and not even trying.

* * *

Emmanuell

I've never been so mortified in my life. I was in a new vehicle with a guy I'd never met. I hadn't taken a real bath or shower in days. My clothes were filthy.

And he had to be the hottest guy I'd ever seen.

Ripper was classic bad boy. Muscles and tattoos everywhere and a full beard that hid scars underneath. One side of his face looked like it had been burned, but there were also gouges in his skin like maybe he'd been hit with shrapnel. Same with his arms. One had scars that went under his shirt sleeve, the other to just below his elbow. All of it was covered with intricate tattoos. All in all, he was as scary as he was beautiful, and I wasn't sure what to do with it.

We pulled into a parking area next to a three-story building. There were five large bay doors that took up all but a small section of the first floor. Off in the distance, it looked like there were more buildings -- houses? -- being constructed along a ribbon of road connecting them all. In the fading light it was hard to tell, but it gave off a gated-community-type feel. Well, except for the loud music coming from the back.

"Party's in full swing," Ripper said as he escorted me inside the building. "You're welcome to join."

"I appreciate the invitation, but given my state of being at the moment, I don't think it's the best idea." That got me a raised eyebrow, but he nodded curtly, then continued inside. Before we got to the stairs, which looked like our goal, a beautiful woman with jet-black hair in tight curls approached us with a warm smile. She didn't look at Ripper, though. She looked straight at me.

"Welcome to the clubhouse." She smiled, her golden eyes bright as she greeted me. "I'm Lucy. Mariana sends her apologies that she couldn't meet you herself, but she just had surgery, and Doc has forbidden her from getting out of bed. To say nothing of Thorn. He's still hovering like she was near death."

Lucy's smile was genuine, and she sounded like she was laughing at the other woman's husband for being a shade overprotective. I wasn't sure what to think. No one had ever fussed over me.

"She could use a private space to rest." Ripper's voice was a low rumble, sending shivers through my body. I had no idea why I was so drawn to him, but everything about him appealed to me. He was everything my father wouldn't have approved of, but I got the feeling there was more to this man than his outward appearance. I also thought that maybe this guy was also the kind of guy my father would have kept his eyes on. Just waiting for an excuse to bring him into his fold just to show everyone else that appearances were deceiving.

"Absolutely!" Lucy took my hand. "I've got the perfect room for you. Fully stocked with toiletries. Do you have a change of clothes? If not, I'll round you up some. Me and the ol' ladies always keep stuff in case it's needed. We even have some really cute maternity outfits. Would you like me to bring you a few?"

"I don't want to be a bother," I said, looking away. "But I don't have anything else. I'd be very grateful if you'd let me borrow a few things."

"You're not a bother at all. I'll bring a couple changes of outfits for you while you freshen up. Ripper, I'll have the girls make her a plate from the party. Would you mind bringing it up to her? She can eat and rest. If she feels like coming down, I trust you'll find one of us for her?"

Ripper threw her a cocky grin. "I'm at your service."

"Yeah? I'll make sure the others know. I'm sure they can compile a list of shit for you to do."

He chuckled. "You know I'm always available to

help out. Even if it involves heavy lifting."

"Is there anything else I can do in the meantime?" None of the offers Lucy made seemed disingenuous. In fact, she seemed like a super nice person. Her smile alone seemed to settle me down.

"Could you tell Doc she needs to see him? Tell him tomorrow's fine. I'd like to get her to rest if she will."

Lucy narrowed her gaze on me. "Yes. She looks pale. Honey, do you want me to have him come up here to see you? I could come with him if you like. That way maybe you won't feel so much like you were surrounded by strange men ganging up on you." She glanced up at Ripper, a clear reprimand. Likely for trying to take over my life.

"I don't think it's necessary," I said. "I'd just appreciate the food and a place to clean up. The clothing will be welcomed, too. But I probably should leave first thing in the morning. I'll clean up after myself, of course."

The other woman looked startled but nodded her head slowly. "If that's what you want. But, honey, do you have a place to go? I mean, I was under the impression when Dazz texted that you were kind of on your own."

"Well, yes," I admitted. "I am. But I've been on my own for several months now. While it's not the ideal situation, I'll be fine."

"Fine and safe and comfortable aren't the same thing, honey." She pursed her lips. "What's your name?"

"Emmanuell."

If Lucy recognized my first name, she didn't give it away in her expression. She just gave me another warm smile and took my hand in both of hers. "Well,

Emmanuell, I know this place can seem a bit intimidating, but it's really not. The club girls can get rambunctious, but are basically harmless. And the guys will protect you while you're here. We're one big family. A little unconventional, but we protect our own."

She had me right up until that last phrase. "I'm not one of you," I said softly. "I don't belong anywhere. Not anymore." I was pretty sure everything that had happened in the last six months was finally starting to hit me. I hadn't let myself think about being homeless or car-less or friendless. *Or* that I was pregnant. Now? I was in a safe place, or at least I thought I was, with the possibility of a real shower and a real meal. Not to mention a real bed to sleep in for the night.

"I'll come get her food in a bit, Lucy," Ripper said. "Bring her stuff to me, and I'll take care of it."

Lucy raised an eyebrow. "Anything I should pass on to Vicious?"

"Yeah. Need a meet with him and Thorn. But not until I get Emmanuell settled and fed."

"I see." She nodded. "I'll take care of everything downstairs, including letting Vicious know you need him. He can tell Thorn. I'd say to text them, but with the party going on I doubt they'd hear you."

"Thanks, Lucy. I owe you one," Ripper said. Lucy held out a key for him.

"I put her on the top floor across from me and Vicious. Figured it would be good if she were close to me. Since most of the other ol' ladies moved out with their men, it's usually just me and Mariana up there. Plenty of rooms available away from the club girls and unattached bikers."

"Good. I'll be back down in a few minutes."

Ripper led me up the stairs to the third floor, then down the hall. He unlocked a door and led me inside. As apartments went, I thought this one was nice. Spacious with a bathroom and separate bedroom, and a combined kitchen and living area made me feel like I was in someone's home for the first time in more than six months.

"This is wonderful," I said, walking around the place. "Are you sure it's OK that I'm here? I mean, I don't want to be in the way or anything."

"You're not," Ripper said. I could hear a note of disapproval. When I looked over at him, it was stamped all over his face. "Get comfortable. I'll be back in twenty minutes with food. I'll set some clothing just outside the bathroom door. Take your time. There's no rush."

"Thank you, Ripper. Please tell everyone taking time out to help me that I appreciate it."

He nodded once, then left, shutting the door behind him.

Chapter Two
Ripper

The second I left Emmanuell's room I was on the phone to Thorn.

"You hear about the problem?"

"Yeah." I could hear the tightness in Thorn's voice. If that was any indication, the man was furious. "Havoc and Beast got Beaner in the interrogation room. They're waiting for me to give the word to clear out the party, so we can get to work."

"You gonna hold off a while?" It wasn't what I'd do, but Thorn was more methodical than I was.

"Yes. I want that little shit to suffer knowing what's about to happen but not knowing when it will. If I'm right, he'll doze off once the adrenaline high wears off. Then he'll be confused and disoriented. It'll be just one more way to scare the truth out of him maybe."

"You gonna need to talk to Emmanuell first?"

There was silence while Thorn thought for a moment. "It would probably be best. I like to hear both sides together, but Lucy said she wasn't sure if the girl was up to it yet."

"I'm bringing food to her room. Maybe if you brought Mariana with you?"

"My wife's still recovering. I'll not have her out of bed until Doc says she's good. I'll bring Lucy and ask Tobias to bring Kitty. Vicious will be a good help, too." I heard Thorn sigh. "This is a fuckin' shit show. Girl's been missin' for months and turns up here."

"Maybe there's more than we're seeing. Though, I gotta admit, I'm solidly in Emmanuell's corner. I don't see anyone with her upbringing willingly being in the situation we found her in. She's the real deal, in my opinion. Only the details need to be hammered out."

"Need you to get on that, brother. It's your territory."

"Already on it. I have some searches going, as well as a little security breaching in her father's lawyer's office and personal accounts. Everything he's into I'll soon know about."

"Good. Give me thirty minutes. I'll meet you in her room."

"Make it an hour," I said. "Girl needs food first. I doubt she's eaten more than snacks or garbage in days."

"That bad?"

"She's tried her best, but she's definitely homeless and penniless. Mentioned coins by public fountains so she's at least learned some of the tricks of being on the streets. My main concern is getting her fed and to Doc. She needs him to check her and the baby over."

"You seem to be taking a pretty intensive interest in this girl. You know her?'

"No." If Thorn suspected she'd gotten under my skin, he'd take every opportunity to throw us together. I might be protective of her -- any man worth his salt would be -- but she was an heiress. I was a scarred biker with one leg. We didn't go together. "I just don't like someone weaker than me being kicked while she's down."

Thorn grunted. "Fine, then. I'll see you in an hour."

There were slim pickings left downstairs, but I managed to round up two hamburgers, a hotdog, and a large spoonful each of baked beans and potato salad. I thought about snagging a soda, but that didn't seem good for the baby. So I grabbed a bottle of water and a jug of milk with a glass. I got a club girl, Retta, to help me take it all upstairs. Didn't take me long to realize my mistake.

I opened the door, and Retta pushed her way inside and put her load on the table. "Wow! Did you get this room all for me?"

"No," I said, hoping she'd take the hint.

"Oh! You're staying here with me!" She threw herself in my arms, fusing her mouth to mine. I grasped her hips and pushed her away, but I heard Emmanuell behind me before I got Retta off me.

"I'm sorry," Emmanuell said softly. "I didn't intend to... That is, I should go. I don't want to interrupt."

"You're not," I said, giving Retta a scathing look. "Retta was just leaving and not coming back. Ever." I swiped my forearm over my mouth for good measure. Retta just smiled and waved. "See you at the party, Ripper."

I turned back to Emmanuell. She had dressed in a pair of white cotton pants that came just below her knees and a pink maternity top with daisies on it. Her hair was shiny and springy with little ringlets as it dried around her face. She looked so beautiful it made my heart hurt.

"Better?" I managed to get out.

"Yeah," she said, not meeting my gaze. "I'm sorry. I don't want to intrude."

"You're not. She's trying to stake a claim on somethin' that ain't hers."

Emmanuell shrugged. "It's not my business," she said softly.

Yeah. Not the way I wanted to start this. She already didn't want to be here. The very last thing she needed was to feel like she was in the way.

"Come on," I said, holding out my hand for her. "I've got you some burgers and hotdogs. Ain't much, but it's filling."

She took my hand automatically. The second she did, I knew I was in real trouble. Her hand was calloused but delicate. Her fingers slim as they closed around mine. The closer she got, the more her scent enveloped me. I wanted to pull her into my arms and kiss her. See if she tasted as sweet as she smelled.

When she looked up at me, her eyes got wide and her lips parted. I couldn't decide if she was afraid or aroused. Not sure she knew which one she was either. Those hazel eyes of hers seemed to beg me to claim her as my own. To keep her safe. At the same time, she had no real idea what kind of mess she'd landed herself in. I could see the internal struggle she had going on. If she'd been used to this life, how an MC worked, I'd have taken her on. But this girl… She wasn't a woman a man could leave when he was done with her. Hell, she was a woman a man might never be done with.

"Food's over here." I wasn't nearly as smooth as I wanted to be. Any tenderness I had inside of me got left in Afghanistan along with my leg. My voice was gruff as I ushered her to the table and urged her to sit. She took one look at the food on the plate, and her whole face lit up. Then she glanced at me. I actually had two plates. One with the burgers and dogs, the other with the sides. So she took one burger and set it on the plate with the sides, then proceeded to cut the hot dog in half.

"What the fuck'er you doin', girl?"

She jumped, her head snapping up so she could look at me. "I -- I was m-making t-two p-plates." She trembled now, her eyes wide and round with fear.

I sighed. "Sorry, Emmanuell. I didn't mean to sound so gruff. That's all for you, honey. Eat as much as you want. I can probably round up some more 'tater salad and beans, but that's all the burgers and dogs."

"No! This is more than enough." She looked back at the plate with longing. "It's not polite to eat without offering everyone in the room something."

"You offered. I declined," I said, my tone clipped when I didn't want it to be. Seeing her obviously hungry but falling back on manners that were ingrained into her made me want to punch something. I didn't need her to think my aggression was toward her. "Eat, honey. I want all that gone when I come back. You hear?"

"I don't know if I can eat it all."

"Just try. You need to eat. I'm sure you wouldn't want to neglect your baby. Right?"

Immediately her hand went to her belly. The look on her face was one of wistfulness as well as a soft sweetness I wasn't even sure she knew was there. She rubbed her tummy absently before sighing. "You're right. I do need to eat."

"Good. I'm going to step outside. I'll be back in fifteen or twenty minutes. Eat as much as you can. If you need more, I'll make sure you have it."

"Thank you," she said. "For everything."

I nodded. "I'm locking the door. I have a key, so no one should be knocking. I don't want you havin' to deal with anyone else, so if someone knocks, ignore it."

She pursed her lips. "That's not very polite."

"Don't give a fuck about polite. I will not have club girls invading your space and making you uncomfortable."

Emmanuell ducked her head, giving a little nod.

Yeah. Retta had shaken her up more than she wanted to admit. Did this attraction go both ways? I thought it might. Which meant I needed to figure out what the fuck was going on sooner rather than later, because I was already making a claim on Emmanuell. I had no idea if she was even attainable.

When I left Emmanuell's room, I went in search of Thorn. I also needed to check my searches. My phone was linked to my computers and would alert me of anything noteworthy, but I had a pressing need to check on it myself. Confirming there was nothing new took disappointingly little time. My office was next to Thorn's, and he was just exiting his office when I locked the door to mine behind me.

"How's she doin'?"

"Got her eatin'. She's falling back on etiquette rather than just rolling with it. Tried to share her fuckin' meal with me instead of just digging in like she obviously wanted to. She's unfailingly polite and more than a little nervous, but I think she's weathered everything all right so far."

"Depending on what we find, this could be a shit show of epic proportions. You realize that, right?"

My gaze snapped to Thorn's. "You don't have to tell me. I know how much trouble the club will be in if this isn't handled carefully. That pissant, Beaner, talking yet?"

"No. But then the interrogation hasn't started, either." Thorn shrugged. "He's not the kind of man to last long under pressure. I don't think he'll break before we start workin' him over, but he won't last long."

"He betrayed the club at the best. Killed an innocent at worst. Somewhere in there, he got Emmanuell pregnant and left her defenseless on her own."

"Allegedly."

I rolled my eyes. "You know Beaner's lying. Right?"

Thorn shrugged. "Don't know. Not looked into his eyes yet. Nor have I talked to your Emmanuell. Though I intend to remedy that immediately." As he spoke, Kitty and Lucy came down the hall accompanied by Kitty's husband, Tobias, and Vicious. Tobias was the VP of Bane. Vicious wasn't a doctor, but he was kind of the moral compass and counselor for the club. He made sure everyone was in a good place. When they weren't, he did everything in his power to make it right. "Thanks for bringing the girls, Vicious."

"No trouble at all. What's going on? Lucy said Ripper picked up a new girl outside the gate?"

"Yeah," I said. "Claims to be Emmanuell Stanton."

Vicious whistled low. "The heiress? She vanished months ago. She wantin' someone to help her get her daddy's fortune? Because that seems more like Wrath's department, I mean, if you wanted to bring Black Reign into this."

"Justice and Mae would be just as suited. Mae has a mean drive when she gets her teeth into something." Thorn grinned, his obvious affection for the younger woman showing. "Justice can guide her through any legal loopholes she encounters."

"Agreed, but she's not mentioned anything about money other than needing her bank card. Can't imagine a standard checking account has millions in it. I don't know what her agenda is beyond getting her purse and suitcase back from Beaner." I scrubbed my hand over my face. "She's holding her own, but she's traumatized. She's not admitting it openly, but anyone in her position would have to be."

"The quicker we get this done, the quicker she can rest. Poor thing looked like she needed it." Lucy was just as emphatic as Vicious. Just... softer around the edges. Lucy and Mariana would be integral to gaining Emmanuell's trust in both the club and me.

I led everyone to Emmanuell's room, knocking before letting myself in. Instead of finding her at the table finishing off her food, she was at the sink, washing the dishes. The leftovers were put away neatly in disposable containers sitting on the counter while she finished. As she looked over her shoulder, her eyes widened.

"I-I'm sorry," she stammered, her movements becoming faster as she hurried to finish the plate she was washing. "I'm almost done."

"What are you doing? You were supposed to be eating." I knew I sounded too hard, but I couldn't seem to help myself. The one thought that kept circling in my brain was to take care of her. She needed food and rest. I'd provided the food, but she'd refused to eat much of it. "It not good or somethin'?"

"No! It was wonderful! I -- I just... I -- It was a lot a-all at once." She looked terrified, her breath coming in little gasps.

"Jesus, Ripper," Vicious said, putting a hand on my shoulder. "Calm down. You're scaring her."

"Here," Lucy said, stepping between me and Emmanuell, gaining her attention. "I'll help you. No sense you doing it all yourself."

Kitty was right beside her. "We can all do this in a third of the time." She smiled warmly at Emmanuell.

I'd have preferred Emmanuell not cleaning up anything. She needed rest, not to worry about the fucking dishes. When I opened my mouth to say something, Vicious put a hand on my arm, shaking his head.

"Bring Emmanuell to the living room when you ladies are finished," Tobias said.

"She don't need to be cleanin'," I muttered. "She needs to be restin'."

"She will," Thorn assured. "Doc will see to it. Right now, let her do this. Trust the girls."

Sure enough, Kitty and Lucy engaged her in conversation while taking most of the work away from Emmanuell. There were only two plates and one glass to wash, but Emmanuell seemed to believe they had to be spotless. When she kept drying the glass, polishing it with aggressive rubs and growing increasingly agitated, Lucy put a hand on her shoulder, taking the glass from her gently.

"It's fine, honey. Let's go talk to the boys. They'll get lonely in there without us."

Emmanuell took a deep breath, nodding. Kitty put an arm around her shoulders and led her to us. I stood, taking Emmanuell's hand and tugging her to sit beside me on the love seat. She sat next to me on the edge of her seat, her back straight. She didn't let go of my hand but pulled it into her lap and covered it with her other hand. The sight and sensation filled me with so much satisfaction I actually puffed out my chest. Thorn smirked. I just met his gaze, raising one eyebrow.

"Why don't you tell us what brought you here?" Vicious said kindly. "I know you told Ripper some of it, but tell me and Thorn."

"I just wanted my purse and suitcase," she said softly, clutching at my hand harder. Her hands twisted in her lap, but she steadfastly clung to me. "I accepted months ago that I'd never have my old life back, and I'm OK with that. But I need my ID and insurance cards. My bank account might be closed, but if not, there's still money in there for me to get a modest apartment or something. My suitcase had clothes in it, though I probably can't wear much now." She looked away. "It took me months to get back home. I walked most of the way. Once I got enough change from a fountain to take a bus to the next town, but why bother? It was better to use it for food or just save it until I needed it. Several places had soup kitchens where I could volunteer and still eat."

"Wait," Lucy interrupted. "You had to volunteer in order to eat?"

"Well, yes," Emmanuell answered, as if it were obvious. "I wanted to give if I was going to take." Thorn raised an eyebrow but said nothing.

"I'm sorry," Lucy said, glancing at her husband. "Go on. Please."

"Once I made it to Palm Springs, I started asking around about Salvation's Bane. It's how I found Salvation's Angels." She shivered. "And the Playground." The Playground was a BDSM club owned by Bane. I'd bet my last dollar that place scared her to death.

"Who led you here?"

"I found a garage called Red's. There was a girl on a bicycle who worked there. Since there was already a woman working there, I asked about a job, thinking I could clean up or help in the office or something. I was told Red only hired people from Salvation's Bane. Knowing that, I figured she was associated with the club. It took several days, but I finally followed her far enough I figured out where the club was."

"Red took the Maybach to the buyer. He didn't

want Rosanna going with him so she's been riding her bicycle to and from the clubhouse," Vicious explained.

"Wasn't she supposed to get a ride from Styx and his woman if she went to the garage?" Thorn shook his head, grinning. Likely because Rosanna amused him, the way she ran circles around Red when Red wasn't looking.

"Yep," Vicious said. "But you know Rosanna."

"Yeah. I know Rosanna. Turned out it was a good thing she didn't follow orders this time," he said. "If she had, Emmanuell might not have made it to us."

"Was it just today you found our compound?" Vicious was careful to keep his tone light, soft. He was always the sensitive one when it came to those in our club who were vulnerable. It was why Thorn had him in this position in the first place.

"Yes. I just kept walking until I found something."

"You realize that wasn't exactly the safe thing to do, right?" That was Thorn. He wasn't short or harsh, just asked a question.

"I didn't feel like I had much choice," Emmanuell said. "I tried to get a job more than once. Actually worked off the books a time or two, but was never able to get reliable employment without identification. And most everyone pays in direct deposit now. I didn't have access to my checking account and couldn't get one without an ID. I did try to open an online account, but apparently, my social security number has been flagged as being stolen or something, and they still wanted proof of ID." She started to hyperventilate, as if merely retelling the event was stressful for her. "I'm not afraid to work," she said defensively. "I'm not looking to cash in anything my father had. I don't care who got his businesses or the house or any of his other assets. I just want my ID and the belongings I had with me so I can build a new life for myself."

Coming from anyone else, I'd have called bullshit, but I knew like I knew my own name Emmanuell was telling the truth. She wasn't like most wealthy women I'd met. Most of them were full of artifice and lived to manipulate. Kind of like many of the club girls. None of them would have been caught dead in the state we'd found Emmanuell in.

Thorn looked at her a long time. Emmanuell dropped her gaze, looking at either the floor or our joined hands. I didn't know which.

"Why?" Thorn said, unexpectedly. "Why would you not be looking to claim your inheritance? It's a lot of money, I'm sure. You'd be back in the lifestyle you've lived most of your life. There'd be no need to get a job or make a new life. You could simply pick up where you left off and live your life in peace."

"That's not what my dad would have wanted." She shook her head. "I have no idea what charity Dad left his estate to, but it was always understood everything would go to the community. I knew this. So did my mom before she died. Dad never wanted me to rely on anything I hadn't earned myself. He said it would make me stronger and able to survive if it was suddenly all gone." She took in a shuddering breath. "He was right." She looked up, meeting Thorn's gaze with a determined one of her own. "I survived six months on my own. And without any of my dad's money. I know it might not sound like much, but it feels like an accomplishment to me."

"I know people who would have done worse." Vicious smiled at her kindly.

"I mean, I know most of the jobs I'd had before

were at my father's offices and stuff, but I would have been content to use the skills I learned at similar jobs, but without an ID there was no way. And with my social security number flagged, I couldn't get a new ID." Her grip on my hand tightened, and she trembled slightly.

"You don't have to explain," I told her, looking at Thorn. "You did good."

Thorn shot me an irritated glance before continuing. "What if I told you, word is your father's will left everything to a corporation managed by your father's attorney?"

She blinked several times. "That wasn't... Do you know what corporation? I-I mean, the last time Dad spoke to me about it, he was going to spread his wealth over several charities."

"It's a new one. LimeLight Division, it's called."

"LimeLight." Emmanuell closed her eyes, her chin trembling as one tear tracked down her cheek. "That was one of my mother's pet projects that never got off the ground. It was supposed to be an educational and recreational center for kids in foster care or group homes, but she died before she could really work with it."

I glanced at my phone, scrolling through alerts until I came to the one labeled LimeLight. "Looks like LimeLight Division was created a month before your father died by one Randal Goldstein. It was set up to be owned by Franklin Stanton and Emmanuell Stanton, but the proper signatures were never filed, and the corporation reverted to Goldstein." I furrowed my brow. "Looks like it was set up that way. If, for any reason, the Stantons never took control of the corporation, it would become Goldstein's..." I glanced at Emmanuell. Her lips were parted, her eyes wide.

"I wasn't in any business dealings with my father. Yes, I worked at his company, but not in any major capacity. I was meant to learn how the place ran from the ground up. If I wanted to work for him, I had to earn my way there. Just like anyone else."

I tapped my screen some more until I found Emmanuell's file with HR at Stanton Industries. The more I saw, the more I frowned. "He made you start in the fuckin' *mailroom*?"

Emmanuell tried to pry her hand from mine, but I held on fast. "Everyone starts in the mailroom," she snapped. "There's no better way to get to know a place than by starting in the mailroom. You learn where everyone is, where every department is. What outside companies deal with which internal departments. Who is the head of each department, and who they correspond with regularly. I learned lots of stuff when I worked there."

She was on the defensive when I'd never meant to attack. "Every company has their own way of doing things. I just never thought your father would make his own daughter start work at his company in the mailroom."

"Like I said. He believed that I needed to make it on my own merit. He gave me help anytime I asked. Help. Guidance. Advice. A nudge in the right direction. But I have always known that any place I had in my father's company would only happen if I earned it."

"OK," I said, trying to soothe her feelings when I usually could give a good Goddamn. Someone got all sensitive, they needed to toughen up. This girl was already tough. Anyone could see it. "I didn't mean to offend you. I just expected he might have let you have a hand in this new company like it looks on the surface."

"No. LimeLight was all my mother's. Dad would never have put anyone in charge of it other than himself. Mr. Goldstein would never have been part of it other than to shore up any legal issues as described in his contract with my father," she finished softly. Ducking her head, she sniffed and wiped at her eyes with one hand.

"Guessing the whole thing is a sham, then?" Thorn's question was directed at me.

"Well, there's no one else named to any board of directors or any mention of exactly what LimeLight Division is. Only that it has an insane amount of money at its disposal." I set my phone down on the arm of the love seat. "I'll have to check bank records to see who has access to it." Advanced searches weren't something I could do from my fucking phone, but I wanted to. I wanted to find the connection to her father's death and this LimeLight Division. Because I had a bad feeling all this was going to do nothing but hurt Emmanuell more than she was already hurting.

"Is this something we need to pursue?" Vicious asked, looking from me to Thorn. "Seems like it's not our business to meddle in."

"Depends on what we learn from Beaner," Thorn said, looking at Emmanuell thoughtfully. "Have you been to see Doc yet, Emmanuell?"

"No." She'd stopped trying to free her hand, but the other one was now clutching at her pants instead of my hand. I didn't like it. "I don't want to put anyone out. I've gone this long. I can wait until I get my purse and my insurance card back from Devan. I'll go to a doctor then."

"You should really let Doc examine you." Lucy leaned forward, resting her hand on Emmanuell's free one briefly. "I'll be happy to go with you, if you like. If nothing else, a quick ultrasound to make sure the baby's doing well. You could see your child for the first time." She said it like it was the greatest wonder of the world. I'm sure it was, though I'd never given that shit much thought.

"I'll think about it." Emmanuell's voice was so soft it was hard to hear. I got the feeling she really wanted to do this but had no intention of going through with it. Probably because she felt like she should pay for the service.

"Doc's gonna see her tomorrow." I gave Emmanuell a firm look. She wasn't bucking me on this. "Until then, she's gonna rest."

Kitty rolled her eyes. "Men. Always trying to boss when they should be minding their own business."

"I know, right?" Lucy gave Emmanuell a grin before standing. "Why don't we make sure you've got everything you need." She reached out to Emmanuell and urged her to her feet. "You boys can see yourselves out. Kitty and I will take care of Emmanuell."

"Like hell," I muttered. Kitty raised an eyebrow at me with a smirk, but I ignored her.

Once they were in Emmanuell's bedroom with the door closed, Tobias stood and paced across the room. "Fuck," he muttered. "This is gonna come back to bite us in the ass."

"That shit hill, Beaner, has a lot to answer for." Thorn sighed as he stood. "We'll give it till morning. Then we'll get everything out of that little fuck we can."

"I'll see what else I can dig up." I had every intention of looking into Beaner as hard as I looked at

Goldstein. My gut was telling me they were connected. "If I'm right, Beaner has put the club in one fuckin' bad position."

"If you're right --" Thorn met my gaze with a hard one of his own. "-- He dies. So you better be fuckin' right."

"I won't come to you with anything less than concrete proof." I glanced back at Emmanuell's bedroom door. "She don't need a bunch of horny bikers makin' passes at her. I want it known she's under my protection."

Tobias snorted. "There's a shocker."

"What?" I snarled at the VP. "She don't!"

"Yeah? Who's gonna keep *you* outta her panties?"

Good Goddamned question.

Chapter Three
Emmanuell

The women of Salvation's Bane were the nicest, most accepting people I'd ever met. They fussed over me, made sure I had several pretty sets of maternity wear, and all the necessary things I'd had to deny myself because of lack of funds. I'd be lying if I said I didn't breathe a sigh of relief that they'd taken over so completely. But I still felt bad about it.

"Really, you guys have done too much. I need to contribute something to repay you."

Lucy leaned in conspiratorially. "You can repay us by keeping Ripper in line."

I blinked up at her. "What?"

"Ripper. He's in charge of the club's cyber security. And he's a bit of a maniac." Kitty sat on the other side of the bed, grinning at me. "He's got a GPS tracker in every one of our cars. Our husband and boyfriends put them in our purses. A couple of them have had trackers made into jewelry to keep on our person, and it's catching on."

"Oh, my God! They want to control you that much?"

"Oh, no, sweetie," Lucy said with a light chuckle. "Not to control us. To protect us. That way they know where we are in case we need help. They already track our phones, but, honestly, it's that way for everyone. Ripper is the chief instigator in that affair too."

"Doesn't that seem a bit creepy? I mean, it sounds very controlling." I didn't want to offend them, but the whole idea of the men constantly tracking the women's movements sounded too much for me. I didn't want any part of it.

Kitty pursed her lips before answering me

slowly. "I suppose if you look at it like they're being Big Brother or something. But they're not doing it to get us in trouble or to make sure we don't do anything they don't approve of. It's just that they're over-the-top protective, especially of the women and children of members of the club."

"Sure, Ripper has every bike tagged with a GPS, but, again, it's for safety." Lucy continued explaining where Kitty left off. "If someone gets in trouble we know about it and can send help. Same with us. More than one of their women has been kidnapped because of dangers following us or to get back at a member of the club. They're understandably cautious."

"You can't tell me they're that protective. No man I've ever met is that protective." It was true. Even my dad hadn't gone that overboard, and I thought he was pretty protective of me.

"Really." Lucy grinned at me. "Because you've met Ripper. And he's probably gotten started with all that stuff for you. If not? Give it time. But I guarantee he's already got plans for a tracker of some kind for you. That man is more protective than all of them combined."

"In fact, I'm pretty sure he's made the rest of them even worse than they were before they met him." Kitty reached out for one of my hands. I sat on the bed on top of the covers with my back to the headboard. The women had propped several pillows behind me, and there was a blanket folded neatly across the foot of the bed. "He's a good man, you know."

"He seems to be," I said softly.

"Are you going to let him take care of you?" Lucy looked at me intently. "Vicious seems to think he wants to."

"I don't need anyone to take care of me." I said it

automatically. It was the way I'd been brought up. My dad was wonderful, and he had looked out for me, but he believed I should be able to take care of myself. I did, too. Because, when the person you depended on left you, you had no one to rely on but yourself.

"Honey, everyone needs someone to look after and take care of them," Lucy said. "The men take care of us, but we take care of them, too. And they take care of each other. We all look after the kids."

"Give him a chance," Kitty said with a smile. "You could definitely do a lot worse for yourself. And your baby."

Immediately, my hand went to my belly. I was already feeling the child kick. Much as I hated to admit it, I really wanted to get seen by the doctor. Lucy wasn't wrong in thinking I wanted to see my baby. Make sure it was doing well.

"What are you hoping for?" Lucy asked.

"A girl," I replied softly with a smile.

"That would be awesome. The men all claim to want boys, but the girls wrap them up so tightly, it's comical. You should have seen Alizay's little girl with Blood and Vicious when she was younger. She had pink glitter fingernail polish out painting their nails. They tried to get her to just do their toenails, but she said their feet were icky and she was not touching them." Both women laughed at the memory.

"They really let the girls do that?" It sounded too good to be true.

"Oh, yeah," Kitty continued. "There have been tea parties as well."

"And don't forget Christmas when they still consider the men with beards free game with the red and green glitter, and that started when Suzie at Bones was still young." Lucy laughed.

"Then our kids get together with the kids of Black Reign and it's even worse. Especially El Diablo's daughter, Dawn. That girl..." Both women laughed before Kitty continued. "She is the most spoiled child in the whole world. And if one of the boys dares tell her no, she runs to her daddy."

"He's never even said a cross word to the boys, but his reputation has them scared to death of him. At least, if they tell his daughter no."

That intrigued me. "How old is she?"

"She's thirteen. And believe me when I tell you, she's a handful." Kitty smiled as she shook her head. "I pity whatever poor man she sets her sights on, because her daddy will kill him if he touches her, but probably if he rejects her, too."

"That sounds... terrifying." But I giggled. If these women were to be believed, this sounded like a wonderful place for a child to grow up.

"Nah. None of the guys would really hurt the boys for trying to date their daughters, but I wouldn't rule out a sound thrashing if they disrespected the girls." Kitty stood and went to the windows, opening them so the breeze came in over the ocean.

"But I'd say that'd go for any self-respecting man." Lucy smiled. "We'll leave you to rest. Don't be surprised if Ripper is a permanent fixture near you, though. He's a good man, but don't go easy on him." She winked at me. "Make him work for it."

When the women left, I scooted down and lay on my side, looking out the window into the night. The moon was a large, golden ball hanging in one corner like a window decoration. It made me smile. The air felt good blowing in my face and over my body. The outfit they'd given me was a soft, light cotton. Though it was hot and humid out, the cotton seemed to soak up the breeze, cooling me for the first time in what felt like forever. I was clean, comfortable, and had a roof over my head where I didn't have to worry about my safety.

The women had given me plenty to think about. Ripper especially. But I had no business thinking about him. If I did, I could see myself getting infatuated with him, and that wouldn't do anyone any good. He was a little harsh, but he'd been so good and protective with me. I got the feeling he wasn't used to soft feelings and didn't welcome them. But he was trying. He'd even held my hand while I'd spoken with his president and Vicious. Plus, he'd taken my side on every single issue. Even with Devan, he'd taken my side from the second he'd realized his club member was the same man I was looking for. The father of my child.

Which was another thing. I worried about what was happening with Devan right now. Or whatever his name was. Seemed it was just one more thing he'd lied to me about. I got the feeling Ripper thought there was more going on than simply a man I hooked up with dropping me off a long way from home with no way back. If I were honest with myself, after everything Ripper and Thorn had told me, I believed it, too.

The door opened, and heavy footfalls approached the bed. I glanced over my shoulder to find Ripper. His gaze was intense as it swept over me. I felt a little exposed and drew my legs up slightly before I stopped myself.

Never show weakness. It will only be used against you.

"You know I'm not gonna hurt you, right?" Ripper stopped beside the bed, looking down at me. My father had taught me to see beyond the surface people presented, but Ripper was still a hard one to read. He kept his emotions close, but I could see something in his eyes he tried hard to hide.

"Yes," I said softly.

"Good." He stepped closer and sat beside me, putting his hand on my arm and stroking in a soothing rhythm. "How're you feelin'?"

"I think it's all hitting me. I'm tired, but I don't feel bad."

"Good. Get some sleep. I'll be in the other room if you need anything." His tone was gruff, but I could tell his offer was more than a token gesture. He truly meant what he said.

"You don't have to do that, you know. I'll be fine."

"I'm sure you will. Still gonna be here in case you need somethin'. I expect you to call out to me if you do. You hear?"

When he would have stood to go, my stupid hand shot out to clasp his. "Don't go just yet, Ripper." I sounded like a whiny child and cringed as I snatched my hand back. "Sorry. Forget I said that."

He grinned at me. "Nothin' wrong with my memory. Tell me what you need."

I took a breath. "I'm not used to people making a fuss over me. It's been nice. You and your club have treated me better than anyone has in a long time. Thank you. For taking me in."

Ripper looked at me for long moments, studying my face. "My name's Gideon Leigh. I'd prefer you call me Gideon in private." He brushed a lock of hair off my face before reaching for my hand. The one I'd grabbed him with. "Now, what else is on your mind." It wasn't a question. He fully demanded an answer.

I knew I needed to be brave. To suck it up. Lord knew I'd heard that enough the first few months I was on my own after Devan had left me alone in New York. No one had been sympathetic. Probably hadn't even believed my tale and thought I was crazy like Devan had claimed earlier.

Suck it up, bitch. No one cares who you are. You're here with us now. Pretendin' to be all high and mighty won't get you nowhere here.

"It's nothing. Just thank you. Gideon." I smiled up at him. I meant it, too. He was gruff and intimidating, but he was a good guy. The second I uttered the words, I knew it had been a mistake.

"Don't lie to me, Emmanuell," he said in a low, deadly tone. "Never to me. I won't tolerate it."

I wasn't afraid of him… exactly. I mean, he looked terrifying when he wanted to, and he wasn't exactly happy with me holding back from him for whatever reason, but if he'd wanted to hurt me he'd have done it a long time ago. Stupid rationale, but I had no problem with it presently. If I admitted what I wanted, would he laugh at me? Deny me?

Ridicule me?

"I don't…" I cleared my throat. "That is, I'd prefer not to be alone." He cocked his head, a puzzled expression on his face. "What I mean is, shelters." I tried to chuckle like it was all a big joke. "They're not exactly, you know." I swallowed. "Safe."

"I hope you don't think you're not safe here, honey. You are." He winced, shaking his head.

"What?"

"Nothing," he grumbled. "Just… shouldn't have called you honey."

I grinned. "Why not? No one's ever called me that before. Kind of nice coming from someone who looks so scary." I shrugged. "Takes the sting out of how gruff you are."

He gave me an exasperated look. "Well, don't tell anyone. My brothers are already givin' me hell." He shifted around, scooting more solidly onto the bed. He kicked off his boots before putting his feet up and turning to face me. I squeaked as he urged me over to my side and pulled me against him, wrapping his arms around me. "There," he said, sounding put out when I was pretty sure he wasn't. "Sleep."

"You don't have to do this," I said, even as I snuggled into him. For the first time since I'd found out I was pregnant, I felt safe. Again, I wasn't hungry. I wasn't dirty. I was in a safe place with privacy. Add to that a crazy-scary biker with a gruff exterior whom I suspected had a good heart, and I could honestly say I'd never been more content in my life as I was in that moment wrapped up in Ripper's -- Gideon's -- arms.

"Know that. Now shut up and go the fuck to sleep."

I giggled. "Isn't that an audio book or something?"

He shrugged. "Don't know. Just know you need sleep. You need to feel safe. I'm here. I'll keep the bad stuff away."

Yawning, I said, "Fine. But don't blame me if I get used to it. This is as close to spoiling as I've ever had." Settling against Gideon's body, I closed my eyes.

Before I dozed off, I thought I heard him say, "Get used to it, baby. Because I intend to do more of it."

* * *

Ripper

I lay with Emmanuell for a long time. At least an hour. In that hour she didn't move a muscle other than to breathe. I'd have lain there until she finally woke if it hadn't been for some motherfucker blowing up my fuckin' phone with texts. Then phone calls. Made me want to punch a motherfucker.

Finally, I took out my phone and scrolled through messages. It wasn't too late. Barely one in the morning. Apparently, Thorn was ready to start the interrogation. Normally, the thought wouldn't have affected me any more than someone saying it was time to take out the trash. Now, though, I was eager to see what Beaner had to say. Didn't mean I wanted to do it right this second.

Never in my life had I held a woman while she slept. Never wanted to. All it did was make them clingy, and I could give two shits. Especially after I lost my leg and got half my body scarred by burns and shrapnel. Any woman who'd been interested had only been in it for the sex. Which was fine by me. We both got off, then she left before she could say something about my scars and piss me off. I didn't want that with Emmanuell. I wanted the fairy tale.

Thorn wanted the information I'd collected on Goldstein and to know if Beaner was tied to him in any way. So far, I couldn't find a connection, but that didn't surprise me. If Goldstein had hired Beaner to hurt Emmanuell, he'd have paid in cash. Most likely, anything tying him to Goldstein would come down to what we could extract from Beaner.

When I thought about Beaner, it was all I could do not to fly into a murderous rage. Not taking into account he might have been part of some kind of plot to hurt Emmanuell's father and maybe even Emmanuell herself, just the fact that he'd gotten her pregnant, then abandoned her with no means of taking care of herself or the baby meant he needed to die. The rest of the stuff was just icing on the fucking cake.

Careful not to wake Emmanuell, I extracted myself from around her. She murmured in her sleep, turning over and patting my side of the bed. I moved my pillow down within her reach just to see what she'd do, and she latched on to it, pulling it close and putting her head on it as she inhaled deeply. Then, with a sigh, she settled. I took the blanket from the bottom of the bed and pulled it over her. The breeze coming in off the ocean had cooled things off considerably. At least for the night. She'd wake if she got too cool.

After tucking the blanket around Emmanuell, I looked at her for a long time. The moonlight shone on her face like a beam from heaven. I'd noticed her beauty right off, but not like this. She was gorgeous. Vulnerable. Before I realized what I was doing, I leaned down and kissed her cheek.

She murmured in her sleep, smiling. "Gideon..." Then her face relaxed, and she slept on.

I was so fucking fucked.

I was also determined to figure out what the fuck was going on with her father's lawyer and how he played into her whole ordeal. If I was right and the fucker had put Beaner up to killing Emmanuell, I was gonna kill him slowly. It wouldn't look like an accident because no one would ever find the fucking body.

When I entered the room where Beaner was being held, the rest of the club was already there. Beaner had been there for four or so hours, and I could see the strain around his eyes and mouth. No one had started on him, but it wouldn't be long.

"Ripper." Havoc acknowledged my entrance. I'd stopped by my office to check the information I'd gleaned that wasn't sent directly to my phone. There was no money trail from Goldstein to Beaner, though I had found where Goldstein had slowly siphoned from a multitude of different sources. Likely it was for cash to pay someone.

"I found a bunch of purchases all over the Midwest from Emmanuell's debit and credit cards, but I can't confirm who made them. I've got a program running for facial recognition on the ATMs from banks I've already hacked into. Sooner or later, I'll find concrete evidence who used her card."

"You got dates?" Thorn sat back in his chair looking calm and collected, not like this whole mess could bring down hell on our club.

"Oh, yeah. Some of them coincide with Beaner's absence."

"I wasn't gone for six fuckin' months. I've been here and done all kinds of stuff for the club! I've gone everywhere you asked me to go! Done anything you asked me to do!"

"Uh-huh," I said. "I'm still collecting data. Can only match you up with a few of those transactions so it could be coincidence, but give me time. I'll find the proof I need to nail your balls to the fuckin' wall."

"I don't even know the bitch!" Beaner snapped, looking at me like he'd love to kill me. Too bad he was tied to that fucking chair.

"Bullshit." I was surprised to find Dazz was the one calling him out. Glad he did, though. I didn't want it to look like I was making up circumstances to fit the crime just because Beaner had pissed me off. "I was there when you first laid eyes on her outside the gate. You know her."

"Which makes Miss Stanton's story all the more believable." Thorn crossed his arms over his chest. "So we're here to find the truth."

Beaner lifted his chin and gave Thorn a mulish

look. Which earned him a sharp backhand from the president.

"You don't ever try to stare me down, you little fuck. Especially when you've bein' a lyin' sack of shit."

"Ain't lyin'," Beaner muttered. Which earned him another backhand.

"Yes, you are. We'll find the truth with or without your help, but we know you're lyin'." Thorn didn't look angry. It didn't seem like it was personal to him. Thorn presented the front he needed Beaner to see. Right now, all Beaner knew was that we thought he'd taken Emmanuell away from her home, knocked her up, then left her defenseless. Beaner had no idea what Thorn was really after. If he did, he'd own up to Emmanuell and point to the fact that she was still alive as proof he had nothing to do with Goldstein or Emmanuell's father's death.

"You have anything else concrete, Ripper?" Thorn raised an eyebrow at me. He knew I didn't, but it was all a mind fuck for Beaner. This whole thing was going to take some time, and he needed Beaner off balance.

"Not yet. Only been workin' a few hours, though. If I can't find anything soon, I'll get help from our sister club. Data, Zora, and Suzie are good at this sort of thing."

"Very well. I want that one stashed and locked down. Beast, he gets three meals a day and a pisser. That's it. No visitors, and he does not get out of his cell for any reason. He has a medical emergency, he fuckin' dies. Get me?"

"Got it, Prez. The storm shelter in the basement should work. It's got several different rooms down there. I'll get a team together."

"Make sure it's patched members who'll take it

seriously. I don't want someone feeling sorry for the little shit and lettin' him out for a day on the fuckin' beach."

"Lock, Poison, and Venus will do nicely," Beast said, grinning at Beaner. "You guys can work it how you want to split your shifts."

All three members gave their agreement. Venus grinned at Beaner while filing her razor-sharp nails. "Little pet needs scratched behind ears," she said with a little chuckle in her soft Russian accent. "I'll take care of this prospect, Thorn. Give him to me."

"Depending on how far we chase this, Venus, you and Ripper can arm wrestle for it." Everyone chuckled. Except Beaner. "All right," Thorn said, standing, rapping his knuckles on the table. "I'm dismissing Church for now. Everyone keep your cells on you. We'll reconvene once we have more information. Also, some of you might be needed later. Don't go far. I expect everyone to be available at a moment's notice."

Once out of Church, I went back to my office. I had several things going. Matching up Beaner to Emmanuell's debit and credit cards was only one of the things I needed. I was also tracking Goldstein. His movements. His cell records. His bank accounts. Everything about the man. Even his family. I wanted to know everything going on with him, LimeLight, and Franklin Stanton. It wasn't going to be a quick job, and I was sure I'd need help. I just wasn't sure I was willing to call in the help I needed.

Contrary to what I told Thorn, I didn't think Data's contacts went far enough. I was certain I'd need Giovanni Romano's help. The tech wizard was the brains behind Argent Tech, the biggest tech giant in the world. He was also an arrogant son of a bitch, and I hated him. Most people did, so I felt I was in good company. But he would be the fastest way to get the information I was after. Besides, it would free me up for a few days to take care of Emmanuell the way she should be. Yeah. My brothers were gonna have a field day with this.

Chapter Four
Emmanuell

I woke up lying on my side with the sunlight streaming through the window. I'd fallen asleep in the exact same position. I'd also fallen asleep with Gideon wrapped around me. Despite having had sex with Devan, I'd never actually slept with a man before. Or cuddled. After sex, Devan had always wanted a cigarette and a shower. Looking back, I knew he'd treated me awful, but I'd enjoyed my time with him. Or I thought I had. It had been the beginning of my downward spiral. He'd gotten me away from my home and anyone I knew, and it had been impossible to get back. At least, it had seemed impossible.

I stretched, and a brawny arm tightened around me.

"Where're you goin', huh?" The sleep-roughened voice sent shivers through my body. I didn't know Gideon. Not really. But I felt safe with him. It was likely a colossal mistake, but I was rolling with it. I mean, I had nothing to lose.

"Just to the bathroom. Maybe a shower. I know I cleaned up last night, but I'd like to again. Just because I can."

He chuckled. "Yeah. I can see where you'd want to do that." When he didn't let me go immediately, I tugged gently at his arm. "Tell me one thing before you go."

"If I can." Even though I had my back to him, I was sure Gideon was frowning at me. Not the answer he wanted, but I could never lie worth a damn. I'd tell the truth, or keep my mouth shut.

"Why were you so upset when I came in and you weren't done doing the dishes?"

I hadn't expected that question. Still, it was answered easily enough. "Some of the places I stayed at had strict time limits on when things needed to be done. There were so many people, if they got behind, it was nothing but a chaotic mess. I learned to be fast and efficient. It was a reflex more than anything else. Then I just didn't want you guys to question me. I was afraid you'd tell me you didn't have a place for me here or that I'd have to..." I trailed off, rethinking what I was about to say. The last thing I wanted to do was insult Gideon or his club.

"Afraid you'd have to do things you didn't want to do to earn your keep?"

"That's a good way of putting it, I suppose."

Surprisingly, he sighed, sounding disappointed. "I can see how you might come to that conclusion, but no one would ever demand that of you. Not me. Not Thorn. No one. If you believe nothing else, believe that."

"I do," I said, meaning it. "Everyone's been so kind. I loved the women I met. They were so encouraging and helpful. I've heard of Salvation's Bane all my life, but never knew you'd be so... I don't know. So much like a family."

"Don't get me wrong. We're not all sunshine and fuckin' rainbows. There's a darker side to us, but we don't involve our families."

"I guess I just thought the place would be one big orgy with drugs and illegal stuff everywhere."

"Illegal stuff," he said with a chuckle. Then he did something completely unexpected. Gideon kissed my neck lightly before giving me a hard squeeze. Then he let me go. I got out of bed and headed to the bathroom as he continued. "All kinds of illegal stuff, baby, but nothing for families to be concerned about.

As to the drugs and orgies? Yeah, some like to get high occasionally. Makes the orgies more fun."

When I gasped and turned to him, my eyes probably wide as a deer in the headlights, he burst out laughing and winked at me. "Oh, yeah. You're gonna be fun to poke. Get on in there and get your fuckin' shower before I decide to join you."

I scrambled out of the bed, needing to put some distance between us. It would be too easy to get used to having the attention of this man, but I knew I'd never be able to keep it. "Not sure you'd enjoy that. Pregnant as I am, I'm not a sight to behold."

"Oh, really?" He raised an eyebrow as if to say, *Challenge accepted*.

I shrugged. "I doubt any man who wasn't the father would find my body sexy right now. Given the fact this baby's father dumped me off almost the entire length of the country away, I'm pretty sure even he wouldn't find me sexy."

"No one's seen you naked since you got pregnant?"

I laughed. "Why would they? Besides, I wasn't that great a catch before. No one wanted me once they found out I wasn't the heir to a fortune." I tried to smile and laugh like it was all a huge joke, but to me, it was a really sore spot. The only reason any man had ever been interested in me was when he thought I was getting my father's money. "Sad truth is, I'm broke. All you get is what you see." I spread my arms wide before letting them fall back to my sides. "Even if I somehow managed to end up with my father's fortune, I know what his wishes were, and I'd honor them. Which means I get nothing. Everything else goes to the community. So what you see isn't all that great. Especially now." I rested my hand on my belly and rubbed. "But I can't be sorry. Though, why this child couldn't have had a decent father is beyond me. He or she deserves a strong, loyal protector."

Ripper got up from the bed and stepped closer to me, stalking me into the bathroom. I backed up slowly, nearly matching him step for step. I wasn't sure why I retreated. I wasn't afraid of Ripper. The look in his eyes, though… Yeah. That gave me pause. Because he looked like he wanted to eat me alive.

"Let's get a couple things straight." He moved toward me until he had me backed against the bathroom vanity. "What I see right here in front of me is what I want. Money ain't got nothin' to do with nothin'. Any man can't see your beauty, courage, and strength and want you for himself don't deserve you in the first Goddamned place. Second, you want a strong protector for yourself and your baby, you got one. I'm takin' that role from this point forward." I gazed up at him. His dark eyes were intense and focused squarely on me. When he stepped into my space, one hand went to the countertop beside my hip, the other to the swell of my belly in a gentle caress. As if the child inside me were fully aware of the situation, it kicked right underneath Ripper's hand. The big man glanced down at my belly, then back at me, a crooked grin on his face. "Looks like I win."

"You win? What exactly do you think you won?"

"You."

Before I could deny him, Ripper bent to take my lips with his. His free arm went around my back, gently holding me still. I didn't fight him. Not because I was afraid of him, either. His touch seemed to ignite a fire inside me, bringing lust so sharp and intense I gasped. Ripper growled, capturing my whimpers with his kiss.

He was gentle but insistent, like he didn't want me to feel trapped, but wanted his kisses from me unless I really, *really* objected. I didn't.

When I sighed, sliding my arms around his neck, Ripper grunted his approval, tightening his arm around me and moving his other hand from my belly to my face. His big hand was callused and rough against my skin, but I loved the sensation. Gripping my chin gently, he positioned me where he wanted me, making our mouths fit together perfectly. His tongue lapped at mine, sending a shiver through me I couldn't contain.

I'd never been kissed like this. Never! All I could think about was trying to get closer to him. Needing to make this last as long as possible. It felt like my body was on fire with need and want. The longer he kissed me, the more I trembled and whimpered. Somehow, my hands ended up fisted in his shirt, holding him to me. The muscles next to my fingers were hard, tempting me to tunnel underneath the cotton and find warm skin.

When he finally ended the kiss, pulling back to look at me, I was so lust-stupid all I could do was look up at him. I was sure my eyes were as big as saucers, my breath coming in little pants.

"Mmm... That's a good look on you, Emmanuell." His voice was raspy and rough. "Like you want to eat me up."

"I -- wh-what?" I couldn't process what he was saying. I mean, I knew he was probably teasing me or something, but I just couldn't process anything beyond the sensual curve of his lips. I wanted them back on my mouth.

"You look like you're starved for a man's touch. Like you'll take matters into your own hands if I don't give you what you want." Could he look any more smug?

I blinked, trying to get my wits back about me. "What exactly is it I want?"

Ripper leaned in next to my ear and growled, "A good, hard fuckin'. Bettin' you'd love to have my mouth on your pussy too. Hell, I'd have a hard time keepin' you from jumpin' me if I laid you out on the bed and worshiped your body all fuckin' night."

"What woman wouldn't?" My voice wasn't as strong as I wanted it to be, but it was the best I could manage.

"Have you had a man do that to you before?" God! Could the man sound any sexier? To answer him, I shook my head, unable to form any more words. He smirked. "Yeah. I could make you scream." Stepping away from me, he turned back to the bedroom. "Go on. You got ten minutes, then I'm comin' in there with you."

I let out a breath I hadn't realized I'd been holding. He looked back over his shoulder and winked at me. That wink had the effect of a bucket of ice water, snapping me out of the sensual haze he'd woven around me.

Turning, I slammed the door, locking it behind me. My breathing was quick and shallow. I could still feel his lips on mine, while he'd looked like he'd been barely affected. Closing my eyes, I took a deep breath. I'd gotten through the previous six months on my own. Learned how to survive with nothing. It had hurt, but it hadn't broken me. Ripper was one man. I'd be fine. I'd resist him, not giving into his charm like I had Devan's, and I'd be fine.

* * *

Ripper

If there was one thing I intended to accomplish while Emmanuell was here, it was to make her understand how beautiful and brave she was. I could tell by the way she responded to my kisses that she hadn't had much affection. I had to wonder how Devan had treated her before he left her. Had he romanced her? Told her she was beautiful?

Had she loved him?

That thought made him want to beat the bloody dog shit out of Beaner. Emmanuell was a beautiful, passionate woman. Those kisses I'd stolen were just the tip of the iceberg. I had no doubt I could have taken things further, but she deserved better than that. When she'd said all that about her daddy's money, it was obvious that was a sore spot with her. Did she truly not see her own worth? How could a woman who'd been brought up in wealth not have a healthy self-esteem? He'd have thought she'd be confident and more than a little self-centered, but she wasn't.

I heard the water going in the shower. I'd never actually invade her privacy without an invitation, but it was Goddamned tempting. There was still time. Girl needed building up both physically and mentally. Right now, though, I needed to take her to see Doc. Then I'd start inserting myself into her life.

Ten minutes later, she emerged from the bathroom dressed in a pale green maternity top with pink, blue, and yellow balloons all over it and lightweight pants that hit her just below the knees. She looked so fucking beautiful it hurt to look at her.

"Come here, girl," I held out my hand to her. Surprisingly, she crossed the short distance and took it. I pulled her into my arms and gently kissed her once. "You good?"

She nodded. "Yeah. I'm good."

I grinned at her. "I need to run through the shower and change my clothes. Then I'm takin' you to see Doc. He's expectin' us."

"You don't have to go with me. I can do this on my own."

"Nope. I'm goin' with you. You're not doin' anythin' by yourself anymore."

The puzzled look she gave me had me smothering a smile. "You're the strangest man I've ever met." She shook her head. "I already told you there isn't any money. There won't *be* any money."

That had me scowling at her. "And I told you I didn't give a fuck about money. Maybe I need to go about this a different way. I already know some things about you, but you don't know anything about me. So let me tell you. I'm a Marine. I work for an independent paramilitary contracting company called ExFil. We mostly do search and rescue, but, from time to time, we're hired by the government for protection detail." Her eyes widened slightly, but she continued to listen. "I'm also a hacker. Nothin' I can't do with a computer. I'm the club's tech guy. I was the one who dug up stuff on you and Beaner and your dad's lawyer for Thorn when you first arrived yesterday."

"Beaner," she said, looking away. "And his name's not Devan."

"No, honey. It's Evan Day. He's been with us a while, so it was a pretty big blow to find out he betrayed the club. And you." That got her gaze snapping back to me.

"Me? What do I have to do with anything? I'm nothing to you guys." She shook her head and turned away again. "Just a stray you brought in off the street."

I went to her, cupping her cheek and turning her

back to look at me. "This club helps and protects women and children. We help and protect *anyone* who needs it. We do not take advantage of a woman, then take her away from her home and drop her off with no means of providing for herself for any reason. That's a line Beaner crossed that he can't come back from. No matter what we find in regard to your dad's death or anything else related to you, he betrayed the club by abandoning you the way he did."

"You know, he could have thought I had my stuff with me. Or that I was rich enough I could get myself out of that jam on my own. Most men don't believe me when I tell them I don't have my daddy's money to rely on."

"That's something we'll look into, but given the things I've already found out, I seriously doubt that's the case. He took pains to spread your trail all over the midwestern part of the country, making it look like you'd just taken off on your own without a care in the world. My guess is, anyone looking for you after your dad died thought you were a thoughtless, spoiled little rich girl who had her hands on the family fortune and split."

She winced. "Yeah. I guess you're right. It was just me and Dad. Probably no reason to think otherwise. Since no one knew anything about LimeLight Division, I could see how people would think that about me."

Which got me thinking. "What about friends? Wouldn't your friends have gone looking for you?"

"Maybe," she said with a shrug. "If I had any close friends. I've been working my ass off, trying to get a good education and work my way up in my father's company. My social life has been nil since before I graduated high school. That little adventure with Devan was the first time I'd done anything like that. If it hadn't been summer break, I doubt I would have. I usually took the summers off to rest and recharge. Not only from school, but from work. I scheduled off Memorial Day through Labor Day. My boss at the company let me because I was the boss's daughter. He probably shouldn't have, but he did. I think he thought I'd do him favors down the road one day if I was in charge."

"And who wouldn't think you'd be in charge one day?" I muttered. "It still doesn't excuse what Beaner did. He's gonna pay for that. As to you being a stray? No. You're not a stray. You're a lost soul who found her way home."

"I got in trouble because I went off with a man I didn't know." She shrugged me off, pacing away from me. "I took off with a guy for a weekend getaway, who talked me into staying after we found out my dad had gotten killed. He kept putting off going back to Florida, telling me he was taking care of things back home. He said he'd been in touch with Mr. Goldstein and that everything was being taken care of. He said I just needed to rest and grieve in private, and that he was there for me."

"Turn around and look at me, Emmanuell." She hesitated but did as I told her. "You got knocked down. Your trust betrayed. But you fought your way back up and kept going. I know what it takes to do that, because I had to do the same. Thankfully, I had my team and my club to help me. You had no one."

She frowned. "I don't understand."

I raised my pant leg, showing her the titanium stick that served as my leg below the knee. "Took a hit in Afghanistan when I was on active duty." I held out my arms for her to see as well. "It's where I got the scars. Combination of burns and shrapnel. So I know what it's like to fight back. To pick yourself up and keep on with life. But I had help. You went it alone. And all you demanded when you reached your destination was for Beaner to give you your ID, your bank card, and your clothes. You didn't demand an explanation, and you didn't demand he take responsibility for you and the baby."

"As if I'd want him to have anything to do with this child," she muttered. "But I hardly think my trials are in the same league as yours. You lost a limb, for crying out loud!"

"Different set of circumstances, but great hardships nonetheless. You're brave and strong, Emmanuell. That means you belong with us. With me."

"I can't stay here, Gideon." I liked it that she used my real name. No one else in my life ever did, and I wanted it that way. I wanted this girl to be different, though. She was mine, and I wanted her to accept me as hers.

"Why not?"

"I can't be here with Devan. I've been pretty civil so far, but the more I think about what he did, the more I realize how much I want to hurt him."

"Oh, don't worry about Beaner."

"Right. 'Cause his name's not Devan. It's Evan. Because I was stupid and didn't even know his name."

"You can't do an extensive background check on everyone you meet, girl. All you can know is what they tell you." I shrugged. "He lied. That's on him. Don't worry about him. You never have to see him again. He's club business now. Salvation's Bane takes care of their own messes." When she opened her mouth, probably to argue, I raised a hand and shook my head.

"Drop it for now. Come with me back to my room while I shower, then I'll take you to Doc's."

I held out my hand to her and she took it. "Fine. But don't think you'll always get to boss me around."

"Keep tellin' yourself that, honey. All the guys around here are bossy. Comes with the job description." That got her to grin.

I led her through the clubhouse to my room, her hand firmly in mine. It got us a few looks from club girls, but if Emmanuell noticed, she didn't say anything. I left her in my room with strict instructions not to leave while I showered.

"Take a look around if you want. You need to get to know me fast, and snoopin' around is the best way."

"Didn't expect that," she said, shaking her head even as she looked around like she was just deciding where she wanted to start.

I chuckled. "Knock yourself out. Give me ten minutes." I snagged clean clothes and headed to the bathroom. The thought of Emmanuell making herself at home in my space gave me the hard-on from hell. Definitely going to have to take care of that, though I had a feeling my dick wasn't going to behave no matter what I did.

I took my time, more for her to pilfer all she wanted without me being right on top of her. I wanted her comfortable and to feel like she could come to me with questions. The best way I could do that was to urge her to get to know me.

Showering with a prosthetic leg wasn't easy. At least, it had taken me time to get used to it. I had a bench in the shower to sit, but mostly I stood. There were also bars so I could steady myself when I moved or take my weight if I slipped or needed to turn around. Not for the first time, I wondered what a woman thought of me only having one leg.

There was a time when I'd thought it made me less. It was what motivated me through rehab and physical therapy after the attack in Afghanistan. I wanted to be worthy of a family. The strong protector I'd always been. I'd had to work to be that man again, and it made me bitter and angry when someone looked at the prosthesis and saw me as less than a warrior. Less than a man. When I'd shown Emmanuell my leg, she hadn't looked at me with pity or even tried to say how sorry she was that I'd gone through something like that. She'd simply taken it all in. She hadn't thought our trials equal, but there was no pity in her gaze. That encouraged me. Made me believe that maybe I could convince her to throw her lot in with me.

I had a bench installed next to the shower so it was easy for me to get my leg on quickly without needing crutches to get from the shower to a place where I could strap on the device and dress easily. It had been so many years now I did it without thinking. As long as I was home. When Cain sent me out on missions, I had to plan for shit like this. Which was why I was never in the field. When I couldn't work from the Bane clubhouse, I stayed in the base we set up in whatever country we were sent to. Wasn't always easy, but I insisted. I was still an incredible asset to ExFil. Thankfully, Cain recognized that. So did my brothers. It had taken me a while to realize it, but they all respected me and my capabilities. Both mental and physical.

Once dressed, I opened the bathroom door and paused, giving Emmanuell time to realize I was coming out. When I stepped out into the bedroom, I found her at my bedside, the table drawer open and an unopened box of condoms in her hand. She raised her eyebrow. "I take it you have visitors often."

I grinned at her. "Nope. I don't bring women here."

She looked perplexed. "So, you have men here, then?"

That made me laugh. "No, sweetheart. I don't have men up here. I'm completely heterosexual. But I don't bring women to my room for sex." I shrugged. "Or for any reason. This is my private space."

"Yet, I'm here."

"Exactly, Emmanuell."

"Then, why the box of condoms?"

I shrugged. "They gotta go someplace. I have a box in the glove compartment of my truck, too, but I'm never in the thing so they're probably outdated by now."

She placed the box back in the drawer and closed it. "You have quite a setup over there." She indicated my computer gear. Yeah. It was extensive. Four monitors with two keyboards and networked systems. I could work and play at the same time.

"You should see the setup in my office. This is nothing compared to that."

"I bet no secret is safe from you." She smiled, genuinely amused.

"Just you remember that." I pointed a finger at her warningly. "I'll know about all your speeding tickets and delinquent library books."

For the first time since I'd met her outside the gates of Salvation's Bane, Emmanuell laughed. Not a giggle or a soft chuckle. She barked out laughter, her eyes twinkling with merriment. By God, her whole face lit up. The whole fuckin' *world* lit up.

"Defender of libraries, huh? I like that."

My breath caught as she continued to smile up at me. Before I realized what I was doing, I'd crossed the distance to her. She still smiled up at me but looked adorably confused. Like she had no idea what she was fucking doing to me.

"You're a stunningly beautiful woman, Emmanuell," I whispered. "So fuckin' lovely."

When I bent my head to graze her lips with mine, she sighed into the light kiss. Her hands went to my shoulders to rest there like little butterflies against me, her touch was so light. I lapped at the seam of her lips carefully, not wanting to scare her or make her think I intended to take more than she was ready to give. She trembled slightly but didn't back off. In fact, she darted her tongue out to brush against mine, and I shivered.

"Mmm…" She moaned into my mouth. The woman seemed like she was starved for a man's touch. My touch.

"Yeah, baby," I said as I continued to kiss her. "Taste good."

Emmanuell sighed and slid her arms around my neck, clinging as we continued to kiss. Lips and tongues clinging and tangling the longer we continued. I could taste her need, feel the desperation for relief in the way she held me to her. There was so much she was trying to tell me in that one kiss. I heard her. But now wasn't the time.

Fuck.

I ended the kiss softly, trying my best to make it so she didn't feel like I was rejecting her. I pressed my forehead to hers, our breathing still ragged. She opened her eyes, looking up at me. I had to wonder what she saw. How she saw me.

"Why'd you stop?"

"Because, as much as I want you, we've got to

get you to Doc's first. Before anything, your health and safety are more important than anything else. Same for the baby. Last thing I want to do is harm either of you because I can't control myself."

Her mouth opened on a little gasp. "So you don't want me now?" Her brow furrowed slightly.

"Oh, make no mistake," I said, taking one of her hands and putting it over my dick where it was hard as a motherfucker beneath my jeans. "I want you now. But I'm not selfish enough to take you before we get the OK from Doc."

She blinked and pulled back slightly. "You're not asking Doc if we can have sex. That's none of his business."

I chuckled. "No, I don't reckon it is his business, but I'm not havin' sex with you until I can be sure I ain't gonna hurt you or the baby."

Looking off she said, "Guess I should have been more concerned about that, huh?"

"Honey, you've lived with this child since it was conceived. You been havin' sex regularly since you found out you were pregnant?"

"No! Of course not! I don't sleep with just anybody! Contrary to how I got in this condition in the first place."

"Calm down. Ain't sayin' you do. Or that it's wrong if you did. Woman deserves to take her pleasure same as a man. I'm just sayin' I'm sure you've had more to think about than if havin' sex would hurt the baby. Even if you had wondered about it and had the opportunity, would you have been able to go to the doctor?"

"No." Her voice was soft, and she looked down at the floor.

I pinched her chin between my thumb and

finger, raising her head back up so she had to look at me. "No one's judgin' you, baby. Least of all me. You're back in civilization now, so to speak. First thing on the agenda was to get food, a shower, and rest. Now, it's time to check on the baby."

"You're right."

I grinned at her. "Good. Let's go see Doc and see how this little one's doin'."

Chapter Five
Emmanuell

How in the world did a motorcycle club have ultrasound equipment? I had no idea. But here I was, in the office of a guy calling himself Doc. I was on an exam table with my shirt up over my belly and the waistband of my pants down under it. Doc squirted a clear jelly onto my stomach, then ran a probe through it. He muttered to himself as he pressed buttons on the machine, taking measurements as he did. He didn't let me see the screen, and when Gideon went to walk around and look for himself, Doc stopped what he was doing and glared at Gideon until the other man raised his hands in surrender and went back to the other side of the table and took my hand.

My heart leapt. Was there something wrong? Once Gideon was back beside me, I snagged his hand, needing something to ground me. Realizing I was taking a huge liberty, I glanced up at him. Gideon just gave me a soft smile, like he was proud of me or something, and enfolded my hand in both of his.

"I'll tell you when you can look," Doc said. "Ain't done."

"Anyone ever tell you, you have the worst bedside manner?" Gideon grumbled.

"More than once. I lived then. Guess I'll live now." He didn't look up, but kept pressing buttons on the ultrasound machine and moving the probe slightly one direction or the other.

Finally, after about fifteen or twenty minutes, Doc pulled the probe away and put it back on its base next to the machine and wiped the goop off my belly with a cloth. "Best I can tell, everything's fine," he said. "I've sent these images to a colleague of mine. I'll know in a minute if he needs any more images. So, while we're waiting, we'll take a look at you, Emmanuell."

"Ain't you gonna tell us how the baby is?" Gideon gripped my hand as he glanced my way. I could almost believe he was as anxious as I was.

"Told you, Ripper," Doc said with a raised eyebrow. "Best I can tell, things are fine. Now. Let's have a look at your girl, hmm?"

"Um, me and Gideon aren't together, you know," I said softly, not wanting Doc to have the wrong impression. "If that's why you're doing this, you should know I'm on my own."

Doc just looked up at me with a smirk. "Right." That was all he said before beginning.

The exam was surprisingly straightforward. Mostly health questions. Taking my blood pressure, temperature, heart rate. He drew some blood and gave me a huge bottle of prenatal vitamins.

"You just happen to have these laying around?" I looked at the bottle in dismay. It probably had five hundred pills in it.

"Had more than one woman around here pregnant at one time or another. Figured there'd be more." He nodded to the bottle. "Take one a day. If they make you sick, let me know and we'll figure out how to manage it. But you need those."

"They gonna make her sick?" Gideon glared at Doc, like the man was going to make me sick on purpose.

"Hopefully not. Sometimes they do." He shrugged. "Then again, some women get sick from everything. Can't be helped."

"Christ," Gideon scrubbed his hand over his face. "We done?"

"No. Need to check one more thing." Doc met

my gaze. "If you'll let me."

I sighed. "Figured this was coming. Not looking forward to it."

Doc tossed me a blanket and stepped out of the room. Gideon looked murderous but resigned. "Don't like another man touchin' you. Especially before I've had a chance to," he grumbled, but helped me take my pants off and tucked the blanket around my hips.

"Didn't you know this was going to happen?" I couldn't keep the grin off my face. Gideon's discomfort made me smile even as it confused me.

"Yeah, well, thinkin' about it and being here when it's gettin' ready to happen is two different fuckin' things."

I couldn't help myself, I laughed. "You need to calm down. This was your idea, anyway."

"You needed checked out."

"You're grumpy."

He lifted his chin stubbornly. "Am not."

The door opened and Doc came back inside. "Are too."

Gideon scowled. "No one asked you."

With a shrug, Doc stepped up to the table. "This won't take long. Normally I'd save it for your OB, but since you've not had any care and… well, just think it's best to do it now." I wanted to question that, but I was too nervous to concentrate on anything else.

The exam didn't take long. Doc gloved up and was extremely professional. Didn't stop Gideon from growling more than once. I gripped his hand and squeezed. The second Doc was done, Gideon's hand went to the swell of my belly, rubbing soothingly.

Doc stood and turned his back, taking off his gloves, then washing his hands. His phone pinged and he took it out to check a text message. His brows furrowed, then relaxed and he nodded once.

"Well, there's good news, what-the-fuck news, and then there's the really horrible news that is really a two-parter."

"Horrible news?" I squeaked about the same time Gideon snapped, "What the fuck, Doc?"

"So, the good news. Everything's fine as can be, given your lack of care, questionable diet, and exhaustion. The vitamins will go a long way toward building you up. Depending on if you can tolerate them and if you continue to eat well."

"So the baby's fine?" I gripped Gideon's hand so hard, I was sure my knuckles were white. I broke out in a sweat and couldn't stop trembling.

"Yes, honey. The babies are fine." Doc smiled at me.

Then it hit me.

"Uh... *Babies*?"

"Twins?" Gideon rubbed my belly just as one child kicked. He looked down at me and grinned. If I hadn't actually been there when I'd gotten pregnant, I'd swear Gideon was the daddy, as proud as he looked at that moment.

"Yeah," Doc said, rubbing the back of his neck as he grinned at Gideon. "That'd be a no. Not twins."

"I don't understand." I looked from Doc to Gideon and back. "If not twins…"

"Right. This is the what-the-fuck portion of the news. You're having triplets. All three appear to be healthy. It's why I wanted to send the images to a friend who's an OB. He's much better at this than me, though I got the basics down. He wants to see you in a week and redo the ultrasound with his equipment where he can see it in real time, but he says things look fine at this point. He estimates you at about twenty-six weeks. He said he'd set your target due date at thirty-three weeks, but he'll get you as far as he can safely."

"So, all that's good. I mean, I can't even begin to wrap my mind around three babies, but I'll figure it out."

"*We'll* figure it out," Gideon said, interrupting me and giving me a stern look.

"Right," Doc says. "Which brings me to the two-part really horrible news."

"Just spit it the fuck out, Doc." Gideon grumbled his order.

"All of your babies are girls."

Silence.

I looked from Doc to Gideon. Doc grinned. Gideon looked ready to do murder.

"I fail to see how having three girls is horrible news," I snapped. "It's mean of you to say such a thing! How dare you!"

"Honey," Doc said with a chuckle. "Don't get me wrong. Everyone here will be thrilled as fuck to know we're gonna have three girls to spoil and adore. Your man, Ripper, there? Yeah. Three girls to wrap him around their little fingers that he has to beat the boys back from. As grumpy as he is normally, expect him to get worse after the girls are born and as they get older. Also expect us all to make fun of him. Heartily. Constantly."

"Motherfucker," Gideon growled.

I sighed. "You guys really have a twisted sense of humor."

Doc blinked. "I have a sense of humor?"

"We done here?"

"Yeah, Ripper. And even though I know you haven't gotten around to asking yet, yes. You can have sex for now. Just be gentle with her, and everything should be fine. Also, don't expect it to continue for long. I expect you'll get cut off pretty soon."

"Good grief," I said, throwing up my hands, my cheeks flaming with embarrassment. "I can't believe you went there."

"What? He was gonna ask it." Doc looked completely unrepentant.

"Get out so she can get dressed," Gideon snapped before muttering, "Fucker."

Doc just laughed and waved at me. "Good to meet you, Emmanuell. If you need anything at all, don't hesitate to ask."

Once he'd left the room, I sat there for a few moments, trying to process everything. "Triplets."

"Three girls." Gideon shook his head but grinned widely before chuckling. "I'm so fucked."

* * *

Ripper

Instead of taking her back to her room, I took her to mine. No way she was staying anywhere other than with me, and I wanted her in my home. Well, as much of a home as I had currently. I'd talk to Thorn about moving us into one of the new houses going up. After the babies were born. I wanted to keep us as close as I could to Doc in case Emmanuell needed him.

"Uh, what are we doing?"

"Takin' you to bed."

She giggled. "I hope that means what I think it means, because I'm anxious to experience what you have to offer by way of sex."

I smirked at her. "Bet you're glad Doc went there now, aren't you?"

"You're such a cad." But she slipped her arms around my neck and kissed me.

"Yeah. Ain't apologizing for it, neither."

I laid her gently on the bed before scooting in beside her, my hand at her waist. I seemed to be touching her rounded belly often now that I'd staked my claim with her. Truth was, I couldn't touch her enough. This taste I was about to get with her was just one more thing about Emmanuell I was going to be addicted to. Her kisses were already working their way into my system like a drug. I could happily kiss her forever.

"This first time's gonna be slow and careful." I brought my hand up to caress her face, my thumb trailing over her bottom lip. "There'll be a day when I won't be so gentle, but I promise you'll enjoy it."

"I have no doubt." Emmanuell's voice wavered slightly, and she trembled in my arms. "I should tell you, I've only ever had one partner. I'm not really good at this." Was that shame on her face? That wouldn't do.

"So?"

She blinked several times, looking at me in confusion. "So, I want it to be good for you, too."

"Baby, it will. No way it could be anything other than fantastic."

"I'm nervous."

"As long as you're not scared. You know I'd never hurt you. Right?"

She chuckled. "Well, considering how you were with me earlier with the doctor, yeah. I know. No way a man sits through that if he wanted to hurt a woman."

"OK, you got me there." I couldn't keep the grin off my face. "But honestly, Emmanuell. Did you have to be pregnant with *three girls*?"

That got a huge smile from her, and I couldn't resist any longer. I leaned over her, taking her mouth in another kiss. This time, I settled in to take her as high as I possibly could.

Emmanuell arched against me, bunching her fists in my shirt. Her little whimpers drove me mad. I wanted to take her hard and fast, but that was something I'd have to put off for a few months. Working her up to that once the babies were born would be a fucking blast.

When my palm slid up to cup her breast, Emmanuell moaned into my mouth, arching to my touch. I squeezed gently, kneading her breast as I continued to kiss her. She was lush and responsive, her body eager for my touch.

"That's it, beautiful. Tell me what you want."

"I want us naked," she panted. "Need my clothes off, Gideon!"

"Yeah, baby. I got you."

I stripped her clothes from her one slow inch at a time, revealing creamy skin underneath the fabric. I kissed both nipples, sucking gently, and her hands went to my hair, tunneling until her fingers tangled there. Her cries and moans were the sweetest music, her body a sensual playground.

I kissed my way down her abdomen until I reached the swell where her children grew. My hands cupped around her, taking in as much skin as I could. Wanting to surround the babies with a layer of protection.

"You know, I'll always protect them," I said, meaning it. "The babies. And you."

"I believe you," she whispered. "At least, I want to."

"Believe it, Emmanuell. I'll be ruthless in keeping all of you safe."

Placing kisses all over her belly, I tried my best to

will her to understand. But, honestly, I didn't fully understand it myself. She'd somehow imprinted on me. Her and her children. The first time one of them had kicked my hand just the night before? Yeah. I was gone then. I knew it and expressed it to her, but there was no way she could fully understand. Or believe. So I'd have to prove it to her. However long it took.

I slid her pants from her slender hips along with her panties. Her pussy glistened with arousal, and my mouth watered for her. Kneeling in front of her, I stroked her, letting my fingers play through her silky folds while we gazed at each other. I brought my fingers to my mouth, bringing all that honey to my tongue. God! She was exquisite!

With a growl, I leaned over her, bringing my mouth to her pussy. "So fuckin' sweet!"

Emmanuell screamed, her whole body shuddering as she reached for my head. Once her fingers closed in my hair, I wasn't sure if she wanted to push me away or hold me close. I'm not sure she did either, because she seemed to do both alternately. I didn't care. I just ate her up.

Her clit pulsed beneath my tongue with each swipe. Her pussy tried to squeeze my tongue every time I swiped through her entrance. Her cries grew frantic, and I latched on to her clit, sucking the little nub until her body tensed and she gave a shrill scream.

"Gideon!"

"Ughh…" I worked her clit with my lips and tongue, needing her to ride out her orgasm to the very end. Once she relaxed, I yanked off my shirt and moved up behind her. "Not takin' a chance on hurtin' you or the babies." I reached over to the drawer and pulled out a condom. Except how the fuck old were they? Fuck! I took precious seconds to check the expiration date, nearly howling with relief when I saw they were good. Then I shoved my jeans past my hips and gloved my cock when it was the last thing I wanted to do. But we hadn't discussed me taking her without a condom yet, so gloved it was.

"How do I… Oh!" I hooked her leg over my arm before guiding my cock inside her and sliding in as far as I could. "Gideon," she gasped. "Oh, God!"

"Just relax," I murmured. "I've got you."

She whimpered, gripping the arm I'd wrapped around her. Looking back over her shoulder, she caught my gaze with hers. Unable to resist the erotic, shocked expression on her face, I leaned in and kissed her gently as I started to move. Carefully, I took her, never taking my eyes from her. With every surge forward, she gasped, her eyes glazing over.

"That's it, baby." My voice was lust roughened. It wasn't as hard to keep focused on her comfort as I'd first thought it was going to be. Not because it didn't feel good inside her. Fuck! She was strangling my fucking cock like nobody's business! But she *mattered*. Unlike any other woman in my life, Emmanuell mattered. I wasn't sure exactly when it happened, when she'd crawled under my skin, but in less than twenty-four hours, she'd become the most important person in my world. And I was going to take care of her and the children she was bringing into the world. "Give yourself to me."

"Gideon…" Her sigh was fucking perfect. A woman being well-pleasured. "God!"

I slid my hand down her body until I found her clit and stroked, her moisture making the flesh slick. Two seconds later, her body tensed and she screamed, arching her back as she came around my cock. Her orgasm triggered my own, and I groaned my release, tightening my arms around her as I emptied myself into that fucking condom. The pleasure was intense and brutal. I didn't want to hurt her, but it took all my strength not to pound into her as I finished.

The feel of her, the way my chest swelled with pride as she came in my arms, was an awakening of sorts. It had never mattered to me if a woman found pleasure. I fucked. If she got off, great. If not? I hadn't cared. But now? There was no way this woman was ever leaving my arms anything other than completely satisfied.

"Fuck, Emmanuell," I panted. "Just… fuck."

She stiffened, looking up at me with wide, questioning eyes. "Did I do something wrong?"

"What? No! Jesus, Emmanuell! I've never experienced anything like that. You were perfect."

"Are you sure? I mean, I didn't do anything but lie there…" She glanced away, and I could see shame on her face. Harder than I meant to, I gripped her chin and turned her to face me.

"Tell me," I snapped. "What's wrong?"

She winced, trying to pull away from me. "Nothing. Let me up."

I took a deep breath, trying to get myself under control when all I could process was that she was trying to get away from me. That primitive caveman inside me rebelled hard.

"Stop," I snarled. She did, but she wasn't relaxed about it. She was stiff in my arms, her body trembling and not in a good way. "Tell me what's going on, Emmanuell. Talk to me."

"Look, I know I'm not great in bed. Just don't pretend something you don't feel. I already told you I don't have any money. I'm not the heiress everyone thinks I am."

Had she stabbed me in the gut, I couldn't have been more surprised. "Honey, money's got nothing to do with this. Not one Goddamned thing. The only thing that matters is me and you. I got my own money. More than we'll ever need. More than enough to take care of me, you, and the girls." I continued to look at her. She still held herself stiffly, not wanting to meet my gaze, but she no longer tried to get away from me. "Now, tell me what you mean when you say you're not good in bed."

She bit her bottom lip nervously. "I'm just not. Devan said I needed to do more than just lie there while he did all the work. But, honestly, I never felt anything like what I just experienced. I didn't know how to fake it, and he just didn't do anything I liked."

I was sure I looked at her in both confusion and anger. "Are you fuckin' tellin' me he knocked you up and didn't even make you come?"

"Well, yeah. He wasn't really all that concerned with my pleasure. And I was just trying to process all that had happened. I hadn't been able to get ahold of Mr. Goldstein, and Devan told me I needed to give it a day or two and take some time for myself." The more she talked the more she frowned. "It was stupid on my part. I should have made my own way back however I could. But I relied on Devan to take care of everything when I didn't know him." Yeah. This wasn't going where I wanted it to go. Her breathing sped up and her face flushed. She pushed at me, struggling to get up. "Let me up, Ripper."

With a growl of displeasure, I released her. Goddamned motherfucking Beaner. For this alone, I was going to kill the son of a bitch. "Emmanuell, I'm not Beaner."

She scooped up her clothes and hurried to the

bathroom without a word and shut the door. I heard it lock, but that didn't bother me. If I needed to get in to her, I'd break the fucking door down if I had to.

I stood, removing the condom and tossing it in the wastebasket beside my bed, then pulled up my jeans. Moving to the door, I put my palm against it. "Emmanuell, honey, open the door." No answer. "Baby, don't shut me out."

"Just leave me alone for a minute. I need to think."

"No, you don't. At least, you don't need to compare me to your past experience with Beaner, and that's what you're doing."

"I'm not comparing you to anything. I'm just using my past experience with life to judge my actions, and I'm being an idiot."

Fuck. "At least give me a chance to prove I'm not like everyone else you've known."

Fully dressed, she opened the door and shouldered her way past me. Tears streaked down her face, and she swiped at them angrily. "Stupid," she muttered as she headed for the door.

"Where you goin'?"

"Back to my room. I'm sorry, Ripper, but this was a mistake and never should have happened."

I wanted to deny her, but I couldn't keep her prisoner. Instead, I ground my teeth in frustration. "If that's what you think's best. At least let me take you back so you don't get lost."

She hesitated, then ducked her head, nodding once.

Chapter Six
Emmanuell

The second Gideon opened the door to my room, I hurried inside and shut the door. Or tried to. The big bastard shoved his foot in the door, forcing me to look up at him. I knew it was a mistake. The best thing I could have done was to just tell him to leave and shut the door, but I couldn't.

My breath caught when my gaze met his. He was intense. Possessive. It thrilled me to have a man like Gideon look at me that way, but how could I really be certain? I was falling fast for the big, rough biker. I'd never felt more alive than when I was in his arms. When he kissed me. He'd taken care of me since he'd met me and even made sure I'd had the babies checked. But how could I really be sure it was me he wanted and not what he thought I had or would get? Just thinking about it all made my head ache.

"Please get your foot out of the door, Ripper." I used his road name purposefully, trying to remind myself I didn't really know him at all. At least, not well enough that I should have the feelings I did for him. Up until right after we'd had sex, I had bought into the fairy tale. Just like I had with Devan. He'd said it was fate we'd met. That I was meant to be with him when I hadn't been with my father when he'd died. I'd been so devastated, I'd believed him. Had let him take control so I could wallow in self-pity instead of going home to assume control of my father's estate until the will could be put into action. I couldn't make the mistake of trusting someone I didn't know again. And my current situation was much more important than the other one. This time, I had three babies to think about.

For long moments Gideon just stared at me. I

was afraid he was going to refuse me, but finally, he removed his foot and stepped back without a word. He held my gaze for several seconds before I could get my wits about me and shut the door. Surprisingly, I didn't feel the satisfaction or relief I should have at shutting him out. I just felt... alone.

For the first time since this whole thing began, I broke down. As I slid down the door, the fight just left me. I dissolved into tears and buried my face in my knees. Tears turned into sobs. Sobs turned into anguished screams. I'd lived homeless for six months. I'd been cold, scared, hungry, and hadn't gotten my babies any prenatal care. I could have been killed. My children could have been killed. And the man responsible for my predicament was in this very place. I was being sheltered by people in his club, for Christ's sake! How safe was I now really?

There was a knock at the door, and I heard Gideon outside. "Emmanuell, let me in." I tried to reply for him to go to hell, but I couldn't get it out. "Emmanuell. Honey. Come on. Open the door."

I had no idea what to do. My mind was in chaos. My heart was aching like I'd never experienced. I'd fixated on Ripper. Embraced his caring like he was the man of my dreams coming in to take all my problems away. But what did I really know about the man? Nothing. Just like I'd known nothing about Devan.

I have no idea how long I sat there, crying uncontrollably. Mourning both the death of my father and the fact that I'd let my babies down by not taking care of them properly. *Triplets*! There were probably any number of things I should have done to make sure they were healthy. I needed to leave, but I had nowhere to go. I'd been gone for more than six months. Mr. Goldstein wouldn't take my calls. I couldn't prove

I was who I said I was. I'd been living homeless or in cheap motels all this time and had learned the hard way that no one cared who I used to be, only who I'd become. Without any way to verify my identity, I had become just another homeless woman. No one cared I was pregnant. No one cared if I had anything to eat or had medical care. Since Ripper had brought me into this clubhouse, with Salvation's Bane, I'd been treated with respect and caring. Like I was someone.

Confusion only made me grieve harder. The babies kicked, which just made me even more miserable. Was I failing them by even considering leaving Salvation's Bane? Was I failing them by trying to kick Gideon out of my life? How much of what he'd told me could I really rely on?

The next thing I heard was another soft knock at the door. "Emmanuell?" It was a female voice. She sounded worried. "Emmanuell, please open the door. We're all worried about you." I thought the voice was Lucy's, but I wasn't sure. Realizing someone other than Gideon could hear my breakdown, I crawled away from the door to sit next to the couch. I was still on the floor, unable to summon the strength to stand. I just buried my face in the crook of my arm, which was around my knees, and continued to sob.

I could no longer hear anyone talking outside the door, but I could hear the gentle knocking. Hopefully, they couldn't hear me either. The door opened, and someone crouched beside me, wrapping a gentle arm around me.

"Get a blanket." I looked up to see Lucy's face next to me. Tears glistened in her eyes as she gave an order to someone. She looked angry even as one tear dripped from her eye. She rubbed my arms and crooned to me softly. "It's going to be OK, Emmanuell.

Whatever is wrong, I'll help you fix it. Me and the other ol' ladies." As I looked up, three more women filed in. Kitty moved in front of me immediately, snatching a blanket from someone. I couldn't see much beyond anything in front of my face. My eyes were so swollen, and tears continued to blur my vision.

Lucy looked in the direction of the door while she helped Kitty wrap the blanket around me. "Spring, thank you for coming."

"Is this Emmanuell? Is she OK? What's wrong?" Spring used a soft, damp cloth to gently wash my face of tears. "Do I need to get Doc, honey?"

"I didn't hurt her," a male voice growled. "I'm the one who called Lucy when I couldn't get her to open the fuckin' door." I looked up to see Gideon standing behind Kitty, looking like he desperately wanted to do something. He clenched and unclenched his fists. When he noticed me looking at him, he crossed his arms over his chest, his gaze fastening to mine.

"Well, something happened," Spring muttered. "When a woman is this distraught and no one died, you can almost bet there's a man involved somehow."

I stirred then, needing to take my gaze from Gideon, but unable to. "It's not his fault," I whispered. "I just need to be by myself for a while." I really didn't. I never wanted to be alone again as long as I lived. But I didn't know these people.

"I think you've been by yourself for way too long, honey," Lucy said, hugging me to her and urging me to stand. The other women helped. There were two other women I didn't know, but they all formed a solid wall around me, helping me walk out of the room and down the hall where Lucy said she lived with her husband, Vicious.

When I looked up at the concerned faces around me, I felt nothing but good will. These women genuinely wanted to help. Then my gaze accidentally went to the door, knowing he'd be there. I couldn't seem to help myself. I was in love with Gideon. He'd imprinted himself on me. I tried to tell myself it was nothing more than infatuation, especially after the explosive sex we'd had, not to mention how gentle and caring he'd been with me. Both during sex and before when he'd insisted I go to the doctor. Did he really deserve my distrust because of Devan?

"I think you need to leave, Ripper," Lucy said, standing and putting herself between me and Gideon. Vicious entered the room and went to his wife, putting his arm around her.

"Don't judge him until you know what happened, honey. I've seen him with Emmanuell, and he cares for that girl."

"I understand that," she countered, "but if she doesn't want him here, no matter what happened, she doesn't have to be near him. We can work it out later, but while she's in my home -- and last I checked this was my home -- I will have the woman pregnant with triplets comfortable and feeling safe. Gideon can sit outside the door if he wants, but he doesn't get to barge in here if she wants away from him."

Gideon looked like he wanted to punch something, but he closed his eyes and nodded once, then turned to walk back outside the door. Vicious sighed heavily, but leaned in to kiss his wife on the forehead. Then he, too, left the room.

"Emmanuell, I know you've met a lot of people, but I have two more for you. This is Venus and Glitter. Glitter is ol' lady to one of Bane's members. Venus is a patched member herself." That startled me. I hadn't realized they let women be members.

"That's right," Venus said. "You need him gutted, you come to me. I have experience in those matters." Her accent sounded Russian. But the most startling thing about Venus was her appearance. She was dressed head to toe in pink leather. But that wasn't all. She also had pink hair and pink nails that looked razor-sharp. Even her eyes were hot pink.

"She's not kidding," Glitter said with a gentle smile. "You tell us if he hurt you, and Venus will take care of him."

"He didn't," I said softly. "I probably overreacted. This isn't his fault. It's mine."

"Tell us what's wrong," Lucy urged, taking my hands in hers. "Let us help make it right."

"Why would any of you do that?" I tried to pull my hands away, but Lucy held fast, holding my gaze with a steady one of her own.

"Because you need friends. Let us be that for you."

"Like I told Ripper, I don't have any money. Even if I manage to get control of my father's estate, I know what his wishes were, and none of that money goes to me. My father wanted me to be able to take care of myself and not rely on his money. He made sure I had everything I needed to survive, but I wasn't the spoiled little rich girl everyone thinks I was. I didn't drive fancy cars or have designer clothing. Even when I accompanied my parents to important fundraisers, I was responsible for my own donation and my attire. They only supplied the ride, and I got to go with them. It was important to my father, and I won't dishonor his wishes just because his lawyer managed to get everything turned over to himself."

"Honey," Glitter said, looking from Spring to

Lucy, confusion on her face. "We just want to help you. This club is a family. Ripper's made it known you're his. He's claimed you. Not as his ol' lady, but we all know it's coming. In our book, that makes you family, too."

"No one here could give good Goddamned about your money or lack thereof," Venus said. "So, if that is your objection to Ripper, you did overreact." She tilted her head as if thinking. "Unless he said something different?"

"No. I just realized that I was under the same roof as Devan. And he'd played me so completely. Devan's here. A member of Ripper's club. Of *your* club. I've been bested once already and have put myself in the exact same position again."

"Devan isn't member," Venus said with a disdainful snort and a shake of her head. "He was prospect. Someone looking to be member. After yesterday, he's no longer that. More importantly, he betrayed club. That carries with it stiff penalty. He's currently in cell in basement, waiting for Ripper and his team to investigate."

"So, an internal investigation." I still wasn't convinced. "What then?"

Venus sneered, looking more than a little bloodthirsty. "Then we take care of him."

"And if this investigation shows I'm lying?"

"We already know you're not lying." Venus shrugged. "Only question is what degree Beaner was involved in Goldstein's takeover of your father's estate, and what, if any, part he played in his death."

I looked at them all helplessly. "I want to believe you. I really do!"

"But you're afraid this is all some elaborate trick to get you to trust us so we can get our hands on your father's money." Lucy quietly voiced what she thought was my concern. She didn't condemn me, just stated what she saw as a fact.

"It's not even that," I said, dropping my gaze. "I'm afraid..." I took a breath. "Devan used me. He made me think he was really interested in me. I bought into it enough I not only gave him my virginity, I never questioned what he told me. That me not being in that car crash when my dad was killed meant we were supposed to be together. He played it out, too. Keeping in touch with Mr. Goldstein, making sure I was in the loop. Because of the accident, not having the funeral right away wasn't unusual. There were medical examiners wanting to investigate and all kinds of law enforcement. Devan convinced me it was best if we just stay away for a while. An extended holiday. I must have gotten pregnant the first couple of days of our stay, because three weeks later, I found out. When I told him, he promised he'd take care of everything.

"Then he said it was time to go back to Florida, and we packed our stuff. We left the hotel late one afternoon and drove for a while, not making it out of New York before he told me he was tired, and we needed to stop for a few hours. I honestly didn't care, but it should have been a huge red flag. We checked into a little roadside motel, but he didn't let me take our stuff inside. Said we wouldn't be there long enough to need it. Just a couple of hours so he could catch a nap.

I dozed off with him, but when I woke, he was gone. He'd left a note on the bedside table that said he'd gone to get us some snacks and to fill the car up with gas and would be right back. But he never showed back up." I started to cry again. "Crying is so stupid," I spat, sniffing and wiping my eyes with my sleeve.

"I understand why you're afraid to trust us. No one can convince you we're not like Beaner." Glitter spoke softly, and I noticed tears glistening in her eyes. "What he did was horrible. No one should treat anyone like that."

"He'll pay for it," Spring said. "But that can't make up for the broken trust."

"I don't know if I'll ever be able to trust again. And that hurts more than anything." I started sobbing again. All the women gathered closer around me except for Venus, who looked angry as hell. She took out her phone, sending a rapid text before putting it back in her pocket. In that moment, I realized what a horrible mistake I'd made. "I've judged everyone here because of the actions of one person," I said softly, my voice still trembling. "I'm so, so sorry."

"Emmanuell, no one blames you," Spring said emphatically. "What happened to you is enough to break anyone's trust. Especially when you're in the arms of people Beaner lived with. Served with. It's understandable -- expected even -- that you'd eventually have some issues. We can't change your mind overnight or convince you to trust us. Or Ripper. All we can do is prove to you all we want is to get to know you better and to welcome you and your children into our family."

"And make no mistake," Venus interrupted. "We will all protect your children and you with our lives. Same as we would for any of the ol' ladies and their children. Whether you choose to be part of us or not, you will always have our protection." Venus meant every word she said. It was written all over her face. When I looked at the other women, I saw that same sincerity in their faces as well.

"Just take a few days to settle in," Lucy said. "Any one of us will help you if you need something. I'll make sure you have all our numbers. Just text if you need us."

"I don't have a phone," I said softly. It was embarrassing that I didn't have even the most basic of things.

"Not a problem. I'll have one for you tomorrow."

"I can't let you do that, Lucy. I can't pay for it, and it's not right."

"We already told you. You're part of this family, Emmanuell. That means we take care of you. And the babies. You can't be without a phone, and the club can provide one. I'll have it to you with all our numbers programmed into it tomorrow." Lucy smiled. "I won't hear another word about it. Now. Do you want to go back to your room, or do you want to stay here with me tonight?"

"I'll be fine on my own," I said softly. "And I need to apologize to Ripper. I was completely unfair to him when he's been nothing but good to me since I got here."

Lucy smiled. "Don't worry about Ripper. He's all in. Probably beating himself up for upsetting you, but he's not going anywhere."

I let Lucy and Kitty take me back to my room. Ripper wasn't anywhere close. Even though I knew I'd driven him away, I still hated that he wasn't right there just waiting for me to jump back into his arms, but I got it. I'd been pretty hard on him when he hadn't deserved it.

When I closed the door, I looked around. Everything I had in this room had come from the club. They'd given me a room of my own, clothes, basic essentials. They'd even started bringing in stuff for the babies. And I'd only been here one full day. They weren't after money. I knew I was young and naive, but these people were a world away from Devan.

I glanced at the clock. It was after eleven, but I could hear the party downstairs. It wasn't overly loud, but kind of beckoned me to check it out. I'd been to a few parties in my life, but I had the feeling this would be nothing like I'd ever experienced. I wanted to go, but, at the same time, was afraid. What if I saw Ripper? What if he was with another woman? I'd rejected him. There was no reason to think he wouldn't kick my ass to the curb without another thought. Wouldn't most men do that? It wasn't like the babies were his or that we actually had a relationship. One day. That's all we'd had.

Deciding to check everything out, I left my room. I wasn't necessarily going to the party, but I wanted to explore. Get to know my surroundings. No one had said I couldn't, so I just wandered around the place, preferring to stay away from the party. For a while at least. I wasn't sure if I was brave enough to tackle that.

"You lost, honey?" A tall, busty woman with long, white-blonde locks stepped in front of me.

"No," I said automatically, holding my hands up and taking a couple steps back. "I was just looking around."

"You're not Bane. You're not allowed anywhere but in the main room. Who you with, anyway?" The girl kept advancing on me, backing me up until I was close to the wall. I put my hand over my belly protectively.

"I just got here last night." I looked around, suddenly terrified I was getting ready to be ambushed. "I'm staying on the third f-floor."

"No one stays up there but ol' ladies and officers.

And you ain't neither." The woman was joined by two more women. They didn't seem as aggressive as the first one, but I still didn't want to be in the hallway with them by myself.

"I am. Lucy can vouch for me. Doc can."

"Yeah," the woman sneered. "We heard all about Ripper taking you to Doc." She indicated my swollen belly with a sneer. "Just 'cause you got yourself knocked up don't mean you're with Ripper. What would he want with a woman getting ready to have someone else's kid?" Her smirk was cruel. "You'll have the fucking kid, then he'll move on when he can't fuck you any longer. Surprised he took you on in the first place. Ain't like you're all that much to begin with. He won't stick around long."

One of the others giggled but kept her distance. "Just long enough to show you you don't belong here. Ain't Rivet right, Taz?"

"Ripper never stays with anyone long, Foxy," Taz said. She looked a little more wary than her companions. "But he's also never taken an interest in a woman like this before. I don't think we need to be doing this," she said softly, backing away. "Rivet, Ripper'll kick us out or worse if he finds out and you're wrong."

As if to press her point to the other two, the first woman, Rivet, stepped close enough to be in my personal space again, stabbing me in the chest with her finger. It was hard enough to make me wince. "Don't think you can worm your way into the club by making him feel sorry for you because of that fucking brat you're carrying. It won't work." She gave me an evil grin. "No one wants you here. Least of all Ripper. I mean, what would a man like him want with someone else's brat to raise?" She shook her head. "No. If he ain't fucking you, he has no use for you. Same as all the other men here." Giving me a once over from head to toe, she snorted in disgust. "Hell, from the looks of you, it won't be long until you're begging off the fucking. How it makes you uncomfortable or what if it hurts the baby?" Rivet mocked me, pretending to be sad or in pain before laughing along with Foxy. Taz just looked at Rivet and shook her head, backing back down the hall but stopping short of abandoning her friends.

"You know him well?" It was a stupid question to ask, but I couldn't help myself.

Rivet laughed heartily. "Oh, yes, baby girl. I know Ripper. He's reclusive. Stays in his office most days. But he's a great fuck. Man loves it rough. He might have shown you a good time, but he's forgotten about you by now."

"If he hasn't," Foxy said with a giggle, "he soon will. We'll see to it."

"We see to all the men here." Rivet shoved me back against the wall, pinning my shoulders there for long moments while staring me down. "You don't belong. Best you pack up and move before you get hurt, baby girl. You and your little brat."

I clutched my belly protectively, the other hand flat against the wall. "I'm not here to cause trouble. And I only stayed because Gid… I mean, Ripper made me. I was going to just leave."

"Well, he ain't here making you stay. I suggest you be on your way before someone takes matters into their own hands," she hissed. "Leave!"

"That's enough, Rivet." I turned to see another woman with long, straight black hair. She was dressed in black leather pants with a matching tank. The heels she wore were positively wicked on the thigh-high black boots. "She's not to be touched. You all know this."

"Yet she's out here alone. Roaming the halls of the club like she owns the damned place."

"She can go where she wants. You three, on the other hand, aren't allowed past your second-floor rooms, and only in designated areas. Which, strangely, you're out of. You know the rules."

"She's breaking them, too! What the fuck, Isadora?" Rivet looked positively livid as she glanced from Isadora back to me.

"She's Ripper's." Isadora shrugged. "Or might be. Doesn't really matter. The ol' ladies have given her free rein of the clubhouse if she chooses, and their men are with them on this. Even Thorn. All you need to do is leave her alone. It's not that difficult to understand or hard to comply with."

"I don't want to be a problem," I squeaked out.

"Too late, bitch," Rivet spat. "From what I heard you've been causing trouble since you got here. Now they've got one of our own locked up, and you're the fucking cause."

"Not another word," Isadora snapped. "You three get back to the party or get the fuck out!"

I was horrified. Were they talking about Devan? I hadn't really thought much about what was happening to him other than what Venus alluded to earlier.

"Want to explain what the fuck is going on, Isadora?"

At the other end of the hall, Gideon stalked toward our little gathering. He had fury in his eyes as he took in the scene. I'd never seen anyone look so angry in my life. Gideon was practically vibrating with it.

"I'm taking care of it, Ripper. These three were

just leaving."

"And they won't be returning," he snapped. "Out with all of you."

"You can't do that!" Rivet marched up to him, and I flinched when Gideon caught her by the throat and shoved her up against the wall. He wasn't gentle about it, either. The woman hit with a thud, grasping his thick wrist with her smaller hands, trying to pry his fist away from her.

Ripper leaned in nose to nose with her and snarled. "Another word, and I'll break your fuckin' neck." He held her gaze for long moments, his hand tightening around her throat. I could see the exact moment Rivet understood the trouble she was in. Her eyes got wide with fear. Then her bladder let go, leaving a puddle at her feet. "Good. Now get the fuck out."

He watched as the three women hurried out. Then he turned back to Isadora. "Get this mess cleaned up. Next time someone gets up in Emmanuelle's face and you're there and don't shut it down immediately, you'll be the one to go."

Isadora met his gaze steadily, but nodded once. She glanced at me, lifting the corner of her lips and winking at me before she left.

"You good?"

It took me a second to realize Ripper was talking to me. Was I? I was shaking. The adrenaline rush I hadn't even realized had hit me seemed to vanish just as quickly, leaving me weak in the knees. Gideon didn't miss a beat. He just scooped me up, holding me close to him. Those strong arms of his surrounded me with heat and protection, and I just lost my shit.

"I'm sorry, Gideon!" I cried. "I'm so sorry!" I wrapped my arms around his neck and clung to him so tightly I was probably strangling him, but I couldn't seem to let up.

"It's OK, baby," he murmured next to my ear. "Everything's gonna be OK. I've got you."

"I'm so stupid. You're nothing like that asshole, Devan. Judging you because I was stupid enough to fall for him is inexcusable!"

"Honey, it's all good. I shouldn't have come on so strong. Even knowing how fragile you were, after we found out about the babies, I wanted to stake a claim on you. Both for you and myself. I didn't want there to be any mistakes." He kissed my temple, carrying me down the hall. "You're mine, Emmanuel. Not anyone else's. Not anyone from your past, or my brothers, and certainly not that little pissant, Beaner. I needed you to know you were mine, and I just steamrolled you into bed."

"I remember being part of that decision. I could have said no." I sniffed, still clinging to him. "The truth is, I wanted exactly what you gave me. I wanted the promises you made. Wanted to be yours because you were so kind and gentle with me. You made sure I was taken care of when I couldn't figure out how to do it myself."

"Someone had to, baby. I didn't do anything any decent man wouldn't have done. Well, other than taking you to bed. Pretty sure I shouldn't have done that. Don't regret it, though, and I ain't takin' it back."

Next thing I knew, Gideon set me down to open the door, and he pulled me into his room once again, shutting the door behind us. He wrapped his arms around me as he rested his back against the door. His chest heaved like he'd been running, and his body trembled around mine.

"Gideon?"

"Just give me a minute, baby."

"Gideon, what's wrong?" Alarm began to fill me. Had he hurt himself?

"I nearly killed that woman. When I saw her back you up against the wall, poking you in the chest, shoving you back and pinning your shoulders. I nearly lost my Goddamned mind."

"She didn't hurt me. Didn't even come close. And she didn't threaten me. Not really."

"I know exactly what she did, sweetheart. I've got the whole fuckin' clubhouse wired. There are cameras everywhere except in the rooms of patched members." I must have looked as shocked as I felt because he gave me a sheepish look. "After Afghanistan, I got a little paranoid. I was vulnerable, and that made my team vulnerable." He shrugged. "I guess I never shook it. I'm not trying to spy on anyone, but it gives me a heads up on incidents like the one back there with Isadora and the other women."

I clung to him, needing comfort, but needing to comfort him as well. "You wouldn't have killed her. She didn't hurt me."

"Yes, Emmanuell," he said emphatically. "I would have strangled the fuckin' life out of her and not batted an eyelash." I opened my mouth to deny his words, but he continued. "And before you say she didn't hurt you, I saw your face. She did hurt you. Maybe not physically, though she shoved you back against the wall, and if I find even one bruise on your delicate flesh, I may find the bitch and finish what I started, but she hurt you. What did she say?" Ducking my head, I tried to turn away, but Gideon wouldn't let me. "Come on, Emmanuell. Just tell me. Don't turn away from me this time." His words were nearly a whisper, but a command. A plea?

"It's nothing I wasn't already telling myself, Gideon." I laid my hands on his chest, feeling the muscles bunch with tension. I looked up at him, needing to see into his eyes. A look of such complete need and possessiveness nearly took my breath. "Why do you want me?" I hated the way I sounded. Whimpering. Scared. Broken. "In all the time I've been trying to survive on my own, trying to prepare myself mentally for everything about to happen to me, I've never let myself sulk."

"I'd think you deserve to sulk if you want to."

"No. It's pointless and did nothing but hurt the people who took me in. And I hurt you."

"Honey, you've known me a fuckin' *day*. That can't negate the months of shit you went through. We've got time. I'll prove to you how much I want to be in your life. If I can't convince you, then I don't deserve you."

Heaving in a breath, I took in his scent. It was soothing, like a gentle caress. I'd never paid much attention to how a man smelled. Well, unless he smelled bad. But Gideon had a wildness about him that called to me. A curious combination of pine, wood, and motor oil. It was oddly comforting. Probably because I wanted him so much. Not just sexually either. The attention he'd shown me over the last twenty-four hours had been catnip to a girl like me.

"Let's talk for a bit," I said, reluctantly pulling away from him, but snagging his hand and leading him to the couch. He came willingly, moving ahead of me to sit in the middle of the couch. I grinned. There was a stubborn set to his jaw as he looked up at me. With a grin, I started to sit beside him, but he just pulled me into his lap and wrapped his arms around me. I sighed contentedly, pulling my knees up and curling against his chest.

"Guess we should have done more of this before, huh?" He rested his chin on my head.

"Talking? Yeah. Probably."

"So, tell me what's on your mind."

I sighed. "I don't really believe all that stuff, Gideon. That you're only with me for my money. I don't even believe the stuff Rivet and the other woman were spouting."

"But you panicked." He didn't sound mad or put out. Just the opposite. He sounded like he finally understood what was going on in my head.

"Yeah. When I realized I was putting myself in the exact same position I had before, I guess I lost my mind a little bit. But you're nothing like Devan, Gideon. I know I just met you, but I was blind not to see it before." Looking at my hands, I took a shuddering breath. "OK, that's not exactly accurate. I did see it before. From the very first encounter with you, you and Devan were nothing alike. When I panicked after we'd had sex, I just…"

"You were trying to protect yourself," he finished for me.

"Yeah. But I hurt you in the process."

"Baby, I get it. And I understand. You're right to be careful."

"I can't stop living because I got hurt, Gideon. I can't give up on good people because one person was an asshole."

Gideon took my face in his hands, leaning in to kiss my lips gently. "We'll slow down, Emmanuell. We've got six weeks before the babies are born, and there's a shit-ton of stuff to do before then. Starting with the doctor's appointment Doc made for you with the high-risk pregnancy specialist. Let's concentrate on that. In the process, maybe we'll get to know each other better."

I smiled, a tear escaping to trickle down my cheek, and Gideon leaned in to catch it with his lips. "I think that sounds just about perfect."

Chapter Seven
Ripper
Six Weeks Later

If there was a hell, I was in it. Doctor's appointments. Baby showers -- yes, there was more than one. Ribbing from my brothers about losing my man card. How was this even my life? Yet, as I gazed down at Emmanuell where she lay on the exam table at her latest appointment, I couldn't find it in myself to hate anything going on. The only dark spot in the whole turn of events was Beaner. He wasn't talking and tracking anything back to Randall Goldstein was proving difficult in the extreme.

"Everything looks good," the doctor said as he offered a hand to help Emmanuell sit up. "You're at thirty-two weeks, and the plan is still the same. I'd like to schedule you for a C-Section so there are no surprises and we can have a team ready to assist with each baby." The doctor was a buddy of Doc's. Guy's name was Jeremiah Redding. Seemed like a decent guy, and he treated Emmanuell with respect and coddled the shit out of her.

"I'm scared," Emmanuell whispered, looking up at the doctor, then back to me. She had a death grip on my hand.

"We'll take good care of you, young lady. I will do everything in my power to make sure you and all three of these little ones are safe and sound." He smiled gently at her, patting her hand. "Tell Doc if you need anything. He can get ahold of me any time of the day or night."

She gave a half-hearted laugh. "How is this all even possible? I had no idea motorcycle clubs were so well connected."

Dr. Redding chuckled. "I'm sure not all of them are, but Salvation's Bane is home to two doctors in our community. With that comes connections. Both men are very respected by their peers, which helps smooth the way." He looked at me. "I can see you've been taking care of your girl. She's in much better shape than she was at our first appointment."

I nodded my acknowledgment. Emmanuell clutched my hand in both of hers now. This was our fourth visit to Dr. Redding in as many weeks. She was still nervous around the man, though she said it was just doctors in general. I got the feeling she was ashamed at how rundown she was when she'd first seen both Doc and Dr. Redding.

"Thank you for taking on my case, Dr. Redding." Emmanuell was always respectful and grateful whenever we were here. "And thanks for not turning me into social services." That got my attention. Dr. Redding just looked shocked.

"My dear, Doc explained your situation. This is in no way your fault. Getting medical care outside of an emergency room without insurance or an ID is difficult nowadays. You had no idea what you were facing at the time. Now you do. And you're doing what I and Mr. Leigh here tell you to. You're eating well. You're resting. You're letting him take care of you. Yes?"

"I just feel so bad I wasn't doing what I should have to keep the babies healthy." She sniffed.

The doc addressed me. "Has she been depressed or is it only when she comes to see me?"

I thought about it. Really tried to remember our interactions over the last three weeks. "She hasn't seemed to be. There's been a lot of baby shit going on, so she's been busy, but when we're alone, she seems content. She smiles and laughs." It was the highlight of my day when she laughed. "Doesn't complain about me smotherin' her with my overprotective instincts." I'd barely let her out of our room unless I was with her. Which was hampering my ability to look into Goldstein, but I honestly hadn't thought about it much other than to email Giovanni Romano and have him pick up where I left off. "Ain't no expert, but she hasn't seemed depressed to me. Just the opposite." I looked at her. "I got the feeling you were happy to be doing something proactive to make sure the babies were healthy. Was I wrong?"

"No! I'm extremely happy I'm doing the right thing. *Now*. I just feel guilty that I wasn't before."

"Honey, you're doing great. I promise." Dr. Redding smiled kindly at her. "You're doing what you have to for these children to make a fine entrance into the world. You're taking the vitamins I prescribed. You're eating regularly from the foods I recommended. You keep your appointments the way you're supposed to. And you've surrounded yourself with good people who are willing to help you and be your support system. That last is the very most important."

He sat on a stool in front of Emmanuell, lacing his fingers together as he rested his forearms on his knees. "I've known Doc for more than twenty years. We were in the Air Force together. Did Para Rescue together. And we went to med school together. I got out after doing my service in the military, but Doc stayed on for a while before leaving to do Emergency Medicine as a civilian. He's one of the best people I know. If he's part of an organization like Salvation's Bane, it's because he believes in it." He grinned. "You may not realize it, but when you stumbled into their compound, you found the best protectors for you and your children you could have possibly run into. Yes, you were in rough shape for a woman carrying triplets when you found them, but you were living in a less than ideal situation." He shrugged. "Now? You're there. With that club. Those men and women. I talk to Doc a few times a week, and he always tells me how well you're adjusting. It had to be scary to put your trust in people you didn't know. But you did. You're doing everything in your power to help yourself and your children." Dr. Redding gave me a knowing glance and a slight grin. "Just keep letting your man help you. I promise you, social services were never even a thought for me. You don't need them. All you need are friends and people who care about you."

I could tell his little speech made Emmanuell feel better, but her shoulders were still slumped. I lifted her hand and kissed the back of it. She gasped and stared at me. So I winked at her. When she smiled, Dr. Redding chuckled.

"I knew Mr. Leigh would be a good influence on you."

"It's Ripper, Doc," I said. "Everyone calls me Ripper."

"All right, then. Ripper." He stood and held out his hand to me. "You're taking really good care of her. Not every man who comes into this office with their woman can say that." He turned back to Emmanuell. "Only a few more weeks to go. I'd like to see you make it to at least thirty-five weeks, but with three babies, thirty-three weeks is usually where we end up stopping. We'll be taking it week by week from here on out. Any change in the way you feel, any discharge that shouldn't be there or bleeding, any pain in your back or abdomen, you tell Doc immediately. He'll either have a look himself or call me. Understood?"

"Yes, sir," she said with a small smile. "I really appreciate all you've done to help me, Dr. Redding. Thank you so much."

"You're very welcome, my dear."

As usual, we stopped to eat after her appointment. She was always so nervous before I could barely coax her to eat anything, but her appetite was always raging afterward. Probably a combination of nerves and hunger. While she was still underweight by Dr. Redding's estimates, she was getting there. She looked a thousand times better than when she'd first come to me.

Of all the places in the whole fucking city, Emmanuell always had a craving for Fazoli's when she'd been stressed or sick. When her appetite returned, she wanted Fazoli's spaghetti and a shit-ton of breadsticks. Even Lucy's homemade spaghetti couldn't satisfy her.

"We don't have to go here," Emmanuell said softly. I was aware she was fragile after the doctor's visit. She always was. No matter how I tried to build her up or how much everyone doted on her, she still felt guilty for the first six months of her pregnancy. Also, I thought the fact she'd lost her father was finally starting to sink in, and she was experiencing survivor's guilt. I hadn't broached that with her, but it was going to have to happen. Lord knew, I had experience with survivor's guilt.

"We do. Got a hankerin' for pasta."

She snorted. "You hate this place."

"Do not. They make a mean lasagna." She was right. I totally hated the place. But she didn't. And I wanted her to have whatever she wanted.

I parked before sliding out of the truck seat. Which was another thing. I'd been off my bike for weeks now. Emmanuell couldn't ride behind me safely, and I didn't want to leave her alone to get my riding fix. Before I could get around to her side, she was already trying to get out on her own.

"Hey, hang on a second!" I trotted to her and helped her slide to the ground. "I told you to wait for me to help you down."

"If you'd drive something other than a monster truck I wouldn't need help," she grumbled. It was a continuing argument. One she only grumbled about right after a doctor's appointment. When she felt so out of sorts. Besides, it wasn't a monster truck. Just an F-150 that was a tiny bit jacked up.

"I'll drive a Bug next time." Standard response.

"Yeah. I'd like to see you fold yourself into stupid Bug." Also standard response.

"Until then, let me help you out. 'K?" I shut and locked the door, then escorted her inside.

As usual, she got a large spaghetti with meat sauce. I got the lasagna and another large spaghetti. Because I knew from experience one wouldn't be enough for her. She glanced at me when I ordered, then ducked her head. Probably embarrassed. I put my arm around her, pulling her to me, and kissed her temple.

She looked up at me, giving me a startled look. I winked at her, and she smiled. I tried not to be overly affectionate with her, but it was clear as water she needed it. Even wanted it. And I sure as hell wanted to give it.

We sat, and she started in. When her first plate was done, I scooted the second one over to her, and she never missed a beat. Once she'd finished the second plate, she sighed and sat back with a sigh. I was still forking pasta into my mouth, taking my time in case she wanted to trespass. We sat side by side, me on the outside of the booth so she could easily help herself.

"You need more?"

"What? No! No. I'm good."

"It's OK, you know. If you want more."

"No. I've had plenty." She smiled up at me gently. "You always make sure I have everything I need. Especially food." She set her fork down and wiped her mouth. "Why are you so good to me, Gideon?"

"Because you're mine, baby. Tryin' my best to be yours as well." Tears sprang to her eyes, and I wanted to kick myself for making her cry. I put one arm around her shoulders and wiped an errant tear with a finger of my other hand. "Don't do that, baby. Tell me how to make it better."

She sniffed, swallowing, obviously trying her best to keep from shedding more than a couple of tears. "How in the world could I have ever said those awful things to you? You've given me more pleasure than I've ever had in my whole life, and I accused you of being a horrible person."

"You know I never held that against you. Not even the second it happened.

"My head was just all messed up. I'm so sorry, Gideon."

"Nothin' to apologize for. I'm just glad you stayed and gave me a chance to prove myself."

She laid her head against my chest, turning her face inward, her body shaking with emotion. "Stupid hormones," she muttered, swiping at her eyes.

I chuckled. "It's all good, baby. Goes with the territory."

She was silent for a moment, picking up another breadstick to munch on while I finished up. "Do you even own a VW Bug?"

I barked out a laugh. "Baby, for you, I'll buy a pink one with a big yellow flower on the side. Just to hear you laugh at me when I try to get behind the wheel."

"You're a wonderful man, Gideon. Thank you for sticking with me."

"I'll always be with you. Long as I live."

* * *

Emmanuell

I was getting clingy with Gideon the longer I was around him. He didn't seem to mind, though. In fact, he was often the one who reached for my hand or laid an arm across my shoulders. He often pulled me in for a hug no matter where we were or who he was talking to at the time.

Once we were back at the clubhouse -- which was a compound, really -- he took me up to my room. Sometimes he stayed with me at night, but he never did more than steal a few kisses. Not since that first time we made love.

"Gideon?" He'd turned to shut the door. When he turned back, he held out his hand to me, pulling me into his embrace.

"Yeah, baby."

"Do you… I mean… Do you still want me?"

He stiffened, pulling back slightly so he could look down at me. "You mean do I still want to fuck you?"

"Well, yeah. You haven't… that is, we haven't --"

"Honey, don't *ever* think I don't want you." His gaze had turned intense. It had been a long time since I'd seen that particular look. Since that first night, he'd been extremely careful, never raising his voice around me. Never showing irritation. Now, he looked like the mere question was insulting to him. "I'm just trying to give you time and be respectful of your condition. The last thing in this world I want to do is make the same mistake I made a month ago." He caressed my cheek before resting his hand on my largely rounded belly. "You're beautiful, Emmanuell. I'll always want you. To pleasure you. But I'm willing to wait as long as it takes till you're ready."

"And if I told you I'm ready now?"

"Hmm…" His gaze never left mine. I could tell he meant everything he was saying. "I might pleasure you, baby, but I'm not fuckin' you until after the babies are born and Dr. Redding gives us the OK."

"He never said we couldn't."

"No, but he didn't say we could. I never asked, and you didn't either."

"But Doc said it was OK."

He shook his head. "He's not the specialist. I absolutely will not risk hurting you or the babies. I lost my leg. Not my hands." His lopsided grin was as sexy as it was comforting.

"I have hands, too," I said, letting one hand slide down his body to close over his cock through his jeans. "And a mouth."

"That you do. Ain't opposed to it. But you still get sick from time to time, and I won't take that chance, either." He leaned down to take my mouth in a deep, but gentle kiss. "This what you want? You want me to make you come?"

"I do." My voice was nearly a whisper. I was nervous. I'd never initiated sex before, and was uncertain how to go about it. "Will you?"

"Honey, I'll give you anything you want if it's within my power. Givin' you pleasure is the easiest because I want to give it to you like I want my next breath."

My heart raced and my breath caught when Gideon scooped me up and carried me to the bed. His strength was so casual and sexy as hell. It made me weak. My arms were around his neck, and I leaned in to kiss him. The second our lips touched my whole body came alive. A little whimper escaped when he swept his tongue inside my mouth, taking me with him on a magical ride.

When he set me on the bed, he pressed me back to lie down. He was half over me, his arms bracketing my body, but he was careful not to let me take any of his weight. He was so careful with me. Like he thought I would break. And, to be honest, he wasn't wrong. Just not in the physical sense.

"You could break me, Gideon," I whispered. "If this doesn't work out between us… I'm so far gone it would break my heart."

"Shh," he said, kissing me gently. "You've got me, baby. I ain't goin' nowhere."

"We've known each other a month and a half. How can you know that?"

He grinned, sliding his hand over my belly in a gentle caress. "I'm forty-two years old, Emmanuell. I've been through hell and back and never in all my life have I even thought about wanting a woman of my own." He shrugged. "If I needed to fuck, I found someone to take the edge off, or took care of it myself. At one time or other, I've fucked several of the club girls here. That's what they're here for. But never in my life have I ever wanted a woman for my own. Emmanuell, I want *you*."

"Never?"

He shook his head. "Never. My childhood was

shit. To say my parents weren't exactly role models is an understatement. When my old man wasn't fuckin' everything in sight, he was beatin' the shit outta my mom and me. And Mom? She was strung out or drunk most of the time. She stayed with my father because he had money to fuel her habits. They had me to have an heir. Beyond that, I was nothing more than an afterthought. I'd always thought that, if this was what a family was, I didn't need it."

"I'm so sorry, Gideon!" I threw my arms around him once again, and he just held me to him. "All those things I said… You know what it's like! You know! And I accused you of --"

"Hush, baby," he said, pulling back to kiss me again. "You thought you meant what you were saying, and on some level maybe you did. But the real reason you lashed out was to protect yourself from a man you didn't truly know. Now, we've had some time together. You've gotten to see how I live and how my club works as a family. Now you're letting me know you're just as gone on me as I am on you." He grinned. "And I'm good with that. Means I'm not as big a pussy as my brothers keep tellin' me I am."

"What? Oh, no!"

Gideon's deep chuckle made my insides melt. How could one man be so Goddamned sexy? Everything he did was an aphrodisiac to me. And it wasn't just physical. He was protective, caring, sweet, gentle. Everything I'd ever wanted but hadn't even admitted to myself because I was supposed to be strong. To survive on my own. Well, I'd done it for six months. And hated every second of it. I never wanted to be alone again.

"Honey, it's not a bad thing. They all knew how much you meant to me. They were just teasing me because I was pretty much gone the moment I saw you. Dazz, the prick, makes it sound like I was worshiping at your feet the second I got off my bike at the gate that night. Embellished something awful. It's great entertainment for the guys, and I can't say a fuckin' thing because it'd be a Goddamned lie. I fell hard. And I'll never regret it."

Leaning over me, Gideon eased my shirt over my distended belly and placed gentle kisses all over it. My hand went to his hair, tunneling there to ground myself. "I'm gonna help you get these girls into the world, and I'm gonna help you take care of 'em. I'll love them as much as I love you, Emmanuell. If you let me, I'll be a good father to them. May not have had the best role model for that, but I'm smart enough to figure it out."

"Oh, Gideon!" Tears flooded my eyes, streaking down my temples. "I don't know of another man alive who'd want to take this on. Three babies? Are you kidding me? And they're not even yours."

"That's where you're wrong. They are mine. The second doc told us what he found and let us see them on that ultrasound, they were mine. No way I'm letting you do this on your own. Even if you don't want me, I'll still be here. For you. For the girls." He shrugged, giving me a sheepish grin. "I'm done for."

I clung to him, crying, unable to stop. It was like a weight had been lifted from me. Worries I hadn't acknowledged disappeared like a feather in a hurricane. Then Gideon kissed me again. This time, it was hungry, stoking the fire inside me he'd been building for weeks.

I tugged my shirt off, needing him to have access to my skin. I was highly aware of how my body had changed over the course of my pregnancy. With three babies inside me, I looked far more advanced than I actually was. This was the first time Gideon would actually see me completely naked.

His nostrils flared as he took in everything from my belly upward. I still had on my bra and light maternity pants. There wasn't a whole lot left about me that was sexy.

"Fuck. Me." He scrubbed a hand over his mouth. "Take off your bra."

I reached behind me to unhook the wicked thing. My breasts had grown, especially these last couple of weeks. My nipples were a dark brown instead of the usual dusky pink. The second I had the clasp undone, Gideon reached for it, pulling it away from my chest and down my arms to toss to the floor.

"You're fuckin' beautiful, Emmanuell," he said, his voice a husky growl. His hands went to my belly, and he leaned in once more to kiss it before sliding my pants from my hips and down my legs. My underwear followed. Then his hand went to my pussy, cupping me there. "There's nothin' more I want than another taste of you. I want to possess you. Make you mine. Keep you in a little bubble so you're always safe."

"Gideon?"

His breathing was deep and fast, like he'd just come in from a run and was catching his breath. "Before I make good on my promise, I've gotta check with Doc first, honey. Last thing in this world I want to do is take a chance with you or the girls."

"But… it's not like we're going to have sex. Right?"

"Yeah, but I didn't get the OK this time, and we're not dealing with a normal pregnancy." To my shock, he shook his head, growling even as he spoke. Then he cupped one of my breasts before leaning in to catch the other nipple with his mouth.

I cried out, arching my back as he pulled gently while his thumb brushed my other nipple. I knew he wasn't going to make me come even as I wanted it with every fiber of my being. To be denied when I was so close seemed like a cruel joke. But the look in his eyes when he'd seen my naked body told me he was in just as much pain as I was.

"Fuck," he bit out, letting go of my nipple with a little *pop*. "Fuck!" He lay beside me, urging me to my side as he wrapped his arm around me while sending off a text with the other hand. "I've gotta get Doc's advice on this. I can't see how it could hurt, but I absolutely will not take a chance with you." He swore again. "Shoulda checked with him sooner. Hell, shoulda just asked Dr. Redding this afternoon."

"I'd have been mortified," I said, trying to catch my own breath.

He turned my head to him and gently took my lips, lapping at my tongue. "You might have been at first. But you'd have gotten over it. I'm not above callin' him myself if Doc can't give me an answer soon. Goddamn, Emmanuell! I want you so fuckin' bad!" He squeezed me tighter. It should have been uncomfortable, but it wasn't. It just felt like he'd wrapped me up in a blanket of protection. His big body trembled around me. I could feel his cock rock hard against my ass, and I wanted to reach back and stroke him, but my arms were pinned against my body. Instead, I wiggled my ass, which made him groan.

"You're killin' me, honey."

"Maybe if I can't do anything, I could get you off."

"Believe me, I would love to see your body

coated in my cum, but if you don't get to, I don't either."

I gasped, turned on so hard and so suddenly I felt my pussy readying for him in a rush. "Gideon! You can't say things like that!"

His chuckle sounded every bit as strained as I felt. "Why not? You don't want to watch as I jack my cock? Don't want me to cover you in my hot, sticky cum? Mark you like that?"

"I didn't say that! But..." I swallowed, my breathing shallow and rapid. "You made me wet."

"Oh?" He moved his hand slowly and gently down my body until he found my pussy with his fingers. One stroke over the top, and he pulled his fingers back with a groan. "Fuck, baby! You're all kinds of wet." Immediately, he stuck his fingers into his mouth, sucking them clean. "So fuckin' good!"

His phone buzzed, and he took it out of his pocket and read the text. His brows drew together as he read it, swearing before turning the phone to let me read it. Yeah. No orgasms until after the babies were born.

"Well, *that* sucks," I said, so disappointed I thought I might cry. "Surely one little orgasm wouldn't hurt."

"Like I'd give you a little orgasm," he scoffed.

That got a giggle out of me, easing some of the sexual tension. Just not much. "I'm not sure I'll survive this," I said with a sigh. "And the really funny thing is, I never really cared before. The first time I've actually had any kind of sexual pleasure since all this started was that first night when we had sex. Then I ruined it."

"You did no such thing. And this is the last time I want to hear about it." He gave me another hard kiss. "If anyone was to blame, it was me. I ain't sorry I fucked you, though. Just sorry I couldn't make you understand everything I was feeling *before* I fucked you." He stood and scooped me up. "Let's get a shower. We can't fool around much, but I can bare myself to you like you have to me."

Well, that wasn't cryptic or anything.

Chapter Eight
Ripper

Just the thought of what I was about to do made me cringe. But I could tell Emmanuell needed this. She hadn't said anything, but what young woman wouldn't be horrified at how her body changed with such an extreme pregnancy? I thought she looked beautiful, sexy as fuck where those babies were growing. But I also was smart enough to know she'd never see herself that way. So it was time to give her part of myself I never showed the world.

"Can you start the shower while I undress, baby?"

"Of course," she said, eyeing me curiously.

By the time she'd gotten the water started, I had my pants down my legs and was ready to remove my prosthesis. I purposefully waited until she was watching before I started sliding the sleeve that went up my thigh, almost to my groin, down my leg until it was inside out and hanging over my ankle. I slid my leg out of the prosthesis and set the artificial leg aside. Then there were two stretchy, cloth sleeves over my leg I had to remove. One of them was just a liner for extra cushion, the other had the umbrella and pin that fit against my stump to hold the prosthesis in place. I tossed both aside.

"Will you hand me my crutches?" I nodded to the corner of the room where they leaned against the wall. Normally, I had them within easy reach, but I wanted to involve her in this. For her to see and realize I was just as vulnerable as she was.

"Of course," she said again softly, doing as I asked. While she did, I finished taking off my jeans and underwear, as well as my shirt. Sure, I was minus a leg below the knee, but my body was still ripped and fit with bulky muscles. Even my thighs were filled out, despite the amputation. I wanted her to see my strength, but I also wanted her to see my weaknesses.

"Thank you," I said with a grin when she handed them to me. I stood, towering over her smaller frame. She looked up at me in wonder, like I was fucking Superman or some shit. I'd be lying if I didn't admit to my chest puffing out just a little. Might have flexed my chest and abs just a little too.

"Wow," she said in a whisper. "You're really built."

"You saw me before," I said with a smirk. "You already knew that."

"Well, yeah," she said, reaching out to lay a tentative hand on my chest, exploring what she found there. "But I haven't seen you like this." She looked up at me. "You're magnificent."

"You sure know how to stroke a guy's ego." I chuckled, urging her into the shower. "Get in. I need help washin' myself."

She gave me a skeptical look. "I doubt that." Then she grinned. "But if it means I get to grope you all over, count me in."

And grope me she did. Lord help me, I loved every blistering second of it. I was hard as fuck but never wanted her to stop.

I moved to the bench in the shower, maneuvering with the bars to balance myself, then just let her take over. She soaped every inch of my skin with her hands. Her touch lingered on my chest and arms. When I stood, she knelt before me and kissed my abdomen, tracing the ridges with her tongue. Before I could stop her, she engulfed the head of my cock in her mouth where it stood out hard and proud between my legs where she knelt.

"Fuck, Emmanuell! Fuck!" Before I could stop myself, my hand had fisted in her hair, holding her still even as my hips thrust subtly. I couldn't stay still, needing to fuck her mouth until I came down her sweet throat.

"Mmm…" She hummed around me, taking me deeper before pulling back. I could see her gag slightly. That was the only thing that gave me strength enough to stop her from taking me over the edge into oblivion.

"Get up here," I said, trying to shake off my need to continue this. To pleasure her like she was doing to me. When she stood, I pulled her into my arms. Her belly protruded enough she couldn't get close enough to take my cock into her pussy. Which was a good thing, because she was trying, going so far as to reach behind her to find my cock. "Uh-uh, baby. None of that."

"But --"

"Doc said it could be dangerous for the babies. You saw the text. I have no idea what placental abruption is, but it can't be good."

She sighed. "Yeah. I remember Dr. Redding mentioned something about it at my first visit. I looked it up, and it's not uncommon in multiple births. I just wasn't concerned about it being associated with sex at the time." She met my gaze with a heated one of her own. "Doesn't mean I can't make you come."

"I already told you, baby. We're in this together. If you can't get relief, neither can I."

"I don't know of a single man in the world who would take that position."

"Now you do." I grinned. "Now. Rinse me off and we'll go downstairs. I need to check on a couple things in my office, and you can come with me. If you want to, that is."

"Sounds like a plan."

* * *

Giovanni hadn't turned up much more than I had on Randall Goldstein. Emmanuell's father had paid him well to be at his beck and call over the years. Not only had Goldstein been Franklin Stanton's personal attorney, but Stanton appeared to be his only client. That was a big flag, but it still didn't prove anything. It also didn't mean that Stanton hadn't left a huge chunk of money to Goldstein in the event of his death. In fact, that would seem to be the likely scenario.

Beaner still hadn't said much, but Thorn had grown tired of waiting on me and Giovanni to turn up information that wasn't there. He'd started the interrogation the day before. From what Beast told me, it was only a matter of time before Beaner cracked. All it would take was enough pain for the man to grow tired of living. He wasn't getting out of this no matter what, because there was no way it was a coincidence he'd carted Emmanuell off across the country. He might not have actually harmed her, but he'd left her pregnant and defenseless. That alone was enough to seal his fate. If it could be proven, or he actually admitted to being in cahoots with Goldstein to remove Stanton's only heir, it was just more nails in his coffin.

"Everything OK?" Emmanuell was curled up on the couch next to my desk, resting. She'd napped about an hour while I puzzled through some of the data I'd gathered.

"There's nothing wrong, if that's what you mean," I said with a sigh, stretching slightly as I looked up from the monitors surrounding me. "Just nothing new."

"I take it you'd hoped for more?"

"Yeah, baby. I know Goldstein's involved with your dad's death, I just can't find anything to prove it. Or even give credible circumstantial evidence."

"Maybe he wasn't involved. Maybe it was all just a big, unhappy accident."

"Maybe. It still bothers me. The timing of LimeLight Division and the fact that you never knew anything about it when it was set up with you as co-founder doesn't sit right."

"It's not something Dad would have done."

"You sound pretty sure about that."

She nodded. "I am. Dad never mixed family and business. I knew he loved me, but it was never implied I'd own the company or anything else at any point. It would surprise me if he left anything to me other than what was already in my bank account. Even the house was supposed to be auctioned off to charity. Anything personal I wanted to keep that might have any value, I had to run by him first."

"And you were OK with this?"

"Absolutely." She nodded emphatically. "Well, at least once I got older. My parents came from a very modest background. I grew up listening to them talk about how some people around them felt entitled to have the best things in life, but they'd never had to work for them. More than one of my father's friends had children who'd gotten in trouble at school or with the law, and money had paved the way for it all to go away. He made it very clear that he and my mother would never go easy on me that way. He told me once that he felt guilty for not giving me everything I wanted, but he was only doing it with my well-being in mind. I needed to know from the start that I had to know how to take care of myself because no one else was going to do it for me."

"Not many young women would be so accepting." Again, it struck me how different she was from anyone I'd ever met. She was guileless and sweet. She'd taken a hit with that innocent trust when Beaner had betrayed her, but I was determined to mend it. And, so help me God, her father's lawyer was not going to factor into her healing.

She smiled at me, that sweet, beautiful smile that turned me into mush. "It was just the way I was raised. I actually saw how some of my friends acted at school, how they bemoaned not getting one expensive thing or another when their parents could have easily given it to them, and it irritated me. It wasn't an attractive look, and I never wanted to be like that."

"Well, you're beautiful, baby. Inside and out. Never let anyone tell you differently. If they do, come get me. I'll make 'em see differently." I winked at her and she giggled.

I stood, moving to the couch. "You ready for supper? I think the club's havin' a cookout. Hamburgers and hotdogs."

"That sounds wonderful. Is there anything I can do to help the club prepare?"

"Not one damned thing. You need to rest and to be off your feet." I scooped her up in my arms, burying my face in her neck and kissing her. She laughed, squirming as my beard tickled her.

The rest of the day was wonderful. I hung out with my brothers, taking their ribbing good-naturedly every time I scolded Emmanuell about trying to get up on her own. Halfway through the evening, I noticed her whispering to the girls around her before she got up and suspected she was doing it on purpose. Still couldn't help myself. I'd call to her to sit her ass down, and the whole table would erupt into giggles and laughter. Followed closely by my brothers' accusations I'd lost my man card. I was on cloud nine. My woman and my club. Soon I'd add my daughters to the list of things in my life. By the time we were ready for bed, Emmanuell's eyes were drooping in exhaustion.

"Did we overdo it a little today?" I asked her gently as I helped her into bed and brushed a stray curl from her lovely face.

She smiled, her eyes already closing. "Maybe a little. But I had a great time. Thanks for everything you've done for me, Gideon. I don't know how I'd get through this without you."

"I'll always be here, baby."

She was asleep before I pulled the covers over her and kissed her forehead gently.

* * *

I woke when Emmanuell gave a sharp cry next to me. I had my arms wrapped around her, holding her to me tightly and immediately loosened my grip on her.

"What's wrong, honey? You OK?"

"I -- I don't know."

"Nightmare?"

"No." She switched on the light and threw back the covers. The sight threw me into a panic. There was blood everywhere. "Gideon?" She looked up at me, her eyes wide in terror. Then a pain must have hit her, because she clutched her stomach and gave another sharp cry, her face scrunching up in pain.

"Don't move!" I snagged my phone even as I started getting my prosthesis on as fast as I could. Doc answered on the second ring.

"Yeah."

"Emmanuell's bleeding and in pain," I said without preamble.

"How much blood?"

"A lot."

There was a slight pause before Doc gave me instructions. "Get her to my clinic. Don't take time to clean up, just pick her up and go."

The seven minutes it took me to get my fucking leg on and get her to Doc were the longest seven minutes of my life. Emmanuell tried to be brave, but she trembled in my arms and whimpered occasionally.

Doc was waiting on me when I hurried through the door. I set her down on the stretcher. Doc didn't explain anything, just hooked her up to a blood pressure monitor, then whipped off the sheet I'd draped over her and cut off her panties. Normally, I'd have beat the motherfucker to a bloody pulp, especially when Emmanuell gave a startled cry and tried to close her legs.

"Shh, baby," I said, taking her hand and gently prying her legs open to assist Doc. "He's got to check you."

"Definitely coming from the vaginal area," Doc said softly.

"Well, duh," I snapped.

Doc didn't rise to the bait, just gently urged Emmanuell to close her legs while he changed gloves and got the ultrasound machine. "There's more than one hole down there, Ripper. Always best to make sure where the problem is. Vaginal area doesn't mean it's coming from her vagina, though. Could still be from her urethra." He sounded more like he was talking to himself than to me, and that he didn't think for one second it was coming from her urethra. "Have you had any pain when you urinate, Emmanuell?"

"Uh, no," she said in a shaky voice. "None."

"OK." He fiddled with something on the

machine and squirted gel on her belly. Then he put the probe on her and moved it around until he found the angle he wanted. He frowned, snapping buttons and switching angles. His frown didn't go away. Doc took out his phone, snapping a few pictures from the ultrasound screen, then made a call.

"Yeah. Did you get them?" Pause. "Heavily. Some of it is external, but I'm seeing internal bleeding behind the placenta. I'm calling it a grade three abruption. Blood pressure is ninety over fifty, and her heart rate is elevated, but she's also been asleep." Another pause, this one longer. Then Doc nodded crisply once. "Agreed. We'll meet you there in twenty."

"What's happening?" Emmanuell was pale, her eyes wide. She winced and clutched her belly but didn't cry out.

"You're getting ready to have these babies," Doc said. He didn't smile or look at Emmanuell other than to pull the sheet back over her and pull up the side rails on the stretcher. He kicked the brake loose and started rolling her out of the clinic.

"Where're we going?" She looked back at me, frantically reaching for my hand. I took it and squeezed briefly before helping Doc guide the stretcher out of the building and to Doc's big Excursion.

"We're getting you to the hospital," Doc said. "It's not the best option to deliver them here as they're not full-term. Besides, three babies are more than I can safely manage, especially in an emergency."

The second we rolled up beside the vehicle, Doc dropped the side rail and motioned for me to take it from there. He ran around to the driver's side and started it up while I got into the back seat with Emmanuell in my lap. He'd used the stretcher to get her to the truck as quickly as possible, so we didn't waste even a second instead of me trying to carry her at a run.

It took us seventeen minutes exactly to reach the JFK North in West Palm Beach. During that time, Doc said nothing, and I didn't ask. Emmanuell sat quietly in my lap, clinging to me until just before we reached the hospital.

"Are the babies going to be OK?" Her voice was tremulous and so soft I almost didn't hear it. "I don't understand what's happening."

"The placenta has detached from the uterine wall. With as much as you're bleeding, we have to get these babies born."

"But will they be OK?" Her voice broke, and I held her tightly, trying my best to comfort her while also doing my best not to fucking fall apart.

"I won't lie to you, honey. This is a dangerous situation. But I truly believe everything's going to be fine. Just hang in there with us." Doc sounded confident, but I could hear the stress in his voice.

Dr. Redding approached us even before Doc stopped the truck. I shoved the door open and stepped out with a whimpering Emmanuell in my arms.

The next thing I knew, Doc yanked Emmanuell from me and put her on a stretcher, and everyone hurried inside. I tried to follow, but I hadn't gotten far when Doc grabbed my arm and took me deeper into the hospital to what looked like a break room inside the surgical area.

"We can wait here until Jeremiah comes for us," he said, referring to Dr. Redding. "He'll get things under control and take care of your girls, Ripper."

"What's happening?"

"She has a placental abruption. It happens with

multiple births sometimes."

"We nearly had sex yesterday," I muttered, scrubbing a hand over my face. "Did I cause this?"

"Don't know. Did you put stress on her abdomen? Did she orgasm?"

"No. I stopped because I hadn't thought to ask the doc if it was OK. We haven't had sex since she first got here."

"Did she orgasm?"

"No. I wanted to make her come, but thought better of it."

"Then I doubt anything you guys did last night caused this. Orgasms in women are muscle contractions. Sometimes, those contractions in the uterus can be enough to cause an abruption, but it rarely happens. In her case, with three babies, she was at high risk anyway. It was probably going to happen no matter what."

"Fuck," I swore as I sat down abruptly in a nearby chair. "If something happens to those girls, I'll never forgive myself. Will Emmanuell be OK?"

"I think so. We got her here fast, and Jeremiah was ready just as quickly as we were. She should be fine. Unless there's something I couldn't see on the ultrasound, the babies should be fine, too." He tried to smile reassuringly. "It'll be a while. Close to an hour."

"How the fuck am I supposed to make it for a fuckin' hour? And why the fuck can't I be in there with her?" My temper was spiking. This was in no way Doc's fault, but he was going to catch the brunt of it.

"Because this is an emergency, Ripper. Can you honestly sit there and tell me you'd be able to stand there with her and not lose your shit? Besides, they'll put her under general anesthesia. No time for an epidural or any kind of spinal block." Doc stood and paced, himself, his nervousness showing as much as mine. "Try to calm down a little."

"I am calm! Who said I wasn't fuckin' calm?"

Doc just raised an eyebrow at me.

It was an hour and a half before Dr. Redding found us. He had a smile on his face, and I stood abruptly.

"Everyone's good. Emmanuell is waking up nicely, and the babies all appear to be healthy. We've got them in isolettes in the NICU for now. They'll have to stay a few days, but I think everything is going to be fine."

"Good," I said, nodding. "That's good." My ears roared more and more with every beat of my heart. "They're fine. They're gonna be fine." My vision tunneled, and everything sounded like it was echoing around me. Then everything went black.

Chapter Nine
Emmanuell

Ripper gave me a grouchy look over his shoulder as he finished changing one of our daughters. They were identical, so we'd taken to dressing them in different colors to keep them straight. Gabrielle was dressed in green, Ava in yellow, and Sophia in purple. I was already finding other ways to tell them apart, but it was hit and miss at best. Gideon did better but pretended not to. I think he pretended to get them mixed up to make me laugh. I was sure as the girls got older he'd do the same thing.

"Three girls," he muttered. "*Three* girls."

It had been two months since they'd been born. Two months since I woke up with blood everywhere. Two months since Gideon had passed out at Dr. Redding's feet after he'd told Gideon we were all OK. Doc had quickly snapped a pic with his phone and sent it to everyone in the club, including me. I hadn't seen it until later, but I'd seen it. He was still getting ribbed about it. Of course, Doc had told everyone it was at the sight of blood and not from relief.

"Could'a been four, Ripper," I said, using his road name. I didn't use it much, but since Doc had sent that pic to everyone, I used it to remind him he wasn't as tough as he wanted me to believe. "Could'a been four."

"No," he snapped. "It couldn't'a been four because I'd never survive four. Gonna be touch and go as it is." He lifted Ava into his arms and brought her to me where I sat on the couch. Then he returned with Gabrielle and Sophia in each arm and sat beside me.

I was recovering nicely. There was no pain, and I'd been given the all clear by Dr. Redding to resume all activities. Including sex. I was looking forward to that part, though with three babies, it was hard to find a time when I wasn't dead on my feet. I'd never have been able to do this without Gideon and his friends.

Ava and Sophia cooed while Gabrielle slept peacefully. They'd been fed and changed. Now it was time for a nap.

"Girls are gonna be the death of me," Gideon muttered, trying to look put out, but I saw the adoration in his eyes. He loved those girls like they were his own. Hell, as far as I was concerned, they *were* his. He'd been in my life far longer than Devan had, and he was actually taking the role of father very seriously.

"For a man who never thought about having a family, you're taking to this daddy business like a duck to water." He just scowled and grumbled. Until Sophia squealed and kicked in delight. Gideon turned his attention back to her and made baby noises back at her. One thing I'd never get tired of seeing was the big, gruff, scarred biker doing baby talk to his daughters.

"Is Daddy's girl happy? She sure is. Yes, she is." I giggled right along with Sophia's cooing, and he turned his head to scowl at me. Which just made me giggle more.

"Got a sitter for tonight, woman. Then you're gonna pay for all the making fun of me you've done over the last two months and three days."

"Sitter?"

"Yep. Vicious and Lucy are coming over with Thorn and Marianna."

"Has Marianna healed from her surgery, then?"

"Honey, it's been three months since she broke her ankle. Thorn still scowls at her when she wants to go out, and she's been dying to spend some quality time with the babies. She hates that she wasn't able to help more when you were pregnant. Now that she's better, she's going to use her position as president's ol' lady to bully you into letting her cuddle the babies."

I laughed. All the women had been wonderful. Their children who were old enough had all taken a turn holding the babies. It truly was like a big happy family. I loved every single one of them.

"She's more than welcome to come visit any time she wants. She and the other women here are so wonderful."

"They think a lot of you, baby."

"I think a lot of them. Thank you for letting me stay here. For bringing me into this family. I don't know what I'd do if all of this wasn't in my life. And you? Gideon, you're so important to me." I ducked my head, needing to tell him yet afraid he didn't feel the same way. Why I was so insecure I had no idea. He'd shown me how much he cared for me every single day I'd been here. But did he love me?

As if he could read my mind, his gaze softened, and he leaned in to kiss me. "I love you, Emmanuell. Been waitin' for the right time to tell you. Thought it would be when the babies were born, but that kinda didn't turn out like I'd planned."

"Babies are like that sometimes." I smiled. "I love you, too."

"Let's put the girls down for their nap. I'll call Thorn and see if they can come a little early. We'll go out on the bike and maybe spend the night in Miami. Would you like that?"

"That'd be wonderful!"

"Good. Let's get them down."

We carried the girls to the bedroom the club had helped get together for them. It had three of everything, all of it color-coordinated as to which item was which child's. Sophia grinned up at her papa before her eyes drifted shut and she was out like her sisters.

Gideon pulled out his phone and was texting when it buzzed. He frowned.

"What is it?"

"Thorn wants to meet with us."

"I don't understand. Aren't they coming here already?"

"Yeah, baby. This is about Goldstein. He wants us in his office." There was a knock at the door. Gideon opened it to find Lucy, Marianna, and Kitty at the door smiling brightly.

"Where are the girls?" Kitty asked excitedly, looking around. "I need snuggles."

"They're asleep," I said with a grin. "I expect you'll be picking them up and holding them now."

"Absolutely!" Kitty and Lucy hurried into the girls' room. Marianna hugged me.

"Thorn said he's in his office. He said not to worry, everything is under control. He also said none of the women were allowed to have any more girls. Said if daughters took away Ripper's man card, they'd take away every man card in the place."

"I caught him talking baby talk to them again," I said.

"I love it when that happens," Marianna said. "Record it next time. We'll have a blast."

"You know I'm right here." Gideon had his arms crossed over his chest, a fierce scowl on his face.

"Yup. Hard to miss that," I said and flounced out the door.

He scooped me up and over his shoulder, swatting my ass as he grumbled down the hall. I squealed and laughed as he made his way down the steps and into Thorn's office. The other man grinned at me before sighing at Gideon.

"I thought I told you to look for your man card. It couldn't have gotten far."

"What's a man card against three daughters? I was screwed from the outset and took it on willingly. Get used to it, prez."

Thorn chuckled. "Well, let her sit down. We have some shit to discuss, and I don't want to do it staring at her ass."

"Watch it," Gideon growled as he let me slide to the floor. Took me a second to get my bearings after being hung upside down, but I managed.

"Not my fault, man," Thorn said, raising his hands in surrender, a cocky grin on his face. "You're the one who put her on display."

We sat and Gideon put his arm around me, kissing my cheek as he did. "What's up?"

"Goldstein wants a meet with Emmanuell."

I sucked in a breath. "What? How did he find me?"

"We finally got Beaner to crack. In exchange for..." Thorn glanced at Gideon before continuing. "In exchange for us stopping his interrogation, he agreed to contact Goldstein and tell him you were here with us. He must know we suspect he had a part in your father's death, so we're not going to grant his request to meet with you alone. The only way he gets to talk to you is here. In our house."

"Is that wise? I mean, I don't want to put anyone here in danger if he thinks he can get rid of me. What if he tells the police you kidnapped me or that it was all of us trying to get my father's money? This could go all kinds of wrong."

"It won't." Thorn said. "No matter what he does, we can control the narrative here."

"What if he brings law enforcement?" I didn't want to meet with my dad's lawyer, but more importantly, I didn't want anyone else to get hurt because of my mess.

"We suspect he will." Thorn shrugged. "Got that covered, too. Trust me, Emmanuell. Everything will be fine, and Goldstein will pay for your father's death."

"You're sure he had a part in it? That it wasn't an accident?"

"It's all circumstantial, but given everything we finally got out of Beaner and the money trail… yeah. He staged it."

I winced, unable to hide my reaction. It was just one more betrayal in a line of them. For me. For my dad. "Why are people so hell-bent on taking things that don't belong to them?" The question was more rhetorical than anything else.

"Good Goddamned question, baby," Gideon said, tightening his arm around my shoulder briefly in a hug. "Good Goddamned question."

As if on cue, Thorn's phone buzzed. The president glanced at Gideon before reading the text. "He's on the way. Says he expects to talk to you and for you to be unharmed." Thorn sneered the last. "As if we'd ever hurt an innocent woman." He muttered the response with a scowl on his face like the very idea was not only distasteful but insulting as well.

"Don't say anything about the girls," Gideon said, looking down at me. There was a sudden, fierce light in his eyes. Like he'd just had a thought that had him wanting to kill someone, but he was trying to rein it in. "Not a word."

I nodded. "I understand. I'm glad you thought of

that. There's no way he knows unless Devan told him?"

"No," Thorn said immediately. "I monitored that phone call myself. He has no knowledge of your girls, and Beaner doesn't know they've been born. We can keep it that way." Thorn pushed back from his desk and stood. "He'll be here in fifteen minutes. We've cleared out the common room for the meet." He grinned. "Expect the unexpected."

"Great," I muttered.

The common room was eerily silent. There were fifteen or twenty men in various places throughout the room. No one made a sound. Thorn, Beast, Havoc, and Justice stood in the center of the room, talking quietly. Gideon led me to a leather couch near where the men stood and urged me to sit before squatting in front of me.

"I need to talk with my brothers," he said softly, rubbing his hands soothingly up and down my thighs. "I'll be right there. I'm not going anywhere. When Goldstein gets here, I'll be right back by your side." Then he reached for me, cupping my face between his hands. "We're in this together."

I was so scared, I couldn't speak. I just nodded. I tried to be brave, but the truth was I just wanted Gideon to take me back to our girls and for all of us to cuddle together under a blanket in the bed where we were safe. There was no telling what Mr. Goldstein would do or say, but I was under no illusion he would be thankful I was back. Even if he was completely innocent in my father's death, he wouldn't be happy about control of LimeLight Division going to me.

It took longer than the fifteen minutes Thorn had expected. An hour and a half later, two cars were spotted coming up the road to the compound. The prospects held them at that gate while Thorn sat in stony silence.

"I hate rude behavior," he muttered.

It was another hour before he agreed to let the Goldstein party in, and only once he'd received a text message from someone. Thorn nodded to Gideon, then to me. Gideon moved to my side and sat on the couch with me, his left arm draped around my shoulders. His right hand rested on the gun he'd placed on the cushion next to him. He was between me and the door, his larger frame likely blocking me from view. I couldn't help but duck into him, resting my head on his chest.

Gideon kissed the top of my head. "I gotcha, sweetheart. It's all gonna be fine."

"I know," I whispered. "I trust you."

Not long after that, Mr. Goldstein entered the room with three other men. All of them were dressed impeccably and looked very full of themselves. Well, all but one. One of them was all business and looked as dangerous as any man in the Bane clubhouse.

"Good evening," Mr. Goldstein said, greeting Thorn. He walked up to the other man and extended his hand in greeting. Thorn didn't take it.

"It was," Thorn said in return. "State your business."

It was hard to reconcile the Thorn I'd grown used to in the months I'd been here with the man confronting my father's lawyer now. That man was crazy scary. But then, so were the other Salvation's Bane members. Up to this point, all I'd seen were the family men here, taking care of their women and children. The side I was seeing now was the side that protected everything they held dear with ruthless abandon.

Mr. Goldstein grinned, silent for a moment before responding. When he did, he tried to goad Thorn. "No need to be rude, Mr…"

"Thorn," he said.

"Surely you have a last name." When Thorn just stared at him, Mr. Goldstein cleared his throat and continued. "Well, it's come to my attention that my late client's daughter is residing here, likely under duress."

"No one in this place is here under duress," Thorn said.

"Why else would she be here? She's the heiress to a fortune. Why would she want to live in a place like this?" Again, Thorn said nothing, just stared the man down. It was obvious Goldstein hadn't seen me yet, and I was eager to keep it that way. "Well? Where is she?"

Thorn glanced back at Gideon. He leaned down to whisper to me. "Come on, baby. I've got you. I'm right here." He urged me to stand and took up a place by my side and slightly in front of me.

"Ah! There she is. Emmanuell, come to me, and we'll leave this place."

"I'm not leaving, Mr. Goldstein."

"Of course, you are. You're coming home with me, and we'll sort out your father's will together."

"There's nothing to sort out," I said softly. "I know exactly what Daddy wanted to do with his money."

"Things have changed, my dear. Before he died, your father was putting together a charity he wanted to put everything into. He named me as managing partner of that company. I'll take care of everything for you, Emmanuell. I just need you to withdraw your court motion to freeze the company's assets."

"I'm afraid I can't do that," I said, taking comfort

in Gideon's hand at the small of my back.

"Of course, you can. Once you get out of this place, away from these people who are manipulating you, you'll see how important it is."

"No one here is manipulating me, Mr. Goldstein."

"You're lying to yourself if you don't think they're just after your money." He looked at me with pity in his gaze. "Just like the other man you took up with the night your father died. Wasn't he part of this club?"

There was a time not too long ago when I'd told myself the same thing. Now, I could see the truth of things. I looked back at Gideon and saw the man I loved with all my heart. The man who'd helped me get my babies safely into the world. Looking around the room, I saw his brothers. who'd given me a safe place to live. Who'd worked to find out what had happened to my father and what part one of their own had played. These were good men and women, and my life was so much better for being here with them.

"He was. I'm still not coming with you." I put my chin up stubbornly. "You're not my friend, Mr. Goldstein, and I sincerely doubt you were ever my father's friend."

"I was your father's best friend. His confidant. He wanted everything to go to LimeLight Division. Just like your mother envisioned."

"LimeLight was my mother's project, but she wasn't able to get it going like she wanted before she died."

"I know. Your father and I worked to make it just like she wanted it. I had just filed the paperwork and was finishing the details when he was killed." He spread his hands out in an innocent gesture. "I just want to see this to the end. To see your mother's legacy brought to life."

"Then leave it like it is," I said. "I'll finish it."

He shook his head. "That's not what your dad wanted, Emmanuell. He and I talked about this at length. He knew you weren't ready to manage something this size."

"Then why was my name on it?"

He paused for a moment, obviously unaware I knew anything about what he'd done. "I don't know what you're talking about, sweetheart. Your father wanted me to manage LimeLight Division. Your name was never mentioned. All his estate was to be liquidated into that charity."

"No, it wasn't," I said. "And the paperwork you filed on LimeLight named me and my father as owners. Why would you do that? My father never talked to me about business." I thought a moment, really looking at Goldstein. "You did it so when I never came forward to take control of the company, you could take control with no questions asked. Only, Devan didn't do what he was supposed to do and kill me. He took me out of state, took any means I had of coming forward with a positive identity, then made it look like I was anywhere but New York. I was supposed to die…" My voice caught. "So you could cash in on my father. Did he not pay you enough? Why? Why would you do this?"

Goldstein glanced around at his associates. One of them stepped forward and whispered something into his ear. Goldstein smirked. "Come with me, my dear. I know you're struggling right now, but once we settle this business with LimeLight, you'll get your half of your father's estate. The second I learned you'd been found, I set you up with an apartment and a new vehicle so you could take some time to get back on your feet. Once you've had time to process everything that's happened, you'll also see that none of this is what you believe. These people --" He indicated the men of Salvation's Bane. "-- They've deceived you. I've known you all your life. You know I'd never harm your father. He was a good friend to me."

"I wasn't supposed to get anything. Everything my father had was to be split between several charities in the community. That's what's going to happen. I'll fight you in court every step of the way." I took a step forward toward Goldstein. "And when I prove that you had a hand in killing my father, I'll personally put a bullet in your head." I had no idea where my outburst came from, but something made Goldstein take a step back, his face going pale.

"I have no idea what you're talking about."

"Yeah? Then you've got nothing to worry about. I'll see you in court."

Thorn stepped between me and Goldstein then. "I think that's your cue to leave," he said, stepping into Goldstein's personal space so the man had to back up a step.

"I'm not leaving without Emmanuell."

Thorn shifted his focus to the one man Goldstein had brought with him who looked like he was taking the meeting seriously. The scary one. "Mr. Black. What's the DA doing in an MC clubhouse?" Thorn's expression held a ghost of a smile. Like there was a joke. And it was on Goldstein.

"I was invited along by Mr. Goldstein here. I work out with one of his partners. They seemed to think my presence here would urge Miss Stanton's cooperation."

"Do you know anything about the death of

Emmanuell's father?"

Mr. Black shrugged. "I know the case was never officially solved. Mr. Goldstein tried to get it ruled an accident by bribing the medical examiner. Unfortunately, the ME is a personal friend of mine and came to me with it shortly after he was approached. We've been working quietly on it ever since."

"What?" Goldstein turned to Mr. Black. "Vincent! We've been friends since you came to the DA's office."

"I have many friends, Randall," Mr. Black said dryly. "Especially when someone wants something. I accompanied you here to see what you would do, and you did exactly what I expected. What would happen to Miss Stanton once you got her away from the protection of her friends and her man? I'm betting the car you purchased for her when you found out she was still alive has a little issue with the brakes. Just like her father's car."

"I have no idea what you're talking about. This is outrageous!"

"Is it? Well. We'll see, won't we." Mr. Black turned to Thorn. "The car's been impounded, and I have a mechanic going over it as we speak. I'll keep you posted, but it really looks like you were right. Keep your girl safe, Ripper. Don't worry about any of this. I'll take care of this scum. Consider it done."

"I owe you, Wrath," Gideon said.

"Just bring the girls to visit Holly and Bella. Holly's dying to get them their own St. Bernard puppies as gifts. To help you protect them, of course."

"Puppies?" I asked, looking from Gideon to Mr. Black. Had he called him Wrath?

"Long story, baby."

"You know these people, Vincent?"

Wrath stiffened, turning back to Mr. Goldstein. "Oh. Randall. I forgot you were there." He waved his hand at the two other men. "Escort him to my office. I'll take care of everything else from there. And just so we're clear, Randall, you're the scum I was referring to."

"What the hell? What's going on here, Vincent?" The two men each took hold of one of Goldstein's arms. "Stop that!" Goldstein tried to shrug them off, fighting them, but it was useless. The men had a tight grip on him. One snapped handcuffs on him, locking his arms behind his back. They forced him toward the clubhouse door. "You can't do this!"

"All evidence to the contrary." Wrath smirked, then he stepped forward and extended his hand to me. "Miss Stanton." I took his hand and he squeezed briefly. "It's been a pleasure. I look forward to meeting under less formal circumstances. My Celeste would love to meet you and your daughters."

"You know about them?"

"I'm with another club in the area. Black Reign. We are allies with Salvation's Bane and have made several friends with this club and their sister club, Bones. When Thorn contacted me, he told me you needed any threat to you gone because of your daughters. He was afraid that, if Goldstein knew about them, he'd try to get to you through them. The last thing any of us will ever allow is for someone to threaten our children." He glanced at Gideon. "Ripper, it's good seeing you." Then he left.

"What will happen now?" I watched as Vincent Black, the District Attorney, aka Wrath, left the clubhouse. Mr. Goldstein could still be heard yelling outside until there was a sickening *thud*, like flesh meeting flesh, and he was abruptly cut off.

"Wrath will take care of him," Gideon said. "He's been getting information from one of my contacts."

"My guess is, Wrath already knows Goldstein is guilty," Thorn added. "Goldstein won't make it to Wrath's office. He'll let me know when it's done."

"Is he going to kill him?" I wasn't sure I really wanted to know the answer.

"Be careful what questions you ask, honey," Gideon said softly. "I'll never lie to you, but you need to be sure you can handle the truth."

I thought about it a moment, really taking my time to consider his words. Could I handle it if they'd ordered a man I'd known all my life to be executed? "If he dies, then you guys know beyond a doubt he's guilty. Right?"

"That's right." Thorn took a step close to me. "We don't harm innocents. And we don't kill for minor infractions."

I squared my shoulders. "If you get justice for me and my father, the least I can do is be brave enough to hear about it."

Was it my imagination or did Gideon's shoulders go back and his head go up? In pride? "That's my woman." He raised his voice so there was no mistaking he was claiming me.

Several men chuckled. Others slapped Gideon's back in congratulations. Thorn just rolled his eyes. "Now that that's settled. Yes, Emmanuell. If Wrath's determined he's guilty of killing your father, or trying to kill you, Goldstein won't live to see the morning."

"What about Devan?" I asked softly. "And no, I don't care for him, and I don't much care what happens to him. But I want to know."

Thorn nodded but took his time before speaking.

Like he was choosing his words carefully. "Beaner's crimes are complicated. It wasn't just his actions against you, leaving you when he knew you were pregnant with no way to provide for yourself in any real meaningful sense. It was his betrayal of the club that sealed his fate. He threw our name around, lured you away from your family, helped everyone think you'd either run off or died, and took an offer to kill you. He just chickened out at the last minute. All of that came back to the club. You turned up on our doorstep. Everyone in the county had been looking for you for months. Just you being here, an heiress to a fortune who'd gone missing, would look bad on us. It could have brought scrutiny we didn't want. It turned out for the best for everyone concerned, but what Beaner did was unforgivable. His punishment is more about his betrayal of the club than anything he did to you. Though, he suffered for that too."

"Suffered. Is he dead, then?"

Thorn nodded his head. "Once we had his complete confession and he did his part to get Goldstein out here, we ended him."

I nodded several times. "I should probably feel remorse or something. But I don't. I never wanted him to have a claim on my girls. Maybe it makes me a bad person, but if he's dead, he can't try to take them away from me."

"As if I'd ever let that happen," Gideon growled. "We done, Thorn?"

"Yeah, Ripper. We're done. Go comfort your woman." He grinned. "Kiss those girls for me." That got good-natured laughter all around.

"Will do, prez."

Then Gideon -- Ripper -- put his arm around my shoulder and escorted me back to our room. After everything that had just happened, the last thing I wanted to do was leave our daughters, but Gideon coaxed me into packing a bag.

"Maybe we'll just take a small road trip this time," he murmured next to my ear. "I've got us a room booked near Miami. Private little place where you can make all the noise you want when I fuck you."

"You sure it's a good idea to leave the girls?"

"Honey, you're a fantastic mom. These babies will absolutely know how much they're loved by both their mother and their daddy. But I want you to know how much I love you, too. You need some rest and some time alone with your man. The ol' ladies got your back. Their men have their backs. Our girls got all of us protectin' and lovin' 'em. Let me give you one night where you don't have to worry. Can you do that? For me?"

The man knew how to get around all my defenses. I absolutely knew our girls would be safe while we were gone. The club would have it no other way.

"Well, when you put it that way," I grumbled even as I smiled and stepped into his arms. He hugged me close, kissing the top of my head.

"Come on, baby. We'll take the bike. You up for that?"

I grinned. "Absolutely."

Epilogue

The ride to South Beach took about an hour and a half, all of which was spent riding behind Gideon with the sea air blowing in my face as we sped down the interstate. The ride alone was enough to relax me more than I'd been in a very long time. I'd had a wonderful few months at Salvation's Bane with Gideon and the rest of the club. But this was the first time I felt like my life was finally settling down. I thought it would bother me more to leave my babies, that I'd worry over them so much I couldn't enjoy myself. While I already missed them terribly, I didn't worry overmuch. They were with a fiercely protective family. God help the little boys of the neighborhood when those girls started to grow up.

Riding with Gideon was an amazing treat. He'd taken me on short rides before, but nothing like this. Sometimes I whooped and waved my hands in the air for the sheer joy of the experience. When I did, he always chuckled, squeezing my knee. I loved every second of it. When we stopped, it was at a quaint little house next to the beach.

"Off you go, little mama," he said, slapping my ass when I stepped away from the bike.

"Hey! What was that for?" I wasn't put out, but I loved playing with Gideon.

"For all the noise you're about to make," he growled, scooping me up and heading inside the little house.

"Noise? What noise?"

"All the screamin' and moanin'. Likely have the police comin' around to find out what the fuck's goin' on."

I laughed, clinging to him as he took me into the

bedroom. "You think you'll be good enough to make me scream, do you?"

"Oh, now you're gonna get it."

Gideon tickled me until there were tears streaming down my face and he'd managed to get all my clothing off. Then he grinned down at me where he'd positioned himself above me, his hips wedged between my spread legs.

Brushing my hair off my forehead, he looked down at me, a little, contented smile on his face. "You're so fuckin' beautiful, Emmanuell."

"I love you, Gideon," I said, brushing my face along his beard over and over. "I love you so much! Thank you for taking care of me when I needed it."

"Honey, I'll always take care of you. Whatever you want. If it's within my power to give it to you, it's yours."

I pulled him down for a kiss. It didn't take long for him to take over, kissing and licking at my mouth, tugging my lips with his teeth before starting all over again. I doubted I'd ever get tired of kissing him. Gideon was mine every bit as much as I was his.

He settled his weight on me, and I reveled in it, clutching him to me while he continued to kiss me. His forearms rested beside my head, his fingers tangling in my hair.

Ending our kiss slowly, Gideon stilled, looking into my eyes. Letting me see his need and love. Of me. I was his woman. He was my man.

"Ain't never lettin' you go, Emmanuell. Got Wrath workin' on the adoption papers. Once you marry me, I'm adoptin' those girls, and they'll officially be mine, too." He said it with a hint of stubbornness, like he expected me to fight him on this or something. I wasn't sure which declaration he was worried about --

that he was adopting my girls or that he intended to marry me. Not that it mattered. I was willing if he was.

"If you're expecting me to argue with you, you're going to be disappointed." I grinned up at him.

"Good. Just so we're clear."

Then Gideon proceeded to kiss my entire body, paying attention to my breasts. They were tender, but large with milk for our children, so I left my bra and nursing pads in place. Gideon pulled them aside to kiss each nipple tenderly, lapping up any leakage I had before replacing everything.

"So fuckin' gorgeous," he murmured as he trailed kisses down my tummy. It wasn't toned and sleek any longer. There were stretch marks and saggy skin, but Gideon didn't seem to mind. In fact, he kissed every inch, every stretch mark. He worshiped my body. My womb. "Thank you, Emmanuell. Thank you for carrying those girls and for letting me be a part of your lives. I swear you'll never regret it."

"I know, Gideon. You're the best thing that's ever happened to me. I love you so much!"

With one tender kiss to my mound and a swipe of his tongue through my folds to tickle my clit, Gideon grunted and climbed up my body to blanket me once more.

"Later I'll take time to love you properly, but right now, I need inside you worse than I need to breathe, baby."

"Please," I gasped. "I need you, too."

Carefully, watching my face every second, Gideon eased his cock inside my weeping pussy. I sucked in a breath, thrilling at his size and length. The first time we'd made love, he'd taken me from behind. It had been easier with my pregnancy. Now he lay fully on top of me, in a dominant position. I could already tell it was going to be my favorite. I loved the feel of his big body pressing me into the bed. Loved looking up at him as he slid into my body.

"Gideon," I whispered as he began to move in rhythmic thrusts.

"Yeah, baby. I got you." He kissed me again, finally settling into a hard, driving rhythm. He went easy until sweat slickened his skin and he had to clench his jaw. I could see the effort it was taking him to hold back and give me the gentle loving he thought I needed so he didn't hurt me.

"I can take it, baby," I said. "Fuck me like you need to. Because I need it too."

That was all the encouragement he needed.

The sex was explosive. He took me higher and higher, my world tilting as one orgasm after another seemed to crash through my body. I screamed just like he'd told me I would. Over and over, I screamed, clutching him to me with my arms and legs. Needing everything he had to give me.

As the third wave of pleasure overtook me, Gideon wrapped his arms around me tightly, squeezing as he pounded into me, taking his own pleasure from my body. When he came, it was with a deafening roar to the ceiling. He filled me with spurt after spurt of hot cum, emptying himself inside me. Making me his.

It took long, long moments for us to catch our breaths. Gideon rolled so that I lay sprawled on top of him, one hand resting on my back, the other possessively on my ass.

"You good, baby? I didn't hurt you, did I?"

I loved him for asking, but there was no need for it. "You could never hurt me, Gideon. Especially not with your love. I'm always here for you to take what you need."

"Same, baby. I'll give you as much pleasure as I'm capable of. If that ain't enough, I'll figure out how to give you more."

"You'll always be enough." I sighed and stretched contentedly. Gideon pulled the covers over us, though it was a wonderful evening. The breeze coming off the ocean through the windows was like a balm to my soul.

"Rest, baby. I've got more for you later. For now, I want to hold you. Here. In my arms."

"Where I belong," I said. The sound of waves crashing on the beach and lingering sea gulls drifted all around us. Gideon stroked my back lazily. I had a man who understood my insecurities and helped me to work through them. He protected and loved my daughters and me. The life I'd once thought was spiraling out of control and into despair was now a dream come true.

I'd never be alone again. And I was surrounded with love.

Marteeka Karland

Erotic romance author by night, emergency room tech/clerk by day, Marteeka Karland works really hard to drive everyone in her life completely and totally nuts. She has been creating stories from her warped imagination since she was in the third grade. Her love of writing blossomed throughout her teenage years until it developed into the totally unorthodox and irreverent style her English teachers tried so hard to rid her of.

Bones MC Multiverse:
- Bones MC
- Salvation's Bane MC
- Shadow Demons
- Black Reign MC

Marteeka at Changeling: changelingpress.com/marteeka-karland-a-39

Changeling Press E-Books

More Sci-Fi, Fantasy, Paranormal, and BDSM adventures available in e-book format for immediate download at ChangelingPress.com -- Werewolves, Vampires, Dragons, Shapeshifters and more -- Erotic Tales from the edge of your imagination.

What are E-Books?

E-books, or electronic books, are books designed to be read in digital format -- on your desktop or laptop computer, notebook, tablet, Smart Phone, or any electronic e-book reader.

Where can I get Changeling Press E-Books?

Changeling Press e-books are available at ChangelingPress.com, Amazon, Apple Books, Barnes & Noble, and Kobo/Walmart.

ChangelingPress.com

Printed in Great Britain
by Amazon